# THE GRAIL AND THE SAUCER

## ROBERT MANIS

# THE GRAIL AND THE SAUCER

CONTENTS

# Prologue

Once upon a time, in a galaxy not so far away from his ex-girlfriend's LA bungalow, a bumbling graduate school dropout was wallowing in self-pity after she had unceremoniously hit the eject button on their relationship. Life was hitting the poor sap harder than a meteor shower on Mercury, and he was teetering on the brink of despair.

But don't desperate times call for desperate measures? So, in a moment of reckless lunacy, he decided to embark on a quest to seek out UFO aliens, in where else but Sedona, Arizona? With UFO enthusiasts abounding and more tin foil hats than you could shake a cosmic ray at, it seemed like the perfect spot for an extraterrestrial rendezvous.

Oh, the irony that awaited! Instead of being whisked away to another planet, he was snatched back in *time* by two Venusians—Talmo and Lamo, smack dab into the middle of Biblical shenanigans. Talk about a rough landing! And he, to make matters worse, was dumped into the sandals of Matthew, one of the dodgiest apostles in the bunch. Imagine the bewilderment as he stumbled through his new life, completely clueless— thanks to the Prime Directive—about his mission in this ancient world.

Lo and behold, after prayer and fasting, and a few New Testament type encounters, our would-be disciple discovered that his grand purpose was to retrieve the mystical emerald tablets for none other than Jesus H. Christ himself. Yes, the followers of the big man upstairs had misplaced these sacred artifacts, while it was up to our hero (me) to jot down His divine wisdom for future generations as well.

Sounds like a piece of cake, right? Wrong! Turns out, being a disciple was no stroll in the mall. And the tablets were as elusive as a shimmer on the sand—what with Romans on the take, and zealots on the prowl. Our hero had to face trial after trial, armed only with a fancy communicator pen, a crystal activator, and a staff that miraculously transformed into a lightsaber.

But the greatest test lay not in the external challenges, no, it was within our protagonist himself. A crisis of confidence raged like a dust devil within his soul. Could he find the strength to persevere amidst all the external chaos and internal self-doubt?

After countless trials, a side trip to 18th century France and whirlwind romances with his soul mate, Elisabet, and his fantasy female Delphine, our hero discovered his inner *je ne c'est quoi* and triumphed over adversity. The choice to stay or return was his for the taking, but in a stunning plot twist, at the last minute he chose the third door, leading to . . .

# 1

# Dungeons and Dragons

Hey do you like barbecues? I used to.

Well, normally. Are you coming to mine? It's going to be right outside of this dungeon in the town square. I'm not throwing this shindig though, I'm the subject of it. Which is a bummer. I'll explain in a minute.

Meanwhile from my cell, I stuffed a shout at the King's jailer as he strutted by. It's pointless. He looked at me, sneered, and rolled his eyes. He has a dark beard and wide nostrils. The dungeon is gray and dim even in the middle of the day. There's a large brown stain on the wall which was probably someone's blood, and the mortar between the stones is dark and flaking. I know because I just flaked some off with my fingernail. Why? To see if I could. The cell doesn't smell good either, mostly like urine I guess, mixed with—Well, not sure I want to imagine. I raised my brows at the jailer, baiting some response.

"I'll be back later," was all he said as he narrowed his eyes derisively at me. But if you're squeamish, don't worry. I have him paid off, and he pretends to torture me while I pretend to scream.

That's because I'm in King Arthur's castle dungeon, awaiting being burned at the stake in three days at high noon. No one I can pay off there, unfortunately. So my views on the subject of BBQ may change. I banged a cup on the heavy wooden cell door which didn't have the same effect as in the movies when you bang a cup on the bars of a modern prison. I'm saying all this because today my strategy is to sound crazy, so they'll release me. Of course, as a strategy, it's pretty nutty, but if you think about it, it kinda proves my point.

Why am I being BBQed? Officially, for being a heretic, but actually for stealing the Holy Grail. And also just maybe for being caught *in flagrante delicto* with Queen Gwenhwyfar, though I swear it wasn't what it looked like.

I was stupidly trying to save that jerk Sir Lanslod, who turns out I knew in a past life and wasn't worth saving then, either. Just makes me a sucker, I guess.

Not that I wasn't attracted to Queen Gwen, but her full name betrays a certain sketchy quality as it means "white enchantress" or "ghost." So don't lose your heart 'cause she'll enchant you then ghost you for sure. That didn't stop Lanslod.  But he was sketchy too, so they had a lot in common.

You probably have some questions. Like who am I, what the hell am I doing here, and wasn't King Arthur just a myth, right? Well, I have the answers for the most part, but first let me describe the set and setting of this situation.

In this particular era my name is Freddie. I'm a time *and* space traveler (they go together, as you'll see), and I'm in King Arthur's dungeon, a basement room in the palace with a stool and a blanket to sleep on or under, with a narrow barred opening at ground level from which I can clearly see people's shoes, and horse's legs and hooves, and whole dogs and cats—all walking on the muddy, rutted street. What I can't see is a market in the distance, although I know it's there. Complete with a mound of half-dry logs for burning folks. You do want to have it in a public place for maximum effect, right?

Most people who walk by actually don't have shoes, they wrap their feet in rags. Well, at least they can afford rags, so it could be worse. The somewhat better-off have a kind of moccasin plus the rags to keep their feet warm, and the wealthiest have boots. You can tell a lot from my small window on the world.

The dungeon is just like you'd imagine, a bunch of cold gray rocks mortared together. With brown stains. That's the setting. The context is—*Yes, King Arthur did exist*. In the sixth century, he ruled over a small but pivotal kingdom near the borders of Wales and Cornwall in West Wiltshire named Cantmell, Frenchified for classiness into *Camelot*, a name that always made me laugh as a kid because it sounded like a place to buy used camels. *Come on down, folks!* There was once a Roman fort there, and Uther Pendragon made it his capital while trying to stave off the Celts, Saxons, and other lowlifes. His plan might have worked if it weren't for Lanslod and Gwen, and for me and that lousy Grail.

So who the hell am I? I'll tell you more in a minute. But first my jailer is here with some food. Probably boiled rodent and turnips. Sounds good, right?

Back now. Well, that was disgusting. But the jailer did bring some good news that my future brother-in-law is coming to visit.

He'd have come with lunch, but they're questioning him right now. Hopefully not by pulling out his fingernails or something.

Okay, so my name currently is Freddie, but you might know me from earlier (or later) productions as Matthew the Apostle or Henri de Saint-Simon the social philosopher. No, I did not play them on TV, rather on time travel, and I was playing for keeps.

You probably wonder what happens to your life when you time travel. Does time proceed without you until you return and then rewrites after you come back to the same moment? Does it stay still and wait for you? Well, it's neither. Time stops for no one, and it can't rewrite either, because that would mean parallel worlds, which can't exist, and rewriting, which can't exist either, because whatever is done can't be done. The fact is, it's all predetermined. So it neither stops nor rewrites, it just is. Time travel and all.

Time travel is how I got here via a spaceship, and time travel is how I will leave, providing my future brother-in-law hasn't lost the refill to my souvenir pen, which doubles as a communication device and triples as a laser. It's predetermined whether he will or not, but unfortunately I don't know which. That's how you can tell if something is past or future. If you don't know, it's the future, but if you can't remember, it's the past. Trust me, they feel different.

Looking around me within the four gray walls, I can see a bundle that contains a change of clothes (my modern outfit) and the staff I carried the bundle on. The staff, however, is actually a lightsaber, which, if there's enough juice in it, I can use to fight my way to my space/time ship, providing I can send a signal with my communicator pen, and the ship is in this time zone to receive it. Otherwise, my message might go to voicemail, and I'll be long since BBQed before they receive it. Actually, if it's predetermined that they receive it, like I said above, then they will receive it, and well . . . I just explained it all a minute ago. There's also a weird cylindrical rod in the bundle that I picked up in 18th century France and probably should have thrown away. Toss it now? Nah, maybe I'll need it, who knows?

You need to understand a couple of things about King Arthur McDragon, son of Uther Pendragon. You did know there were dragons back then? You didn't? Well, there were a few. I know because I fought one. Well, kind of. It wasn't what you'd expect. Not even close. Light years away in fact.

The old St. George vs. dragon legend got so much traction because it is one of the many versions of the old-world story of the conflict between Light and Darkness, kind of like Ra and Apepi, and Marduk and Tiamat—you know all about them, right?

All woven on a worn tapestry of historical this-and-that. Tiamat, the scaly, winged dragon, and Apepi, the powerful enemy of the glorious Sun God, were both made to perish in the fire that St. George sent against them and their friends—or maybe it was their *fiends*, haha. Remember? Not to mention, Dadianus, also called the "dragon," with his friends the sixty-nine governors, also destroyed by fire called down from heaven by the prayers of St. George, and blah, blah.

So all in all, I think the dragons were probably more real than St. George. That was the view of my comparative religion professor who had a thing about the dude. Though not about the dragons, of which he had no idea, ha.

The local version was started by Guy of Warwick who used it to justify grabbing some land just west of York, which was then called Eboracum. Much later, his great-great times whatever grandson Tom Malory juiced up the King Arthur oral history and turned it into the stuff of legends, probably for similar ulterior motives. Arthur's dad took the name Pendragon, meaning "first dragon" because it signaled power when he grabbed it back from Guy. Whatever.

While I'm sitting here on a stool, waiting for my brother-in-law to-be to maybe help me escape from a horrible death by fire, let me explain why it's all predetermined.

Let's start with Quantum Mechanics, since that's the religion everyone seems to believe in, in your time period. The big problem with quantum theory is that it actually seems to work. But it really shouldn't. It shouldn't because the whole thing is a goddamn paradox. Let me explain. Quantum Mechanics shows that light is both a particle and a wave at the same time. But that should be impossible because a particle is matter, and waves are energy. And it makes a big explosion when you convert one to the other. The problem is that light behaves like a wave when you don't look at it, but it behaves as a particle when you do. In other words it acts differently when you're watching, just like people do. But light doesn't get embarrassed—which is the main reason why we act differently.

So the standard interpretation of this phenomenon is that the observer affects the observation. But that's nutty for a lot of reasons. One reason was suggested by the physicist Erwin Schrödinger, who proposed an experiment using a box containing a cat and a vial of poison gas. The experiment would be set up so there was a fifty percent chance that a random single particle triggered the release of the gas. But according to the theory, the experiment wouldn't actually work until someone *observed* whether or not the particle had released the gas. Which meant that the cat was neither living nor dead until someone looked at it. And what happens if the result is just recorded on a video camera—is that cat in suspended animation until someone watches the video? And what if it's Friday afternoon, and no one watches 'til Monday? That's a long time for the cat to be in limbo. And what about this: What if the video was viewed by a rat? Or a spider? Would they trigger the collapse of the wave into particles? And what if some guy named Wigner told his friend to do the experiment. Would his friend collapse the wave, or would it take until Wigner found out? In case you're wondering, Wigner was this smart dude—in fact, he was the physicist who proposed this riddle.

Finally, some genius (I use the word sarcastically) proposed this whole idea of parallel worlds, that every possibility caused a whole different world to branch off. Unfortunately, that spawned a zillion science fiction episodes on Star Trek and captured the imagination of physicists who were mostly all fanboys, after all. Finally, in 2035, the physicists realized that they were just jerking off because it was all predetermined, and the photons did whatever they did, and that cat was either alive or dead, and that was that. That's what my Venusian buddies told me, anyway, to keep me from asking too many questions.

Okay, hold on now, the jailer just hollered out that my half-brother is here. He's not actually a half-brother but hey, close enough. The jailer announces the visitor not out of politeness, but because if the guest is important in any way, he doesn't want them to be embarrassed if you're defecating in the corner.

After a minute, my potentially future brother-in-law Dag showed up, smiling. That's if I live. He's usually smiling because that's his job. He's the court jester, which, though not particularly important, is the best job in the world much of the time and the worst job in the world when you're not in the mood. Actually, as you might realize if you ever thought about it, jesting is not a full time job. It's evening work, and most jesters have a day job too. Dag's is washing dishes. It's great for me, though, because he's got inside knowledge from the throne room or the kitchen nearly all the time, whereas I'm only in the room when Arthur convenes the Oval Table.

Yes the table is oval, not round. It was round for a few weeks, but Arthur didn't like the conversation being dominated by Sir Bors who was always telling long stories that went nowhere. So Arthur carved the round table into firewood and replaced it with an oval—with him at the head and Sir Bors at the foot. It's been said that's where the word "boring" came from, but it's probably just a coincidence, haha. You'd have thought the knights would've been outraged at the bait and switch since they'd been promised equality with Arthur—symbolized by a table with no head , i.e. round—but no one protested, proving that even anarchists need organization. Or that boredom is a bigger motivator than pride.

Dag is tall and thin with a large mouth, the better to make the wry faces a jester makes to get laughs amongst the knights. Arthur doesn't like that kind of humor, he likes puns—of all things. Once Dag got a laugh from him by grabbing a bun off the

Oval Table and, pretending to thoroughly peruse it, finally concluded, "The bun is the lowest form of wheat."

That's a pun on the old saying, *The pun is the lowest form of wit,* which apparently was old even back then and got a great laugh from Arthur, groans from Bors and Galahat, and blank stares from Lanslod and the other knights. They are not too bright as you can tell, but decent with a sword and rich for the most part.

But more about me. I'm average height and build, dark hair, elegant nose. I look the same as I always do, whether I'm in biblical, modern, or current times. At least, to me. That's because I am the same, though a little worse for wear from the anti-matter exposure it takes to go backwards in time. Also there are slight molecular rearrangements to make me look a little more like the dude I'm dropped in to replace. My name (or his) officially is Sir Escobar. It's Spanish. First name, Frayim. I'm a Spanish Jew but have told everyone I'm from Galilee to make it seem like I'm holier, or at least have an excuse to be Jewish.

I could do that because I just came from Galilee via time/spaceship, so I can describe it unbelievably well. They haven't figured out why I have a Spanish name though, the dopes. The name Escobar means "from a plain of thorny bushes"—*Spanish broom,* to be precise. Frayim is a diminutive of Ephraim. It's Hebrew, meaning "fruitful." It indicates an intense personal nature. According to Merlin, who was also real and who looked the name up in his book of names and spells, and read it to me:

*Your feelings and emotional desires are strong. Your creative nature and ambition drive you to pursue success to the extent that you sometimes jeopardize your personal well-being. You are too cer-*

*tain of yourself, and you are not open to the views of others or responsive to their desires or needs.*

*Also, this name does not incorporate qualities that enable you to be diplomatic and to compromise. In all your work and activities, you are inclined to be rather unsystematic and disorderly. These characteristics spoil stability, progress, and accumulation, even though you may put forth intense effort. You are often preoccupied with the desires and demands of the moment. Temper and indulgence could become serious problems in your life.*

All those things are true. Which is why I'm in the dungeon awaiting BBQ. Also why I prefer to be called Freddie, instead of Frayim, plus that name also reminds me of a frying pan. Actually, I don't, because Freddie is like a 1940s dorky name. But *he* did. I would have chosen Francisco. Or Frankenstein, haha.

Anyway, Dagen, my future brother-in-law, or Dag as most call him, had a report.

"Freddie, the King is willing to be merciful and pardon you. You just need to return the Holy Grail." He smiled with his big wide mouth in the most compassionate and understanding manner.

"I can't," I sighed.

"Why in God's name not?"

"It's a long story . . ." I looked up at the ceiling, which was not stone but wood, cross beamed and stained black.

"Tell me . . ."

"I can't." I kept my eyes aimed at the ceiling, so I didn't have to meet his gaze.

"Why not?"

"That's a long story, too," I offered, shrugging.

Actually, it's not. The Holy Grail can't be returned because it no longer exists, having been repurposed for a bigger, higher purpose. And I can't tell him that because of the Prime Directive which states that knowledge about the future cannot be shared if it benefits any human, cat, or dog. Horses are okay because they are necessary to get around. I'm not sure about any other animals.

I am called *Sir* Escobar because I am rich enough to own a horse and a sword, and some chain mail, and a squire. Sure you are supposed to be knighted, but that can be bought or faked. Really, that's all you need to be a knight. Well, that and an ability to BS and fight if someone calls bullshit on you. So my name Frayim was actually a plus, I mean if you believe in numerology, or *namer*-ology, haha, or whatever the heck Merlin's book was based on. Which everyone here goes along with, as well as every other superstition under the sun. Which is not to say it doesn't work—as with my name, astrology, and a little magic. Big magic is harder, of course.

Big magic, in fact, is only accomplished by people with friends in spaceships. Fortunately, that's me and Merlin, too. He's the guy who called me here via my friends up there. Unfortunately, I need a refill to charge my souvenir pen that also acts like a communicator, and guess what? Dag didn't bring it.

"Dag, where's my pouch?"

"Sorry, Freddie. They wouldn't let me bring any of your possessions until you told me where the Grail is. I *was* able to bring you a little bread . . . "

I grabbed it and put it down on my stool. "And what if I *did* tell you where it is?" I can tell him, but it won't help him.

"Well, maybe if you tell them, they'd let you have your pouch—but maybe not. They are knights, after all."

Knights being the most devious, nasty fellows on God's green earth. Which is why Arthur decided to develop a code of chivalry to mellow them out. Which is why the knights turned on him, which is another reason why I needed to steal the Holy Grail. Unfortunately, Arthur hasn't wised up to the plot because the knights are such good liars. But I'm getting ahead of myself.

"How about this," I submitted, "They let you bring my pouch, and when I tell you where the Grail is, you can give me the dang pouch. They can even send a knight to accompany you."

"But they'll ask me, how I can be certain you will tell them the truth?"

"Tell them I'm willing to swear right then and there on the Holy Bible."

"Verily, that should work."

I'm telling you, it's hilarious that people as devious as the knights would be that gullible. But even more than being devious, they are superstitious. Nothing is more important to a knight than two things: Number One, upholding an oath, and Number Two, not having anyone step on your shadow. I've made the mistake of the latter, with the result being a match on the field of honor that I barely survived. The oath you can get out of, by another oath to a higher ranking thing or fellow. Of course, there's nothing higher than the Holy Bible. 'Cause if you break it, you go straight to Hell. Or so they think.

I know otherwise because I wrote the dang—I mean, blessed—book. Well, the book of sayings it was based on. Like

I said, Matthew the Apostle. Back then, I scribbled down some sayings and left them to my girlfriend Elisabet. I was on my way back to see her when I got sidetracked by an interesting opportunity. Like Merlin's book said: . . . *In all your work and activities, you are inclined to be rather unsystematic and disorderly . . ..*

'Nuff said.

Also there's the matter of reincarnation. Some people prefer to believe in heaven and hell, but that's oversimplified. Hell is just a room in Saturn where after you die, they make you look at the consequences of your misdeeds. Not pleasant. In fact, it seems like eternity, but it's not long at all. The problem is, once you've seen those things , it's kind of hard to let go of them, and that can last a long time. What can be even worse, though, is they *also* make you look at all your missed opportunities. For most people, that's far more bitter—when you realize that the sorry mess that was your life can't be blamed on anything but your laziness, doubt, and cowardice. That's torture, for sure. Unfortunately, most people respond by going to the other extreme in their next lives, so that is when they get to do the misdeed torture. And then the cycle continues. Really, if the Saturnian Lords of Karma who run the place were into repeat business they couldn't have designed a better system. Maybe they get a commission or something.

Actually, *Lord* maybe isn't the best word for them. Being here in old England, I have discovered that the word is *hlafweard,* which sounds like "half-weird" but means "guardian of the bread." And *Lady* means "kneader of the bread." I've noticed bread is a big deal around here. Better than rodent and turnips, for sure.

About then, the jailer came in stroking his dark beard, and told us that Dag had to leave. But there were other visitors on their way later. Hopefully, one of them is Arthur or Queen Gwen telling me I'll be pardoned. But I doubt it. Meanwhile, I'll use this opportunity to write all this down. How? Using my souvenir pen. Despite needing a refill, it can write forever, thanks to a miracle Joshua H. Christ performed back when he did the loaves and fishes. Unfortunately, he didn't know or didn't choose to extend that timeline to the pen's other abilities.

Dag left after embracing me and telling me to buck up. I bucked up enough to pull my blank scrap of parchment out of my bundle, and started writing all this down. Fortunately, I can write really small. Which, if there were someone literate enough to read, their eyesight would not be able to decipher. Paper is still rare around here, apparently. I got in the habit of journaling when I was back in biblical times, and now I can't do without it.

After an hour or two, the jailer shouted, announcing the visitors. "Two ladies to see you, you piece of scum." Wow, he was in a bad mood. Or maybe he was jealous, forgetting I was due to be burnt to a crisp in a couple days.

A minute later, he ushered them to the door.

"The Queen and her Lady. Bow, you weasel," he said.

I bowed. He wrestled with the door, unbarred it, and brought in two chairs. Queen Gwen and her Lady, Aelfhere, who happened to be my fiancée and was the real reason I was naked in the queen's bedroom, sat down. The Queen looked concerned, her bright blue eyes, high cheekbones, absolutely white as snow skin, and strawberry blonde hair made her look seriously like a descended angel. She had a few crow's feet at the corners of her eyes that made her look wise, which she probably was, and also kind, which she was not, as far as I could tell. She truly was the fairest in the land even at almost forty, and it was no wonder Arthur and Lanslod—and every other clod in the kingdom who had eyesight—was in love with her, except me. I was only in lust, and that was just when I let my guard down, which was rarely, but it did happen and that was how she convinced me to take the fall for the jerk Lanslod. She frowned with concern and my fiancée just looked embarrassed. It was surprising that Arthur even let her see me after what had allegedly happened, but maybe he assumed Aelfhere would chaperone her, when really, it was the other way around.

"Dear Freddie," she pronounced, furrowing her elegant eyebrows. "I so appreciate you keeping my and dear Lanslod's secret. And I am so sorry to see you in this situation. I only wish I could pardon you right here and now."

Okay, that was clearly off the table, then.

"If you would only return the Grail, we could perhaps just execute a peasant and pretend it was you, while spiriting you off to Winchester or somewhere you prefer." Winchester was currently the largest city on the island since London had been abandoned by the Romans a couple hundred years ago.

"My peasant or yours?" I asked, knowing full well I couldn't give her the Grail but not being able to tip my hand if I wanted to get out of this.

"Well, it was assumed it'd be yours, but I suppose that's negotiable."

"I can tell you where the Grail is if you return my pouch, as I've said to Dag."

"Yes, we saw him earlier."

"So is it a deal?"

"It's up to Arthur," she paused and looked upwards, "Who will ask Gawain the Pure, who will ask Galahat, who will probably ask his dad . . . Lanslod." She frowned. "Who will probably say no." She shook her head. "He hates you, you know."

Aelfhere looked pained, kneading her hands worriedly. She was always a quiet girl with a sweet but sad look as if she knew the world was just too cruel for someone like her. But it made her wide face a little prettier. Which was a plus because the Queen's Ladies had to fit in a narrow slot of prettier than most but not any competition for the Queen.

"Why don't you tell us first, and we'll give you the pouch after we get the Grail?" she asked.

"The knights," I replied.

"True." Everyone knew that the knights were lousy rats. Except Arthur, of course.

"But as I told Dag, I'm willing to swear on the Holy Bible that I'm telling the truth."

"Oh. Well, in that case . . . " Gwen's face brightened. Her eyes sparked and the crinkles around them momentarily vanished. I'm telling you, people think if you lie on the Bible, you'll get smitten by a lightning bolt. Which can't happen, unless you have a friend in a spaceship. I have two, but I don't know if the ship is even around, and won't find out until I get my pouch with the refill.

My two "friends" are named Talmo and Lamo, originally from Venus, but you might know them as Kasper and Mateno from our previous production known to history as "the Life of

Jesus," where they appeared as a couple of magicians bowdlerized into "wise men" in the Storybook version of events. I say *production* because, well, we made it go down in a certain way that it wouldn't have. You'll thank me for that (I hope).

Actually, I'm not sure if they are really my friends or are just using me, but I guess I'll find out. I'll tell you more about them later, but right now I have to chat a little more, then say goodbye to the beautiful ladies who have just given me hope I might survive.

Or not. The jailer just appeared, smiling like a snarky Cheshire Cat, informing the Queen that Sir Mordred was waiting to see me.

"Oh no," Queen Gwen sighed, "We must depart immediately." She wouldn't want to be caught dead in the same room as the king's illegitimate son and mortal enemy. She extended her hand for me to kiss, which I did, and then I kissed the cheek of poor Aelfhere who hadn't said a word the whole time. She looked so worried, it made me feel even worse.

"Love you," I said as nonchalantly as possible and started to give her a hug.

She tensed up. "Freddie, be reasonable for once," she pleaded.

The jailer harrumphed, so I broke away.

The minute the ladies left, Mordred stormed up to the door. He was in a bad mood. The jailer let him in wordlessly. He was in his early twenties, dark hair with bangs, dark mustache, and thin beard with big eyes that would have been soulful if he wasn't always angry. He had a right to be though, and I kind of sympathized with him. He was the illegitimate and incestuous son of Arthur and Margause of Orkney who was serving as a spy upon the young king and didn't know they were related when she seduced him.

That wouldn't necessarily have been incest nowadays since they were cousins, but once it came out, Mordred was hounded mercilessly by the other young knights. We could maybe have been friends if he wasn't so hot-tempered. I'm hot-tempered, too, in this lifetime, so it's probably for the best. I understand the most likely people to murder you are your close friends—Well, after your parents, children, and spouses, that is.

"You can't give the Grail back to Arthur," he blurted out. Obviously, he believed the Grail would help him overthrow Arthur and, conversely, could help Arthur defeat him. It wouldn't do either, even before I cannibalized it, and especially not now. But no point in saying that, right?

"The Queen has made me promises if I return it," I replied.

"Which she won't be in position to fulfill," he retorted, glaring.

"Well, can you get me out of here?" I glared right back.

"Yes, soon. But I need the Grail. Tell me where it is."

"I've got two or three days before they incinerate me—I can't believe you're that close to being ready to strike."

"I could be," he stroked his wispy goatee, trying to look inscrutable.

"Well, the Grail isn't that close to get it and come back in time," I countered.

"I see." He paused to consider, "Well, I may be able to spring you before then."

That would be great, I thought. Or not. Because right then, the jailer returned with half a dozen armed men. They took positions at the end of the hall.

"Sir Lanslod has sent some added protection in case someone tries to attack you for defiling the Queen," the jailer said.

As if.

Mordred turned to the guard. "I'm leaving," he said. Then back to me. "I'll be back," he said, a bit sadistically, I thought.

The guard laughed. "I really don't think you handled that very well," he said.

Like I'd listen to him. He didn't even go to college, haha. He turned away and opened the cell door across from me and pulled out a ragged, emaciated old man with hollow eyes. He crumpled to the floor. The man didn't look like he would live too much longer.

"In what way?" Might as well ask. The jailer straightened himself up.

"You need to show some loyalty. My opinion. People trust them which is loyal."

Like I'd listen to him.

At that moment, there was a howl from another cell and the jailer turned away. I took that opportunity to grab my piece of bread from the stool and throw it to the old man. His eyes widened in surprise, and he grabbed it and snarfed it up in a couple of huge bites. And nodded to me gratefully. Hey, we were both going to die soon probably, but that bread might make the difference for him. And my stomach was the one that was probably more able to digest those dang stewed rodents and turnips.

# 2

# Surf and Turf

*One Month Earlier...*

After an evening of time traveling, I found myself in a familiar, unfamiliar place. A lodging in a *burh*. Not a castle, despite what you've pictured about King Arthur, because castles weren't adopted until the Norman invasion some 400 years in the future. Until then, there were burhs, which were fortified towns with earthen and wood walls and sometimes stone. They looked a lot like forts in the American West, except burhs had mounds called *revetments* surrounding them that acted as barricades. Cantmell had stone walls with wooden parapets. But not so classy as you've pictured. Inside the burh walls there are most businesses, such as the inn where I'm staying. Some structures are made of stone, especially the two-story ones, but many are wood, almost like log cabins. Most have thatched roofs. But they don't have the cross hatched walls, like you see in pictures of Merrie Olde England. No, that was much later.

I was time-lagged, so I staggered onto my luxury bed of feathers that promptly collapsed flat, so my butt hit the floor. Apparently, I was supposed to fluff it before I lay down. The smoky wood smell of the room wrinkled my nose. I felt dizzy and exhausted as if my very cells had been turned inside out. Which in a way they had because they'd been converted temporarily to antimatter and then back. Fortunately, I'd been decomplexified first, so it wasn't fatal. I decided to take the opportunity to fold up my clothes because nothing is worse when you are hung over from time travel than seeing your dirty clothes strewn across the floor. Well, actually there are many things worse, but it does stick out at you, so I always do try to fold my clothes. Small mercies can be helpful.

I slept deeply, but fitfully if that makes sense, and woke with an anti-matter hangover to beat the band. *Shite, merde, frickin' A, dang it,* and *hell's bells* were the first words out of my mouth. I would have said worse, but my time traveling "sponsors" have told me that cursing cancels out several minutes of mantras, and you need to achieve 72,000 minutes of mantras every lifetime if you want to move spiritually forward, and more if you know better. I know better, at least some of the time.

Looking around me, I can see my modern clothes, neatly folded, thank God, neatly centered on a chest facing walls of rough wood, almost like a log cabin except flattened. And a sword of Damascene steel hanging by its handle from a hook next to the door, shining in the morning sun—which had just appeared from behind a rain cloud—a saddle, a suit of chainmail, a pitcher of water, a stool and table with a half loaf of stale bread and a half dried sausage on it. All of those possessions of the dude I replaced, who presumably is in cold storage on the spaceship while I perform my expected tasks that I don't know yet, because I can't be told anything important by people from the future due to the Prime Directive. But hopefully, I'll be able to piece it together from people here now, to perform the task for which I've come. Since it's all predetermined, I'm certain to succeed, unless of course I'm predetermined to fail in which case I don't know why I was brought here, but I will eventually find out.

Next to my clothes are my souvenir pen and a weird, steam-punk cylinder I used to charge some crystals for Joshua H Christ 600 years ago. I should probably throw the latter out, but then whenever you throw something away, the first thing you know you need it the next day.

Let me get you up to speed. In modern times, I was a graduate student specializing in the history of science. I got interested in pseudoscience as well, especially UFOs. I started to suspect that UFOs were real, though, and since I couldn't find a job, I went to Sedona, Arizona, to see if I could spot one. Unfortunately, I succeeded. I met two fellows from Venus who tempted me into a journey—not to outer space but back in time. I was part of the plan, it seems.

They have phasers, light sabers, replicators, and holodecks, just like in sci-fi. Their most important technological advances are, however, the complexifier and anti-matter. The complexifier enables people to come from other planets where the temperature is too hot or cold and the density too great or little by expanding or contracting the distance between molecules. In other words, turning you from gas to solid and vice versa. It also enables time travel by decomplexing you enough to not turn into a black hole when you approach the speed of light, which would've made your mass infinite as relativity predicts, or explode when the anti-matter drive kicks in, enabling you to go backwards in time as anti-matter particles like to do. They also have a babelfish, which is not a real fish, but something you put in your ear that enables you to understand the local language mostly, except for some jokes, which it tends to mistranslate. Just like in that *Hitchhikers Guide to the Galaxy* book. Author was on to something, I guess.

The plan was to go back to the era of Joshua H. Christ, replacing Matthew the apostle who'd accidentally been eliminated, and then finish his mission which was to write down some sayings and encode them with directions to the emerald tablets, then to be hidden in the ruins of Megiddo (also known as Armageddon) and a pyramid. They chose me to replace Matthew because I happened to be a reincarnation of him and wasn't going to amount to much anyway in my current lifetime.

Anyway, here I was in Cantmell in an inn with my horse and squire sleeping in the stable, about to answer the call of King Arthur the Just (everyone wants a cool moniker to give them cachet) for all local knights of honor to join him in establishing a more perfect kingdom. I (or the dude I'm substituted for) was in the neighborhood having completed an assignment for a local earl, when "I" (Escobar) was struck down by a random bug, creating an opening for the other me to step in just as I was returning to biblical times to my sweetheart Elisabet where I'd get martyred in a couple years. It was really a dismal choice between living a long pointless life in modern times or a short exciting one in the past.

After getting faded with my Venusian "friends,'" the short exciting one seemed more tempting—with a stop off in Camelot as a bonus, there to hang out with my other sweetheart Delphine (currently known as Aelfhere) and see what she was like a third of the way between when I met her at the well in Capernaum and when we had a brief but intense flirtation in pre-revolution France. One has a lot of romances over the lifetimes, but many of them are with the same people, so you get a chance to chip away at making them better. Although I have to say, my decision might have been biased by the Venusian dudes for their own reason—it's hard to tell, since they play their proverbial cards close to their respective chests allegedly due to that dang Prime Directive.

The Prime Directive limits what they can tell me when they put me in the information headset during time travel to get me up to speed. So I know enough to play Trivial Pursuit in any location I visit (if they have the game or some version of it, which they usually don't) or to make conversation in a tavern (usually helpful in getting the lay of the land), as well as seemingly random stuff about the rest of the solar system that someone somewhere deemed significant but not likely to bias our actions. So I know a lot about Atlantis, Lemuria, Shambhala, and other supposedly mythical places, as well as life as gases on other planets. I guess they consider it "cultural literacy."

Timothy, my squire, has just knocked timidly at the door. I think it's who it was—that's who came to mind after I thought for a second. I expect he has some news regarding meeting King

Arthur, so I need to let him in. He's a thin wisp of a fellow with long earlobes, I abruptly remembered. I opened the door.

"My liege," he said with a little bow. I do enjoy the sound of it. You should try it, it makes the whole day better to have someone call you that.

"Yes, squire, what have you found out?"

"I have informed the palace of your return to Cantmell, and they request your attendance tonight for a small feast and a discussion of the day's problems. RSVP."

"I'll come, what's the dress code?"

"Same as usual, a light coat of mail, no helmets allowed though. Wear a clean surcoat as well." Surcoats were the cloth shirts worn over the armor usually displaying one's seal or heraldry. I think Arthur started it because no knights wore them outside Cantmell. Rumor was he insisted on them because he was near-sighted and hated to be embarrassed by confusing different people.

"Where, pray tell, is my surcoat, then?" I had already scanned the room and not spotted it.

"I sent it to be cleaned. It will be returned when it's fully dry."

"Good boy. Someday you'll be a fine knight, once you master the nine agilities and skewer a person or two." Timothy was nineteen, just a couple more years to go. The nine agilities, I somehow knew, were riding, archery, swimming and diving, climbing, participation in competitions, wrestling, fencing, long jumping . . . and dancing of all things. That was only important if one of your family members was a rich knight, though. Otherwise you could probably skip it.

Timmy's family was noble but a little poor due to them picking the wrong side of a feud and losing most of their land . . . just another futile, feudal feud. Say it three times real fast. Not quite a tongue twister but fun to say. Anyway, it seems he was a perfectly fine page but then when it came time to squire at fifteen, he couldn't find anyone due to his family situation. Fortunately, I (or my double) happened along and was in need of a sidekick, so I took him in. Tall and gangly, he was decent at long jumping, not so good at dancing or wrestling. He will have to slay a "dragon" or something if he wants to actually ever achieve knighthood, but I'm not the one to tell him.

After he bowed and stepped out, I reached over to try the bread, but it was hard as a rock, probably a couple days old. I figured I'd better go to the tavern for some ale and bread, and any info I can obtain. I didn't know where it was but guessed there would be one within a block or two, and I could ask. I scrounged around for some coins and found a few Kentish silvers and one Northumbrian. It'd work. I didn't put on any mail, just belted on a sword over my tunic, a fur pelt over my shoulders for warmth, and for good measure slipped a knife into my boot once I'd finally gotten it on without Timmy's help. I swear, time travel makes my feet swell.

Sure enough, when I went out into the slightly muddy street, I glanced each way and saw a tavern in either direction. Smoke hung heavily in the streets, coming from many hearths in the town, maybe weighted down by the English humidity. I flipped a Kentish coin, but couldn't tell whether it was heads or tails, so I went right. Where a couple of drunks were already fighting in the light spring drizzle, which had just restarted. In my modern life, I would've gone the other way, but the scene aroused my curiosity.

As I neared, I recognized them, or should I say Freddie recognized them, as two local knights, Agravain and Balin. They were drunk as skunks, spotted with mud and rolling around on the ground. A couple of townspeople were gawking and laughing which was dangerous because at any moment one of their friends might come by and run them through for being insolent, or the two knights might forget their grudge and get together and attack them. Agravain, a redhead and the bigger of the two, was drunker, and every time he started to pin the smaller one, he got dizzy and lost his focus. Then dark-haired Balin would push him off and roll on top, until Agravain would summon his strength and roll him back over. I'm not sure how they'd gotten so drunk by mid-morning, but presumably they'd started very early if not the night before.

The townspeople started placing bets of small coppers. Agravain was the favorite at first, but then we could see him starting to tire out. A fat man placed a big bet (a silver) on Balin, and then the bets started to shift in his favor. Then a tall guy placed a bet on Agravain right when Balin started to favor his wrist as if it might be sprained. Then the money started to shift back until Agravain moaned.

Finally they both rolled onto their backs trying to catch their breath. After a moment, Agravain remembered he had a knife and started to pull it from his belt, but right then, the tavern owner, a big brute in his own right, appeared in time to kick the knife out of his hand. Agravain gave up then, and they both lay back in the mud, panting. The townspeople protested, not knowing how to settle the bets.

"What was the fight about?" I asked the taverner, as he pushed aside the fat man who'd bet on Balin and headed back in.

"Who knows? They're knights." He then noticed the long sword at my side and added, "No offense, milord."

"None taken," I said and slapped a Kentish coin into his hand. "Your name is Joseph?" I suddenly remembered him. He nodded. "Serve me breakfast, good man." He nodded, then bowed slightly and gestured for me to enter.

I walked into the dimly lit tavern—*dimly lit* because the only lighting in these places is the window (or windows). Here there were three, narrow and tall, with wide[MR1] [nm2] sills, shutters, and curtains that looked like cheesecloth. Probably to keep bugs out. Glass is rare, though I've heard that the nobility in some kingdoms in France have them. At night it's even more dimly lit because shutters are closed, and the only light is from the fireplace. Don't believe those movies where there's braziers blazing everywhere and candles lit in every room. Too expensive. No, one reason it could have been called the Dark Ages was the lighting was never good.

I sat right next to the window to make sure I could see what I was eating and drinking. No worms in my bread and no flies in my ale, if you please. I'd really would've liked some coffee, but that was a pipe dream. After a minute, the ale and black bread came with a mug and a wooden plate. Next would probably be some local hangers on showing up, but that would be fine, I needed some of those to help figure out my next step. Like I said, the Prime Directive prevented me from knowing anything particularly useful. But so far, it was helpful in terms of knowing the names of some of the actors and some of the props.

I started thinking about Arthur the Just which got me into some nicknames I could attach to myself. Sir Escobar the Something wasn't going to be any good, it was too long—and those stupid knights couldn't tell the difference between my first name and last. Last names weren't common in England, mostly it was place names like Kenneth of Kent, or Marcy of Mercia, or Angela of Anglia—the population being low enough to have only one person so named per town. I could sympathize now with what Asian people have to deal with in modern times, having people always confuse the two. Frayim wasn't going to be any good either. Really, Freddie was by far the best alternative. Sir Freddie the Ferocious was pretty good but would get me into even more fights than I would already be in, and I had a mission to accomplish, although I didn't know what it was.

Other folks' names? Agravain the Aggravating. That was pretty funny. Lanslod the Clod. Balin the Boastful. That was probably accurate because most knights were. Bors the Boring—that was too obvious. Bors the Bloviator was great but over their heads and wouldn't translate well. I seemed to have a chip on my shoulder about the knights, but I didn't know why. Yet. The population seemed to share it as well. Interesting.

Then I started thinking about modern Round Table jokes I'd heard—like this one:

Lesser known Knights of the Round Table:

*"I was the knight no one expected to see on the battlefield."*—*Sir Prize*

*"I shall see you around."*—*Sir Cumference*

*"We shall fight on land or sea."*—*Sir Fenturf*
*"I was the knight who was afraid to fight."*—*Sir Render*
*"I was the unbelievable knight."*—*Sir Real*
*"I was the knight that drank too much."*—*Sir Rhosis*

Sir Fenturf was my favorite, just thinking it made me laugh. And of course my name could be one also: *Sir Freddie*—ready to hang ten at Pipeline. Get it? Say it fast a few times. Actually the bread and ale was hitting the spot. I felt better. Dark bread and dark ale probably had a couple nutrients here and there. After a while, a moderately disheveled local sidled up to me. He had messy blond hair with a cowlick and freckles partially hidden by a dirty beard.

"Buy me a drink, good Sir?" he asked.

The Kentish silver I'd spent entitled me to a day's worth of drink the way I figured, but I couldn't afford to be too drunk when I got to the Oval (not Round) table. Because there'd be a lot more drinking there, for one thing. For another, I had to keep my ears and eyes open, and for yet another, the morning's events already showed that the knights themselves were not great at self-control. So no point in not spreading the cheer around—I bought him a drink.

"Indeed. What's your name, my poor peasant friend? And what do you have to say for yourself?"

"My name is Berthulf. And I have a sorry tale to tell ye, full of injustice and woe."

"Pray speak."

"Ah, the knights, the wretched wizard Mirdynn, and the witch Mirgan have all conspired with my master, to turn me out from the lands which mine family farmed." Mirdynn was the real name of Merlin. Thomas Malory used the wizard's revised name when he wrote *Morte D'Arthur*, which popularized the legend, because he'd translated the story from the French where the name had been changed. Mirdynn sounded too much like someone full of *merde*, if you know what I mean.

"My sympathies. How so?" The fire in the back crackled almost as punctuation.

"'Tis a long story, but . . . " I looked past him at the fire, which snapped again loudly as if it noticed.

"The short version, and I'll buy you another drink . . . "

"As you wish." He bowed slightly. "The knights envied my master's land and so bought him out but didn't want me on account he said I did no hard work."

"What about Mirdynn and the witch Mirgan?"

"Oi, I just added them to make the story more enticing."

"Tell which knights, and I will buy the drink nonetheless." He was pissing me off, but I kept my head. I resisted the temptation to pick him up and toss him onto the fire. Hmm, that wasn't like me. The temptation, not the resistance—to be clear.

He nodded, "'Twas Lanslod and his son Galahat." Ha, then maybe the drink was well bought. "Why did they desire the land?"

"I believe they thought it contained secret wealth. But I know not what."

I resisted the next urge which was to bang his head against the table for exaggerating and not knowing a potentially vital piece of information. I definitely seemed to have a hot temper in this time period. The opposite of my modern personality, but perhaps explaining the (somewhat) hot streak I had centuries later as M. Saint-Simon. If Freddie was my previous incarnation, that is. Not sure about that. With all the restraint I could muster, I ended up giving him a not-that-gentle pat on the back while cursing him under my breath. I then ordered him another ale and took my mug to another table, lest he regale me with the long version of the story.

I'll use this opportunity to tell you more about my background. I was born in Connecticut in the mid-1980s. My father was a nerd, and my mother was kind of a hippie. My parents split up when I was thirteen, because my mom joined a Jesus cult, and my dad had an affair. Not sure which happened first. Then I moved to California with my dad who'd gotten a tech job in San Fernando Valley. Right about when I was eighteen, he met someone new and started a new family, which left me as the odd teenager out. Fortunately, I inherited most of his nerd brain, and got a scholarship to the university, followed by a fellowship, and then an assistantship. So I guess it wasn't illogical, after all, for me to apply to a spaceship, right?

The spaceship used anti-matter to go backwards in time, like anti-matter likes to do. That's after decomplexifying to allow it to go closer to the speed of light without gaining infinite mass and creating a black hole. One has to also find the Earth which is rotating, revolving, and meandering through space: 67,000 mph revolving, 490,000 mph meandering toward the center of the galaxy, and so on, which is why time travel requires a spaceship, not a DeLorean like in *Back To The Future*. Point of all this being: I was an unemployed, perpetual student with no ties, so I was in perfect position to either join a cult or hop a UFO. In a way, not that different from being a knight errant in the sixth (or was it the seventh?) century—though I was currently under oath to King Arthur in exchange for a small plot of land somewhere, complete with some peasants and a place at the Oval Table. Huzzah!

I decided to order some *briw* with my bread and brew. Briw was broth, usually served for dinner, but they started brewing the briw early. I wondered if they had any Brie to eat with my bread, brew, and briw. Probably not. Brie was French and the Normans weren't due to invade for another few centuries. Too long to wait. The briw was still a little watery but okay for dipping the bread.

I looked out the window. Lanslod was striding by with his teenage son Galahat. They were in full mail and surcoat with their noses in the air. Perhaps it was due to the smell because someone had just dumped a chamber pot into the street from upstairs. No sewers in this town, which is why I should remember to walk near the center of the street, horses be damned. I gestured out the window to him, wanting to find out more about his land purchase, but he glanced at me and turned away without acknowledgment. I guess he didn't like me any more than I liked him. Well, I'd find out one way or another.

Lanslod stopped to help up Sir Agravain but left Balin in the mud snoring. He wiped his hands on the side of Agravain's horse that was tied up nearby. I think it was Agravain's but really could have been anyone's. Agravain wiped his face with his sleeve, staggered to his feet, then headed inside the tavern. I motioned him to come, and he stumbled on over, then motioned to order a wash basin and ale and bread. The tavern keeper brought the wash basin and a cloth over first, and Agravain wiped his face again and his hair and hands while harrumphing a half-hearted apology for his appearance.

Well, it was really a string of mumbled curses uttered in an apologetic tone, but I got the point. The polite thing to do now was to offer condolences and a brew, but I was trying to moderate my consumption for the reasons I mentioned, and the fact that I'd just time travelled and wasn't sure about my tolerance under the circumstances. He looked at me expectantly. Heck with it.

"Good fellow, may I purchase you an ale?"

He nodded. "I think upon you favorably," he said, which meant thanks, I think, and lifted his mug to me. He'd had it strapped to his belt. I guess he didn't trust in the County Health Department here. The tavern keeper noticed his upraised mug and poured it full from a clay pitcher. "On my dime," I said, which, after I said it, realized it wouldn't mean anything, but he seemed to understand, so maybe my babelfish translated it.

"How fare you this day?" I offered, as if I hadn't witnessed his earlier drunken brawl and stupor.

"I'm stinking drunk and mad as hell," he replied. He seemed sober enough now, I thought.

"Do tell me your predicament, if you desire."

"I have tried to collect a gambling debt from Balin, but he claims to have no coin." Most of the knights were inveterate gamblers with dice and various other things.

"I assume that you need to collect for some pressing financial need."

"That is so. I need to pay back Lanslod from gambling the night before."

"Well, as he helped you up, I assume he would look accept-ingly on your delaying payment for a time."

"Not so, I must pay by tonight or forfeit some land nearby."

"That seems harsh—what land is it?"

"A small plot by the river. It only has a couple dozen peasants, but their revenue keeps me afloat so to speak." He looked down.

Out the window, a young man, probably a squire, was help-ing Balin onto a cart. Balin shouted, "Where'd he go, the don-key's ass?" Which, since a donkey was a kind of ass, would've made him an ass's ass.

"It appears Balin is calling for you." I nudged him.

"Bah," he sputtered. "I'm in here," pushing aside the cheese-cloth, he shouted out the window. "Come in and get me if you dare."

Balin staggered towards the inn, but his squire restrained him and was rewarded with a swing at his face that fortunately missed. He then fell back into the cart.

"Is there a way to get funds to pay Lanslod back?" I inter-jected, trying to distract Agravain, so he didn't run out to taunt Balin.

"Only gambling. Do you have any silver?"

I should have figured. No good deed unpunished. I had only two more, but on the other hand, he would owe me a big fa-vor—*if* he remembers. I considered for a moment, then slapped a Kentish coin on the table.

"You must regain your honor," I said stoutly. "Honor" being the number one road to destruction in ancient societies. But also a temptation hard to resist.

"I think of you favorably, good sir." He tapped the coin to his forehead in a kind of salute.

"You will be at tonight's supper, I assume?" I didn't want to come in cold.

"I wouldn't go if I could help it, but it's mandatory—don't you remember?"

"Yes, but I don't remember why," I offered.

"The Queen requires it, and of course pussy-whipped Arthur does whatever she says." I sincerely doubt he said *pussy-whipped*, but that's how I heard it.

"But why does she want it?"

"Who knows, perhaps another stupid quest . . ."

"Not again," I sighed convincingly.

"I know, first a dragon's egg, then a unicorn . . ."

"Next she'll want milk from a witch's tit." I was spit balling here.

"Ha, you forget, she already did that one. At least it was easy, since Mirgan had just given birth again. The witch likes to sard, you know. It was a lot harder to fake the dragon's egg and dress a pony into a unicorn. At least I didn't waste time searching all over Albion like the other knights, the suckers." *Sard* meant the same as a later, more famous four-letter word, I assumed, since *sard* sounded like *sword*, like the F-word, which then meant "to stab."

"So you think . . . another quest?"

"Probably. She says it develops character. But I think she just doesn't like us drinking and gambling and fighting here in town."

"Indeed. On that note, allow me to buy you another ale before I leave."

"I again think of you favorably, sir. 'Til tonight, then."

# 3

# Queen's Gambit

As I lay on my fluffed up, deluxe feather bed awaiting the call to assemble for supper with the knights, staring at the dark beams of the ceiling, I thought of the moments before the spaceship left Sedona again for here. Memories tended to pop up rather randomly after time travel, I noticed, usually the most unimportant first, but I figured I'd better let them play out and if possible, write them down.

We were kicking back in the ship after smoking some killer Martian marijuana, and the sound system was playing these weird interweaving sonics that took you into some interesting mental places, when Talmo turned off the music and out of nowhere said, "Do you want to play some ping-pong?"

"Seriously, I totally do—Do you have a table?" I loved playing ping pong in college especially when I was stoned. I glanced around the ship's bridge which gleamed like stainless steel but was some material unknown to me. It was softly luminescent and utterly unworldly. Couldn't see anywhere they could've stored a table.

"We can replicate one." He turned to the control console.

"Why not just simulate one in the Holodeck? You have one of those too, don't you?"

"Oh no, wouldn't go near them. Too addictive. We told you what happened to the Neptunians, right?"

"Oh yeah, they stopped wanting to do anything else, right?"

"Couldn't even get them to reproduce. Real life sex was too boring." Talmo waved a wand-like apparatus that he'd pulled from underneath the console, and a regulation table appeared. Wow.

"Hey, I have a question. What does the replicator make stuff out of? It's not out of thin air, right?"

"Absolutely not, we have a reservoir of miscellaneous matter on the ship. It replicates things out of that."

"But where does the matter come from? Do you load it up when you refuel?"

"Not at all, we recycle. Much more efficient."

"In other words, garbage?"

"Pretty much, plus a little sewage. Although not much— since we are gaseous beings that's mostly farts." He shrugged. "Volley for serve," he said, as he tossed the ball up. It hovered magically for an instant, but after all I was stoned. I hit it with a wicked spin, and it sailed across the net where he slammed it back, but I returned it in a smooth motion as if automatically. So fun.

"Hey, did we ever introduce you to our super bad advanced android robot?" He paused with the ball in his hand. I shook my head.

"Well, I think you'll get off on him, too," Lamo added. He slapped one finger onto his wrist, which I knew acted as some kind of remote, and a very handsome, perfectly human-like, dark-haired android appeared, bowed slightly, and said in a perfect George Clooney voice, "Hello, I am Doltly."

"Uh, *whut*?"

"That's what we named him," Talmo said. Then served a whiffer right by me. "Your serve."

"But why?" I spun a possibly illegal serve and watched it swerve in mid-air.

"To remind us. You know the first law of robotics, right?" He returned it with a little less on it.

I nodded, "I think so. A robot shall never harm a human?" I tried to slam but almost missed the table.

"No, that's the second law. The first law is: Computers are dumb." He returned it with a counter spin.

"I kind of remember something like that. But don't these androids have artificial intelligence and neural nets, and that kind of thing? I mean, we've been working on that since the nineties. And by your time, I'd have thought . . . " My return missed the table, and he caught it in his hand.

"Nope, that's almost as dumb as Doltly." He tossed it back for my serve.

"But in my time, people were already worried about what they called 'The Singularity,' which was when computers would become aware and intelligent. Then they could eliminate all the humans." I tried a speedy sideline serve.

"That's the reason for the second law, for sure, but they could only eliminate humans through a programming error or conflict."

Lamo chimed in: "Robots aren't alive, so they can't have subjectivity and therefore consciousness. People love to anthropomorphize." Talmo tipped the ball gently just over the net, it glimmered briefly, and I had to rush in to tip it back.

"A worm has more consciousness than a robot," he added. "Look, you've advanced to the point where you have voicemail, right? A critical point in the advance of civilization, certainly."

"Absolutely, all historians in our era concur on that point," Lamo agreed, nodding. "Point of fact, instead of dating eras AD and BC we date them AVM and BVM." He paused, "Well, we don't really use the same initials since we don't have the same language, but the point is the same." Talmo spun his return and I tipped it back again.

"But you don't think your voicemail is aware, do you? Even if it sounds like a real person?" Lamo asked. They both looked at me. My tip was too high and Talmo slammed it back in my face.

"Ha. Of course not."

"Then how could you imagine a robot could achieve consciousness?" he asked. I caught the ball in my hand and bounced it on my paddle a few times, taking a break. "Hmm," I muttered cleverly.

"Quantity does not change quality," Lamo observed.

"What do you mean?" The ball seemed to float every time it bounced above my paddle. Fascinating.

"No matter how long something is, it doesn't make it wider, right?"

The ball suddenly floated upwards. I looked up. Talmo was waving his paddle at it. The ball wandered over to his paddle. That was weird.

"What about water changing to steam? Isn't that a qualitative change?" I remembered that from solid state physics.

Talmo replied, "Yes, but not the same thing really. Adding more water doesn't change anything. Changing the temperature does. That's a different variable. So no matter how powerful a computer is, it can't obtain consciousness. A computer isn't more conscious than a calculator, and a calculator isn't more conscious than an abacus."

"And calculating is a different quality than being aware," added Lamo

"Computers are dumb because they only do what they are told, even when they are told to 'learn.' They learn what or how they're told to," concluded Talmo.

"And here's the final proof . . . " Lamo turned to the robot. "Doltly, would you like to get stoned?"

Doltly smiled intelligently and replied, "I can't because I don't have a mind with which to get stoned. However, I can do a reasonable simulation. Here's a sample: 'Whoa, have you ever really looked at your hands? I mean *really* looked?' Would you like to hear more of the same?"

"No thanks." Lamo said, and turned back to us laughing, "He's so lame."

"But he's great at calculating. Or anything that can be algorithmed. Even poetry, prose, hip hop. Doltly, calculate the square root of negative one."

"The number can't be calculated but is referred to mathematically as '*i*' which stands for imaginary number."

"You can't ever fool him. Now make it into hip-hop."

Without pausing, Doltly launched into a poetic hip-hop rhythm, spitting out the words:

"A square root of neg *one*/Is a calculation that can't be *done*/Can't be ended, can't be *begun.*/You might think an imaginary number is a crazy kind of notion/But it helps to describe periodic motion."

"What do you think?" Lamo asked.

I rolled my eyes. It wasn't like I wasn't familiar with AI since Chatbots took over everything including the government last year. "We have AI in my time period, you know."

"That's good, that means it was predetermined when we leaked it in our last visit. Anyway, what did you think?"

"Not bad, but he's no Pitbull," I replied.

"Of course not. Android means *man*-like, not *dog*-like."

"No, I mean the rapper."

"Oh, we're not that up on 21st century Earth. In fact, except for picking you up, we tend to avoid it."

"Why?"

"Except for all the war, disease, and famine—nothing in particular," he deadpanned.

"Right?"

"Do you want to try one?" He motioned towards the android.

"Sure. Doltly, how long will the solar system last?" I asked.

"About 395 and half more Earth years."

"What, I can't believe it, I thought we were going to save it." I felt suddenly sick.

"Sorry, I assumed you meant the solar *panel* system of the ship." The robot continued nonchalantly, "The planetary system surrounding the sun will last 3.2156 billion more Earth years before the sun explodes. However, the local life forms will have evolved past physical existence 1.07 billion years earlier."

"That reminds me of a joke," Lamo said, "A guy is listening to a planetarium lecture, and the astronomer tells the audience, 'The sun will likely go out within four billion years.' The guy stands up all agitated, saying 'How long did you say?' The astronomer repeats, 'Four billion years.' The man sighs and starts to sit back, 'Phew, I thought you said four *million* years.'"

"Haha. You guys are real cards."

"Maybe we should get moving," Talmo said. "Otherwise, Doltly will ask to play the winner. He never loses. And he's programmed to act very disappointed if you turn him down." He pulled out the wand-like device, waved it, and the table disappeared. "It also de-replicates. On Mars, before they added that function, they replicated so many things, they had to rent a giant storage locker on Uranus."

Back in my room, Timmy knocked on the door. It was getting dark, and with no heat but from the fireplace, I closed the door quickly behind him.

"It's time to go to the supper," he stated. Across his forearm, he had draped my clean and dried surcoat, showing my emblem which was two crossed swords over a thorny bush. The bush looked pretty amorphous, almost like an amoeba. I guess Freddie didn't have a good artist.

"Hey Timmy, do you remember who designed my emblem?"

"Yeah, it was my mum."

"And a great job she did," I responded. I guess Freddie was economizing.

"I'm thinking of jazzing up my emblem, what do you think?"

"Too expensive, don't you remember? That's why you asked my mom." I was right. But then I had an idea.

"What do you think about me putting the words *Joseph's Tavern—A great place for ale and bread* on my surcoat? Joseph would probably pay quite a bit to have that endorsement."

"I don't think so," he replied. "You've noticed there's no words on his sign, just a picture of a pig? Joseph can't read and neither can most of the knights except Arthur and Lanslod and Galahat."

"Too bad." Another idea ahead of its time.

I already had my mail on, so I had Timmy help me with my boots. Then he placed the surcoat on me and straightened it.

"You look dashing, Sir."

"Naturally," I responded, unsure whether one ever thanked one's underlings. Probably not.

"Well, point me in the right direction, and I'll be on my way." That was allegedly a joke, but I was serious. Not being the original Freddie, I wasn't sure where the Palace entrance was.

"To the right and then right again when you pass the gryphon on the rooftop," he humored me. Gryphon would make a nice emblem if I could find the right artist. It's an eagle with the body of a lion, for you non-gryphonologists in the audience.

Just as I passed the gryphon, which leered ominously from above, Balin caught up with me, looking much recovered, but limping just a little. He called out.

"What ho, Sir Escobar?" I think that meant *What's happening,* or maybe *What are you doing?* I thought about saying *Nothing much,* but if it was the latter then I'd sound stupid since I was obviously doing something. Maybe the babelfish wasn't working well.

"Heading to the supper, Sir Balin," I chose. "How fare you?"

"A bit stiff from fighting this morning, but otherwise fit." He stretched his arms as if to demonstrate.

Pretending I hadn't seen the fight earlier, I asked, "With whom and why?"

"Agravain, because I had no money to repay him."

"But how? Surely you have means."

"I do. But I have lost much to Lanslod, and can't collect taxes for another week," he sighed.

"Lanslod must be an excellent player, then?" I asked as we entered the Palace. A couple of guards lounged lazily just inside. Balin nodded at them, but they didn't bother to reciprocate.

"Or a better cheater. I'm inclined to believe the latter but don't dare say so, or he'll challenge me to a duel, trial by combat. Or worse." He stroked his beard.

"What could be worse? I hate dueling—all that hacking at each other," I found myself saying. Interesting.

"Who doesn't? . . . but the Queen loves to watch it."

"I just wish we could do it on horseback, that would make it so much better," I ventured.

"Absolutely, but it would never catch on." He shook his head as if the idea was utterly ridiculous.

"Ah, here we are," Balin said as we reached the room with the Oval Table.

"You go on," I said. "I need to piss." Mostly I wanted to enter alone in case Agravain was still angry at Balin. I found a dark corner and started to piss.

"Good idea," I heard from behind me. "Takes longer to fill an empty vessel than a full one. It reminds me of the time . . . " It was Sir Bors, and I needed to stop him.

"Ah, Sir Bors, begging your pardon. But I've heard we may have another quest to fulfill. Have you heard that?" Stick to yes or no questions.

"I have not," as he started to piss. "But it occurs to me . . . "

"Hold that thought," I interrupted, "For I see Sir Agravain, who owes me money, and must reach him before he enters."

I dashed off, leaving him hanging, so to speak. That one part of him, anyway.

I entered the room which was lit by a roaring hearth fire as well as some candles sitting in the middle of the Oval Table. Arthur and Queen Gwen were seated at the head. Arthur looked to be about Gwen's age—no more than forty. He must have sired Mordred at around sixteen, I guessed. Arthur had an ermine pelt on his shoulders, as did Gwen. Not white ermine but light brown, a.k.a. English stoats. So they were wearing stoat coats, haha. They both had cheesy little crowns that looked like they came from a high school prop room, but the Queen's had a nice sized ruby in the front. She was wearing a white dress, low cut, with a Roman style *chiton* over it and some pearls around the neck, and Arthur a red velvety robe. The dress looked lovely, but honestly she would have looked good in anything. In fact, she had a radiance and poise that outshined anyone I'd ever seen in all three lifetimes I'd experienced. It was hard to take my eyes off of her, but I forced myself.

Next to Gwen was seated Lanslod, then Galahat and Gawain. Lanslod was speaking with his nose in the air, so I guess that was his style and not the due to the chamber pot earlier. Unless the piss smell from me and Bors had gotten through. I sniffed but couldn't smell it, what with the smoke from the fire and candles. Gawain had a holy expression pasted on his face, eyes tilted upwards towards the heavens. Seemed tiring to me. The ventilation was a little poor, but at least the room was warm. On Arthur's side was Sir Kay, who I seemed to remember was Arthur's foster brother, then Sir Bedivere, a handsome fellow who unfortunately only had one arm, then Agravain and Balin. Apparently, the two had made up or worked out some arrangement. There was an empty seat next to Balin, so I sat there. After a minute, Bors slid into the seat at the foot of the table, and tried to start a conversation with the knight on his left, but the fellow turned away to look at the King and Queen just as Arthur had planned it.

"How are you and Agravain doing?" I asked Balin.

"Better," he smiled, "We both realized out problems are due to Lanslod, so the solution will be to no longer play or pay him."

"But Agravain's land?" I let that slip out. But he didn't notice.

"A problem, to be sure." He shook his head. "Probably only to be solved through trial by combat."

"Yikes, don't we have courts here?"

"This *is* the court. Do you think we solve problems over supper?"

"Of course not, it requires a trial with a judge."

"There *is* a judge for trial by combat. Queen Gwen."

Wow, she was a little bloodthirsty for such a lovely woman. Looks aren't everything. I looked over at her and next to her but behind a little, I noticed a familiar face. It was Delphine. My past flirtation from the well at Capernaum and the future one in Paris. Sitting behind Gwen. She had a rounder face than Gwen and fuller lips, and looked to be twenty at the most. Her name was currently Aelfhere, or so a memory bubbled up, along with other memories of stolen kisses, fevered secret embraces, and the like. My face flushed. She waved a dainty finger at me and smiled. My heart warmed, and I bowed a little.

"Are you and Aelfhere an item?" Balin, noticing, asked.

"I think so."

"Then be careful. Queen Gwen involves her Ladies in her plots."

I changed the subject. "You should tell Agravain to do the trial on horseback—I heard Lanslod is clumsy on his horse."

"Haha. You don't let go of an idea. Sure, it'd be entertaining to watch, but it'll never happen." He took a big swill of ale and wiped his mouth.

Just then the servers started bringing in the food. Pheasant and boar and legs of lamb. Very Paleo. Then parsnips and turnips in some sauce. Yuck. I reached for my ale.

As I drank, I started to recall memories of Aelfhere. See, generally memories are from the person I replaced. I suspect they may be uploaded from that person's brain, hopefully when the person is already dead or at least unconscious. The thought of it happening otherwise gave me a shudder. Alternatively, the memories could be in the headset that the Venusians give me that is supposed to provide background knowledge.

So I remembered that Aelfhere was born on Twelfth Night, which made her a Capricorn. Her parents were landowners of moderate wealth which was ideal for a queen's lady. She was very sweet, but underneath I suspected—or rather, Freddie suspected—that she was quite calculating. That fit with being a Capricorn and also with Balin's warning. Freddie didn't care, having totally the hots for her, but I needed to be careful. She was extremely demure, well-mannered, and charming, all of which were perfect qualities for a queen's lady. But I also suspected that along with the calculating-ness, she had some fire beneath the surface. But that part would only make things more fun.

After dinner, I slouched back in my seat, watching the shadows from the fireplace. It was considered rude to the King to get up from the table and make conversations with others so long as he was sitting, and I was talked out with Balin. I looked over at Sir Bors, merrily chattering away at his neighbor who was slumped down with a beaten expression on his face. At the table's head, Queen Gwen was raptly listening to Lanslod bragging, if the position of his nose was any indication, while Arthur slouched, clutching his ale in a death grip. Aelfhere was leaning forward, chatting with another lady, and sneaking looks at me and smiling. Hopefully, I'd get a chance to talk with her a little when the supper broke up. Arthur reached over and tapped Gwen on the shoulder, but she ignored him. He tried again with similar results. Finally he grabbed her shoulder and turned her to him, and whispered something to her. She reddened in response and faced the table.

"Be quiet," Arthur shouted over the dinner noises. The table fell silent, except for Bors who kept talking for nearly a minute, before noticing. "The Queen has an announcement to make."

"She's getting a divorce," Agravain mumbled, before Balin shushed him. Divorce was forbidden under church law, but that made it even funnier.

Gwen stood, her cheeks still flushed from the reprimand by Arthur. I guess he had really read her the riot act.

"Gallant knights, I . . . " she fumbled for words,

"Want a divorce . . . " Agravain whispered, laughing.

"Shut up," Balin said, a little too loudly, making the closest knights turn to us. Agravain made a face showing that despite being shushed, he was unrepentant. Then he winked.

"I want to ask you . . . ," she paused again, then tried a different tack. "Sir Lanslod has told me of a holy relic, perhaps the holiest of them all, that has made its way to our land. It is the Holy Cup encrusted with precious rubies that our Lord drank from at his last supper, and that Joseph of Arimathea brought to England centuries ago. It is called the Grail due to the blood-red rubies symbolizing the blood of our Heavenly King."

Now I happened to have been at that dinner as Matthew, and I can tell you that number one, Josh didn't drink from a jewel-encrusted cup, and number two, Joseph of Arimathea wasn't even there. It is possible that Joseph helped bury Josh—I wasn't there for that part— but no way did Josh carry the cup from that last supper into a Roman jail, trial, and execution. Nor was it likely that anyone else did, given that we were all running for our lives, cowards that we were. So this "holy cup" was a fake of some sort, but I knew gems and crystals figured into Josh's mission in various ways, so I kept listening.

"I am asking my gallant knights to participate in a quest for this Holy Grail, that the honor of our Kingdom be known throughout Christendom."

Always with the Christendom thing. Didn't anyone tell them about honoring diversity?

She continued, "The knight that obtains the Grail shall be given the honor of wearing my ribbon!"

She smiled, and held up a light blue ribbon. The knights cheered. Whoopie Doo, a ribbon! That might have motivated me in first grade. Naw, kindergarten.

And then it was time for entertainment, so Arthur stood a little tipsily and announced, "And now, a fellow that needs no introduction, our very own Dagen the jester!" He paused, but there were only a few claps, more groans, and some catcalls.

"No puns," Galahat shouted out.

"Hear, hear," several others seconded. Then they sportingly started calling out Dag's greatest hits, and cheering and booing the various suggestions: "Do Mirdynn!" "How about the witch?" "Do a dog!" "The wide-mouthed frog!"

Then a chant arose, "Wide-mouthed frog, wide-mouthed frog, wide-mouthed frog . . . "

They'd heard the act a dozen or more times but apparently never tired of it. Forgive me for repeating it if you've heard it, but it was indeed a classic passed down by generations of wide-mouthed jesters. Dag downed his ale and launched right in:

"Once upon a time there was a wide-mouthed frog who decided to see the world. He left his pond to explore. First he met a bird. 'Hello,'" Dag said, slurring his words by opening his mouth almost to the widest possible extent, "'Who are you and what do you eat?' The bird said, 'I'm a bird and I eat worms.' 'The frog replied, 'I'm a wide-mouthed frog, and I eat fli-i-i-i-i-es . . .'" Dag opened his mouth even wider. "Then he met a cow, and the frog said, 'Who are you and what do you eat?' The cow said, 'I'm a cow and I eat grass.' 'I'm a wide mouthed frog and I eat f fli-i-i-i-i-es . . .'," opening his mouth wider yet. "Then he met a cat, and asked, 'Who are you and what do you eat?' The cat said, 'I'm a cat, and I eat mice.' The frog answered, 'I'm a wide-mouthed frog. and I eat fli-i-i-i-i-es . . .'," Dag said, opening his mouth still wider. "Then he met a snake, and asked, 'Who are you and what do you eat?' The snake replied, 'I'm a snake, and I eat wide-mouthed frogs'." Dag pursed his lips up as tiny as possible and whispered, "'Oh . . .'"

The knights guffawed, slapped their knees, and cheered as if they'd never heard anything so funny. Like I said, they aren't too bright. Dag took a bow and then started juggling while making funny faces. The knights were rolling in the aisles more or less, tears streaming down their faces.

As things seemed to be breaking up, and the King had stood up, I arose and slid over to Aelfhere, "Is it possible for me to see you tomorrow?"

"Freddie, you know you can't come and see me in the palace. But maybe I can come see you for a little bit during the Queen's nap." I started to kiss her cheek, but she pushed me away. "Not in public—I keep telling you that."

Oh well, another complicated love affair. It seemed like I had a bit of a pattern. I wondered if Elisabet was around in this lifetime. Something told me no, she wasn't. Well, I'd only be here for a few weeks if my last couple adventures were any indication. Best not take things too seriously, which is good advice, even if you are around for a full incarnation.

"I know," I said, even though I didn't know until she told me. "But tomorrow is the longest time," I added a pout and some puppy dog eyes for effect. She smiled, saying, "Verily, you are a sweet pea." I made a little bow and smiled back. "I will come after dinner or send a message," she said.

Dinner was lunch, apparently. She gave me a little air kiss and turned back to Gwen who was just reaching out to her.

I turned around to see Sir Bors approaching, then glanced all around for a possible escape, finding no one but Lanslod nearby. I headed toward him.

"Hello *Escobar*," he said, accenting the first syllable in a voice dripping with iciness.

"Hello *Sir* Lanslod," I replied, moving the emphasis and iciness to the Sir, which implied a sarcastic lack of respect to him or maybe a chiding reminder of him to respect me. Hard to tell. Nuance can be lost when time traveling.

His expression shifted in a way difficult to discern. "Would you like to join us for some games of dice?"

Ah, perhaps his plan was to indebt me like he did with Agravain and Balin.

"I shall decline, I do not like to gamble."

"Yet since gambling is forbidden to the common people, it is a point of honor for a knight to never decline. Just as he would never decline a challenge to combat." He looked around, making sure others had heard him.

He was practically calling me a coward. I felt a hot surge in my chest and was about to strike out at him, when Dag behind him, shook his head, mouthing "No, no."

"Do not mistake my hesitation for cowardice," I firmly asserted. "I have no head for numbers, and today I've drunk much ale. Another time I will satisfy you, providing the stakes are not excessive."

"I will take you up on it," he replied. I should have just let myself be cornered by Bors.

But no, it's never too late to be cornered by a bore like Bors. He'd come up right behind me, tapping me on the right shoulder. I turned to the right to see who it was, and he stepped to the left. I swear knights were about as mature as first graders. But again, maybe it was a new trick back then.

"Freddie," he took a deep breath. Bores always presume to call you by the most familiar name. "Have I told you that Arthur's illegitimate son is due to return to the burh shortly?"

No, you did not. And that is actually interesting. But before I could encourage him to speak, he turned away. "Oh. I forgot to finish the story I was telling Gawain! Be back shortly."

Goddamn it. Ooops, there went several minutes of mantra. That's what they told me on the ship. Your mantra was the only action you could do that—long-term—actually benefited you, and swearing tended to cancel it out. Maybe I could do a few minutes before I went to sleep. If I did twenty minutes a day, I could do my 72,000 in ten years. Of course, if I went back to Elisabet's time, or even stayed here, I doubt I'd last that long. Maybe I should have stayed in my own time after all. I wondered what happens if you don't do enough. Do you get a lesser incarnation or just not move forward? But since it's all predetermined, maybe you stay the same but just feel more screwed up. Oh well. This predetermination thing is hard to figure out. Impulsively, I touched my nose three times to see if I had free will. Nothing stopped me, but maybe I was predetermined to do so? *Whatever*! I shrugged a bit hostilely to myself.

Arthur's illegitimate son was Mordred. That I remembered from the movie *Camelot* or something. He would lead a rebellion against Arthur and/or Lancelot. Couldn't remember exactly, but Lanslod wasn't much like in the movie except for the handsome part. I wonder if he's having an affair with Gwen right as we speak. I looked around the room but didn't see either of them. Maybe they'd already snuck off somewhere.

I'll bet Aelfhere knows all about it, though she might be sworn to secrecy, who knows. I don't recall my role in *anything*, anywhere, so that's no help. But anything that I knew in history will probably turn out to be wrong—that's been my experience, so far.

Well, the pieces seem to be falling into place, fingers crossed, so maybe it'll all work out anyway.

# 4

# Don't Say Gay

I decided to start the day out with breakfast in bed. Well, not really—but the next best thing. I had to get out of bed to go get it, but since I was a little hung over from the previous day's ale drinking, I decided not to hit the tavern right away. In fact, I'd discovered that my lodging place, known as the Queen's Inn, offered meals, so long as you were there at the right time and weren't too particular about what you stuffed down your gullet. I was hungover but fortunately had overcome my time/space lag.

So I decided to check it out. The inn's main door was right next to mine, so I went out and right back in. Apparently I had a luxury suite, as I not only had a feather bed but a separate entrance. Inside, the other residents were gathered around a table eating and drinking. A single small glass-less, even cloth-less window, plus the fireplace illuminated the room slightly. Some smoke from the fireplace didn't like the chimney, so it hovered near the ceiling. I coughed. The residents were drinking river water and sipping something halfway between oatmeal and soup, in very coarse stoneware bowls on a thick picnic-style table.

"Yo, what're you eating?" I said heartily.

"Pottage, of course—Have some?" A thin, squint-eyed man responded.

I bent over and smelled. It was not unappetizing, but then it wasn't appetizing either. Definitely a gray area. I sniffed the water, too, while my head was bent. Smelled like algae. Possibly the tavern was a better idea. Just then, the matron of the place came up and introduced me to the others.

She was white-haired and chubby with a red nose and cheeks. "This is Sir Escobar, who has been here these last few weeks in the annex. He's finally come to dine with us. Give him a warm welcome."

The six residents all applauded as if my appearance had somehow validated their very existence. There were five men and a woman, all mousy and thin. Their clothes were pretty threadbare and featured numerous patches. The matron introduced me around the table to all six, but their names didn't stick in my head for even a minute before they departed to wherever non-memories go. I sat, and she poured me a glass of river water and ladled me a bowl of pottage.

The squinty man chimed in, "If you come tomorrow, there will be bread and cheese. The King lets us bake in one of his ovens once a fortnight. And on Friday we will have fish, God willing, as it's our day to fish in the King's river. And finally, the following day we might even have rabbit or a rodent, as that's our day to trap in the King's woods. Really, it'll be a great week."

I dipped my wooden spoon gingerly into the pottage.

"So the king owns the ovens, the river, and the woods hereabouts?"

"Of course, and he owns the air too, which is why we can't eat doves or pigeons except once a fortnight."

"Once a fortnight?"

"Yes, every 14th residence has its chance each day. It's very fair. That's why we call him Arthur the Just, you know."

"What if you can't catch anything on your day?

"Well, then it's just pottage and *briw*, of course. It's almost filling, you know."

I tasted the pottage. It wasn't terrible. But it wasn't good either. Basically it was watery oatmeal with bits of parsnips and turnips—again. I swished it around and could see no meat. Probably just as well.

"Would you like some water?" I declined. "In a few days, we will make cider . . . " he offered.

"Your day in the King's orchard?" He nodded.

When I got up to leave, all my housemates stood up and bowed. I opened the door out, noticing another typical drizzly English day and dodged right into my doorway where Timmy was huddled.

"The lady Aelfhere is inside, my liege." Love that!

"Thank you, Timmy, I won't need you. Is there anything at the palace tonight?"

"Yes indeed. A message was given to me that there will be a planning meeting to organize the quest."

"Organize? I assumed quests were kind of like personal individual things."

"Yes, but the King felt the last quest lacked organization. So we will get organized."

I shrugged and opened the door. Aelfhere was sitting primly at the table, looking off into space. "I've come as you requested," she said. "But I shan't be able to stay long, as the Queen's naps are often short."

"That's too bad, I was hoping to spend some quality time."

"Quality? Oh, you mean caresses," she blushed. After a pause, she offered, "Two days hence, the Queen will entertain Sir Lanslod, so she will send me out on errands, and you may caress me as much as you like." She was exceptionally cute and charming, but I wondered how much personality she had in this lifetime. In the 17th century, as Delphine, she was a real sparkplug.

"That will be nice, I know these rough quarters are hardly fitting a gentle woman such as yourself."

"Freddie, you know such things as these are not important to me. I can endure them until we marry at your castle in Galilee."

Uh-oh, it appears my alter ego told a bit of a whopper, in that there would be no castles in Galilee until the Crusaders built one in Tiberias in the 12th century. Perhaps he actually had a plan to obtain wealth and build one though, who knows. Or maybe she just meant a burh and the babelfish mistranslated.

"What's the news in the palace today? Anything interesting?" I asked, changing the subject.

"Yes, Sir Mordred has arrived and has started some kind of trouble, but I don't know what." So Bors was right. Perhaps I could find out more at the organizational meeting.

"Anything else?"

"Yes, Sir Lanslod has challenged Sir Agravain to trial by combat over a debt. But the King has postponed it until after the quest, because no knight may have blood on his hands for the quest and Lanslod is expected to both win the contest and find the Grail."

"Was that the Queen's request?" She nodded.

I said, "Come here and let me have a few brief kisses before you depart." She came over, sat on my lap and kissed me. Kisses that were both familiar and different from the ones I experienced in Paris eleven centuries later. They were a bit rawer and more passionate but less sensitive. It was as if one's talents developed over the lifetimes. But there was an innocence now that was charming to make up for the difference. She kissed me harder and then stood up.

"I must go. But perhaps I will see you in the hallway tonight." She smiled and gave me a parting peck on the cheek.

I lay around after she left, trying to piece together my mission. Lanslod was clearly up to no good, between boinking the Queen and trying to get the knights all indebted to him. Mordred would be plotting to overthrow the King, or even assassinate him. The Grail was clearly a part of the situation, but the question of whether it was a fake or not—well, that wasn't clearly a part of its significance, at least at this point. Agravain and Balin seemed like good fellows—if they stayed on good terms with each other and if Agravain survived his duel with Lanslod. Bors was a nuisance but clearly plugged into the palace gossip. Galahat and Gawain seemed to be part of Team Lanslod.

What was Gwen and Arthur's role? It almost seemed like Arthur was a figurehead or dupe but maybe there was more to it?

And Gwen, was she just a gold-digger who worked her way up to the top of the heap? She did not have a hard edge to her eyes, but it was really difficult to look past so much beauty and grace to see what was truly inside.

After a while, there was a knock on the door. It was a messenger boy, telling me to come down the street to Joseph's tavern to meet Kasper and Mateno. Kasper and Mateno were the aliases of Talmo and Lamo back in Josh's time. Why were they reusing those names? And why did they not just come to my door?

I told the boy I'd be there shortly and closed the door.

It was still drizzling, so I dressed up like before with pants and tunic and pelt. By the way, it's not like in the movies when you wear a pelt. You don't wear it fur up, so it looks fancy—you wear it fur down, so it's warmer. Duh. Except when it's ermine, I guess, and you want to show off. It took me a while to pull on my boots which made me realize how important a squire was in the life of a knight, for that reason alone.

I stepped out into the afternoon drizzle, and made my way to Joseph's place avoiding mud puddles and horse droppings, and especially where the two combined. I realized they never showed you that in any movies about the olden days. I recalled seeing something on PBS that by the beginning of the 20th century, New York City was producing 2.5 million pounds a day of horse manure. That was almost half a pound for each and every man, woman, and child each and every day. Add that to another pound of poop humanly produced, and that was a lot of crap, so to speak. At least they had toilets by then for the most part. We didn't. Which reminded me. I jumped to the middle of the street, remembering the chamber pot dumped out of the 2nd floor window yesterday.

I managed to make it to Joseph's without stepping in any puddles or poop, or being run down by horses. I opened the door and right away saw Kasper and Mateno sitting by the window where I was the day before. Apparently they too had concerns about eating the food in dim light. They had beards again, unlike on the ship, and were clothed somewhat similarly to how they dressed in Josh's time, but with trousers replacing the robes and caps replacing turbans. They waved me over.

When I sat, Kasper slapped me on the back. "What ho, Freddie? Just dropped in to check on you."

Still not sure of the precise meaning, I answered as with Balin. "I had a pleasant meal at the inn, and spoke to the Queen's lady, Aelfhere today."

"A sweet girl," Mateno acknowledged. "Making any progress?" I wasn't sure if he meant with her or in general. I chose the latter. "I'm starting to get a bit of the lay of the land but haven't really figured out my purpose yet."

"As you know, we can't tell you," Mateno commented.

"Unless you say please, and it doesn't advance civilization in any way or benefit any humans, cats or dogs," Kasper added.

"But horses are okay. I know. Please, *please* will you tell me something about my mission, just to get me started? And by the way, why are you still called Kasper and Mateno?"

Mateno replied: "Too many cover stories get confusing. We switch to Smith and Brown after 1200. We can ride that for almost another millennium or so. But I think we can give you a couple hints, right?" He glanced over at Kasper.

"Sure. As you've probably already figured," Kasper explained, "Gwen and Lanslod are having an affair, and Mordred wants to assassinate the King. It's tricky whether it's better he succeed or fail because both options have some bad effects. Even more important is who succeeds the King, whether it's now or later. It can't be Mordred or Lanslod. The Grail is important too, but we can't tell you why. You need to remember these places—Glastonburh and Salisburh. You should probably try to contact Mirdynn, but that might be hard because he's busy practicing astral projection. Have you tried this cider?"

I shook my head. They passed me a mug. I took a swig, and it was darned good, and packed a good kick, probably 7 or 8 percent alcohol. Burhs, as you know, were fortified towns, so in modern terms, that would be Glastonbury and Salisbury. Glastonbury was a powerful spot for some reason I couldn't remember—maybe the Grail? And Salisbury plain was maybe where Stonehenge was located—or was it?

"This is great cider. Is it from the King's woods?"

Kasper and Mateno laughed. "Hardly. He doesn't let the peasants in on the best days. But we replicated a great batch and switched out Joseph's barrels. It'll probably only last a week, so get it while you can."

After I left the tavern, I got in a nice nap, and before I knew it, Timmy was knocking on the door, telling me to get ready for the planning meeting.

"What's the dress code tonight?"

"Chainmail and surcoat plus your helmet and sword."

"Really? I wonder why."

"No idea, but the messenger said to be sure to bring them."

I looked over at my sword. It was a beautiful weapon of damascene steel with a handle engraved with some kind of swirly curlicues. It was a lot heavier than the swords I practiced with in France or the lightsaber I had in Josh's time. Hopefully, we wouldn't have to do any demonstrations until I had a chance to get used to it. Or worse yet, any trials by combat. Or any other combat, for that matter.

"Hey Timmy," it made me think, "When was the last war, hereabouts?"

"Quite a while ago. At least six months."

"Oh," I felt like the wide mouthed frog. "Who did we fight against?"

"Kent, of course. They are the most powerful so they're always trying to expand. They grabbed some lands to the east. Before that it was some Celts."

"What happened?"

"We lost, but put up a valiant effort."

"How did we do against the Celts?"

"We lost, but . . ."

"Put up a valiant effort. Do we ever win?"

"Generally, no. We just don't have enough knights. That was why Arthur put out the call for knights to join the Round Table."

"Which is now oval. How many came?"

"Just you."

"Seriously? I can't believe it!"

"Well, you can probably count Mordred, since he's back now."

"So we literally have a dozen knights?"

"No, there's a few score in nearby estates, but they don't come here unless Arthur pays them. And Arthur prefers to save his money . . . And his food."

"Well, that's no way to run a railroad!" I snorted.

"What kind of road?"

"Never mind."

I followed the same route to the palace as the night before but didn't meet anyone on the way. The two guards outside waved me in, and right inside to a curved stone stairway. Having always been fond of spiral and similar staircases, I thought I'd pause to explore. I realized that except for the two fellows in front, there weren't any guards, so it wasn't really much of a risk. Perhaps the people loved Arthur so much he didn't worry, or perhaps he was confident enough in his ability to defend himself. Or maybe he was just sloppy. Of course, there were always a few knights hanging around shiftlessly, so maybe that was enough protection. I always liked looking down from above, so I climbed all the way up until I reached a stout wooden door with an iron knob. I glanced down and saw that no one else was entering, so I tried the door. The knob turned but it was bolted. I could hear voices within. Gwen's and Arthur's. They were having an argument. I pressed my ear close.

"You embarrassed me last night." That was Gwen speaking.

"You embarrass *me*—always flirting with Lanslod and quoting his conversations." I pressed closer not wanting to miss anything.

"Who else should I quote? You never talk to me."

Typical marital dispute, I thought. He's going to say *I'm busy, I'm trying to run a kingdom, you know.*

He said, "I'm busy trying to run Cantmell, aren't I?" Pretty dang close. Now she's going to say *-Maybe if you didn't spend so much time . . .* doing something or other, who knows?

She said, "Maybe if you didn't spend so much time praying . . ." *Whut*? I wouldn't have guessed that one.

"I'm trying to be more holy, like you *used to* want."

"And your damn falcons." Well, that was a little more normal.

His voice raised. "Leave them out of it!" Of *course* he said that.

"And gambling with Lanslod! You could have bought me another pearl necklace!" Her voice was rising, too. Lanslod probably also had Arthur in debt.

Then there was a crash. Something was thrown. Couldn't tell who or what.

Then there was silence. Finally, Arthur said, "We need to go, the knights are here for the meeting."

I crept down the stairs just in time to see Sirs Kay and Bedivere entering the palace, Kay with his helmet in one hand and his other on his sheathed sword, while Bedivere, being one armed, carried his sword in hand but his helmet crooked on his elbow.

"What ho, Escobar," Sir Kay bellowed, "What are you doing, you greasy Jew?"

Maybe I had a guilty smirk on my face or maybe he was an asshole. I was used to insults, being called a greasy Spaniard once or twice in Normandy. But why? I didn't grease my hair. I guess it was my olive complexion.

"Nothing, paleface. You speak with forked tongue." I used to watch Lone Ranger reruns as a little kid. Came in handy. I stepped back in case the fellow drew his weapon.

But Bedivere stood in his way. "No quarreling," he said. "Our meeting is due to start, and I don't want to miss any of it— for I aim to be the one who finds the Grail."

He looked me over. Then, calmly, "Perhaps you will do us the favor of standing aside, since Sir Kay is intoxicated and requires extra space."

Graciously, I took one more step back, did a mock bow, then waited until they were well ahead. I congratulated myself on my restraint, until I realized that my snarky comment, even though not understood, could still have provoked a clash since Kay was drunk. And maybe even sober if he was as much of an ass as he seemed. Well, I guess I can still give myself a C plus, ha.

When I got into the oval table room, all of the knights were seated there, talking loudly with one another. Gwen and a fellow in religious garb sat behind Arthur, along with Aelfhere. The only space open at the table was next to Bors, unfortunately. Fortunately, he was already talking to the knight next to him, who already, too, had a pained expression. The room was lit, dimly as usual, by the also usual fire and by candles on the table near the front wall. The usual smoke also caught in my throat, so I fought the usual cough. Didn't work. There was a deerskin nailed and stretched on the wall, and Arthur was writing on it with a quill or something. Gwen was leaning forward, talking to him softly, apparently telling him what to write. Two knights were conversing, just the other side of Bors and I heard the name Mordred, but couldn't make out what was being said. Amidst the shadows cast from the candlelight, it was a little difficult to make out what Arthur was doing all the way from where I sat at the very foot of the table, but by squinting I saw it was a rough map of the English island. Not that much like it actually, but it *was* long and tall with some protruding parts that looked like Cornwall in the south and Scotland to the north. Actually, it looked like a squirrel sitting on its tail, but that's just me. There was a small circle approximately where we were located geographically that represented us. Really pretty minor league, if I had to describe, sad to say. Arthur started drawing lines outward from the small circle, kind of like a football playbook.

He turned to us with a serious expression. "Before I begin, I would like Bishop Wulfric—fresh from Dorchester—to say a few invigorating words to inspire us and increase our faith." He turned to the bishop, who a-hemed and stepped forwards. He was a mousy man with thin lips and nostrils that flared, wearing silk and a pointy hat. One thing I've noticed about organized religion is it's all about the hats. Unless they shave their heads, or the tops of them, into tonsures like the monks. I wonder why that is? I guess if it was about the feet or armpits, no one would notice how holy you were. I wondered if the reason why Christianity took a few hundred years to take off was that they hadn't yet gotten hats.

The bishop pursed his lips then spoke, as his bored guards leaned against their lances lazily. "Noble knights . . ." He paused for dramatic effect. One of his guards yawned. "I wish to impress upon you the importance of this *most* holy quest. Christendom is threatened from many quarters. From without, the Danes.

And an even *worse* scourge from within. Knights, I speak of the unholy deeds of the effeminate, who rot our land to its core."

The effeminate? Did he mean gays?

"Even now the effeminate spread from taverns in Winchester to my own city and beyond. As with Sodom and Gomorrah, it may cause our country to burn . . ."

Yep, it was the gays. Clearly the cause of all the world's problems. Excepting plague, poverty, war, and famine, not to mention injustice and treachery. Oh well. He started droning on about the various sins of the effeminate and the virtues of manliness, and my mind started to wander.

I started thinking about the anti-matter drive on the ship, wondering exactly what happens when an anti-particle and particle meet: It would have to give off energy because of the impact. And it must result in the creation of at least two photons because the colliding antiparticles are destroyed and thus must have no net momentum, whereas a single photon always has momentum which would be contradictory. *Now would the photons be photon and anti-photon?* That seemed obvious, but since photons are chargeless, the photon and anti-photon actually would be *identical*—except for their opposite momentum. Dang! I wished I took more physics but that would have meant less time for smoking pot.

I smoked pot because I was depressed because college was a big impersonal institution and I felt lost. Then I was depressed because I couldn't find a job in my field despite all my education which is why I was tempted to board a spaceship. Well, that's way ahead in the future and back in my past. I have bigger fish to fry. Well, more immediate fish to be precise.

My awareness returned to the room where the bishop was winding up to a thrilling conclusion. " . . . but we have a chance to change our course," he practically shouted. "Finding the Grail will elevate our holiness to an unprecedented level, so high that the bestial effeminate will depart our shores or burn. Join in this quest to save our lands!"

The knights gave a rousing cheer. The bishop folded his hands and gave a slight bow. His guards pretended to look interested, but clearly they'd heard this all many times before. They adjusted their grips on their notched spears almost in unison.

King Arthur stepped forward. "We will send everyone in different directions and to different places. First, who would like to go to Winchester? Raise your hands."

Everybody but me did. Winchester was the party capital of England as well as the actual capital of Wessex. Didn't matter to the knights that the effeminate were out in force there. Or maybe it was an added attraction to find out what these monsters were really like. Also, King Cenwalh had recently constructed a small but beautiful cathedral now called Old Minster to placate the bishops as well as a row of whorehouses to placate the knights. The knights started clamoring noisily and even trying to push down each other's hands.

Queen Gwen stood, and the knights quieted. She asked, "Is there anyone whose first choice is not Winchester?"

Silence. Finally, I raised my hand. "I'd like to go to Glastonburh or Salisburh." Several knights chortled, and others rolled their eyes.

"Is there anyone else that wants to go to either place?" No one volunteered. "Then you may go to either or both, as you choose."

Perfect. Gwen drew arrows in their direction on the skin, and I think scrawled the letter E next to them. But I couldn't be sure because shadows from the candles flickered across the skin.

"Does anyone want to go to Lindisfarne?" That was the holy island, a good candidate at least on paper for the Grail. There was half-hearted stirring. Finally Gawain raised his hand. There was some chuckling but not as much. Maybe ''cause it fit his image. Most of the knights were holding out for Winchester or somewhere similar. Gwen realized that as well. She frowned.

"You realize that only one of you will go to Winchester, right? So you had better start picking your second choices, hadn't you?"

"Eboracum!" Agravain immediately shouted out. Now called York, it was where Emperor Constantine was crowned in 306 AD, but though it had seen better days, was still known for its whorehouses as well. Gwen put the appropriate letters next to arrows that were already drawn in those directions.

Balin chimed in, "Legacester!" That was modern Chester. Gwen wrote a B next to that arrow. A safe bet because it was the nearest big city with plenty of taverns. Unfortunately, right on the border of Wales, so subject to military draft by the king of West Mercia, but hey, otherwise probably worth the risk.

Pretty soon all the assigned places were taken by the various knights except Arthur and Lanslod, who everyone assumed both wanted to stay home to protect Gwen, especially from each other.

Then I realized: Since every photon emitted had to be eventually absorbed, the photon paradox probably proved that the universe was expanding and space cooling, although at this moment I can't remember why. I jumped up and almost blurted something out before I remembered where I was and that anything I said would be seen as gibberish at best, and witchcraft at worst. Which raised an interesting question in my mind: Was homophobia somehow related to witch-hating? It seemed possible, since gays were effeminate and witches were women, and manliness was the order of the day. Wow, a lot to think about. I wish Talmo and Lamo had left me a bud or two. Anyway, I quickly sat back down, mumbling, "Never mind."

As the planning meeting broke up, Aelfhere came to me and shyly said, "I will come to you tomorrow after dinner." Which meant after lunch. "But first I must discuss something very important with you."

"Go ahead."

"Not here, privately. Let us walk down the hall." I nodded and we walked through the dim hallway.

"Before we marry, there is something I must ask you . . ."

"Of course, verily. What is it?"

"The wizard Mirdynn visited the Queen last week. And he foretold some troubling events. He said that Mordred would return and that his return would cause a schism amongst the knights. And that many of them would turn against the King."

"Yes, and it wouldn't take a wizard to foretell that would happen after Mordred came."

"He said that the queen would be forced to choose between Lanslod and the King, and whomever she chose against would die."

"That makes sense. The Queen is well-loved and could sway both the knights and the people. Not that the people count, of course. I'm assuming she will choose Lanslod—Is that right?"

"I believe so. Although she would prefer the King not die."

"Of course. And your question is whom shall I support?" I stared down at my feet, grimacing.

"Unfortunately, yes. I love both the King and Queen, but my love and duty are greater to her. Will you support her whatever she decides?"

"You know I don't like to get involved in politics . . . " I raised my head and looked her in the eyes.

"But you must choose. Mordred says whoever is not for him is against him."

"And how does Lanslod figure in?"

"Lanslod would reign with the Queen if Arthur dies. But not if Mordred overthrows Arthur first." She pursed her lips.

"So it seems like the Queen should support the King."

She glanced both ways before responding in a low voice, "Lanslod believes the knights will prefer him to either Arthur or Mordred."

"That's probably true. But it's no indication of how things will turn out."

"Yes, the Queen knows that. But she's in love with Lanslod, and if Mirdynn is right, siding with the King might mean Lanslod's death."

"Maybe not, if she can convince Lanslod to side with the King. Has she asked you to sound out the knights?"

She nodded, "Yes, but subtly. With you, I can be more direct."

"Well, I don't know. I don't like to choose. Seems like a lose-lose proposition."

"What do you mean? One can only lose once."

"Never mind.  I can't decide."

"But you must." She turned away. "I must go back. You will tell me when I come tomorrow."

That sucked. I hated decisions. Especially choosing sides. In graduate school, there were two star professors in my department. Naturally, they hated each other. They competed in literally everything. Including graduate students. They each wanted the best of them on their team of assistants. So they threw parties in the first semester to get to know us. Then they tried to recruit us as research or teaching assistants. Whoever you chose would be your mentor and help you get grants, dissertation ideas, etc. But the other would become your enemy and try to thwart you in all of those. It was good preparation for feudalism, I guess. I knew plenty of students who got caught in the middle. Myself, I opted out as soon as I could and got a job in the social science lab, outside of their reach. But that meant I had no mentor at all, which didn't help me overcome my procrastination, and I never finished.

Yeah, indecisiveness was the big weakness of my modern self. I could never decide anything and usually ended just throwing my hands up and acting impulsively, as if I hadn't thought things through at all. My decision to get on the time/spaceship was a perfect example as was my decision to stop off here. That's why I liked the concept that everything was predetermined, because it let me off the hook. But on the other hand, there were choices to make, and they didn't seem to be conditioned. And on the third hand, Talmo and Lamo had a full time job "correcting" others' previous actions. And on the fourth . . . Oh no, I had to stop this. I started tapping my hand on the wall to see if it was predetermined when I would stop. No, it seemed like it was my choice but was that a good indication? Probably not. At least debate the present matter! Comparatively, that was simple. Both sides sucked. The knights were crooked, mean, and exploitative. Arthur was a weak idealist, who would be exploited by whoever came next, even if he defeated Mordred and the knights. And Mordred, from what I remembered as Freddie, wasn't as bad as people said. As Freddie, of course, I was a knight errant knocking about different kingdoms, avoiding exactly this kind of political conflict. When there was a choice between two sides, my choice was neither. I left.

But now I was here on a mission. Whatever it was. And I couldn't leave anyway. But it meant thinking clearly enough to pick the right course.

Which side did Aelfhere prefer? The Queen's. But the Queen hadn't decided either. And wouldn't the Queen follow the general decision of the knights? The knights didn't respect Arthur and would obviously choose Mordred. I'd even heard them mention his name at supper. And what about Lanslod? What was his play? Was he lobbying people too? Or was the Queen lobbying on his behalf? Would my vote make a difference? Or would it just be a question of whether there was a black mark against my name if I picked wrong when the decision was finally made.

I'd made my way down the stairs and was now at the palace entrance. Faced out into the dark. Still no other guards. Did that mean the knights had already decided against the King?

I stumbled down the street lost in doubts and second guesses. It was lit only by the moon and an occasional candle on a windowsill. After quite a bit, I found myself in front of the sign of the Pig, the tavern right by the inn. I'd probably been walking in circles for a while. I considered going in and having some ale. But then I thought better and turned around. There was a river a few blocks away, I suddenly remembered. Maybe I could stand on the bridge, and watching the water would clarify my thoughts. Or I could jump off. Ha, I'd tried playing the suicide card before. Before Sedona . . . and Joshua H. Christ. No point in being redundant. I wandered through the gates out of the burh. There were a few houses outside and then the river.

By the time I got to the bridge, I'd had another thought. I looked over the edge at the swollen waters and watched the current eddy around some branches. A little bit of light from the crescent moon reflected in the ripples. Maybe the Queen was just testing everyone's loyalty?

Naw. Not likely. She was torn between two lovers, the King she'd married and owed everything, and the conceited handsome jerk who'd seduced her.

Who would be the worst king? Maybe that was the right strategy, starting from the worst possibility and working backwards. Lanslod would be worst, for sure. Mordred might be next worst, being so aggrieved. But on the other hand, Arthur wasn't likely to last long, and whoever succeeded him might be worse than Mordred. Possibly a lot worse. I stumbled to the middle of the bridge and looked down. A small log careened through the water, briefly caught on a rock, then broke free.

The only person who was good and pure was Aelfhere. All right, that's my decision. Whatever Aelfhere wants, I will do. And Aelfhere will follow the Queen. And the Queen hasn't decided. Or hasn't told anyone. Nevertheless.

I felt calm. I picked up a rock and dropped it in the river. It made a satisfying plunk.

# 5

# Witch Came First?

I was awakened by Timmy who urged me to dress rapidly for riding as we need to perform an errand, though he was reluctant to tell me exactly what. He'd left the door ajar, but that wasn't why he was hesitant. Eventually, I wormed out of him that we needed to travel into the hills to meet a witch. It took a little more to get out of him why, which was that Aelfhere had sent a message that she wasn't coming, and in fact thought she might be pregnant and wanted some abortion herbs. He was embarrassed to have to talk about the subject.

I was torn between two feelings. Anxiousness about the pregnancy and disappointment about not being able to tell her about my decision. Well, I'd write her a note.

Apparently Freddie (me) and her had gotten carried away with the caresses one day, and she was late with her moon, which is to say her period. We had planned to delay intercourse until at least after the engagement, but the engagement would require permission of the King and Queen, and there was no way the Queen would let go of Aelfhere at the moment, and eventually the pressure got too much and Freddie wanted to put it in for just a moment, and you know how *that* goes. I felt like kicking myself, but it wasn't my fault, because this happened a millennium and a half before I was born. I also felt like kicking Freddie, but that would have meant kicking myself and like I said . . .

Then I wondered if aborting Aelfhere's pregnancy would be aborting an ancestor which would create a time travel conundrum. I survived one of those in Josh's time, but they were pretty unpredictable. On the other hand, impregnating a Queen's Lady without permission might have severe consequences including banishment or execution, which might also create a conundrum as well as ending my life and squelching my mission, whatever it was. On the third hand, abortion herbs might not be safe and probably weren't, so that could create a conundrum if I were descended from a later child of hers. But on the fourth and final hand (four hands being necessary to play bridge, haha), there was no necessary reason that I was anything but a spiritual descendant of either Aelfhere or Freddie, in that there was no reason reincarnation followed family lines. But then the space guys had never said I was a reincarnation of Freddie, like I was with Matthew. So I had nothing to go on at all. I guess the best thing was just to move on and see what happens.

"Who are we going to see?"

"Well, I considered if you were going to see a witch, you might as well see the best." Timmy replied.

"And who would that be?"

"Why Mirgan La Fay, of course."

"I know the name. Tell me about her."

He shifted uneasily. "She is a witch. She has great powers. She can kill a man with a single glance. Or poison him or bewitch him. She can fly, and she can swim."

"She can swim?" Odd thing to say. Although obviously that was more plausible than the flying part.

"Yes, which is all the more frightening as drowning is the only way to kill a witch." I guess this was before burning witches at the stake became so fashionable.

"I see. But she has good qualities because we are going to see her. Right?"

"Yes, she has the greatest talent with potions. She can heal a person of most anything. She can brew herbs to win anyone's heart. She is kind to children, and she has many of her own. And she is a friend to all creatures, be they great or humble. And she listens to them and converses."

"That sounds fine," I said, dismissing most of what he said. "And where might we find her?"

"In the hills. Some ten miles away." That would be two hours each way, more if there's a steep climb.

"Can we expect bandits?"

"Always."

"Then shouldn't we be accompanied?"

"Already arranged. I have talked to Sir Agravain's squire and the four of us will make the journey. You will treat for supper at the tavern in exchange." That seemed fair enough, although Agravain did already owe me a favor. But I guess I could save that for later. Some whacking sounds were coming through the still partially open door. Distracting. I kicked it shut.

"When?"

"They will be here shortly with the horses. I will go to the tavern and obtain some bread."

"I'll get the bread—I need you to send a note to Aelfhere." I reached into my pouch and fumbled around. There was that silly cylinder, which I needed to throw out eventually but not today, and my souvenir pen which I grabbed and wrote on a small piece of parchment: *Whatever you do, I will do.* I folded it and handed it to him. He placed the note inside his top shirt, then bowed and turned.

I went indoors to put my tunic and mail on, and struggle with my boots. By the time I had finally succeeded, the whacking noises had gotten louder punctuated with loud grunts. I ambled across the street to the tavern to get the bread and for a quick ale. As I approached, I noticed a somewhat familiar figure next to the doorway, standing with a sword in his hand -in front of a large coatrack, or so it seemed, partially blocking the left tavern window. Except it was way too big to be a coat rack, too thick and with longer arms. What was it? Actually a tree. Its leaves and smaller branches had been trimmed away.

The man nodded to me, then motioned me over. Who was he? He had a thick, strong body with long, curly blond hair pulled off his face by a leather string headband. He was dressed like a knight in mail and surcoat, which I couldn't distinguish from the angle I was approaching by. He was young, early to mid-twenties. I racked my brain. As I neared, he turned a bit, and I recognized it to be Gawain. He was wearing his surcoat which pictured a lion holding a cross in front of him, as if warding off vampires. Or so I thought. He also wore an extremely large wooden cross around his neck, maybe nine inches long and four or five wide. It almost obscured the lion. Kind of stepped on the punch line, if you know what I mean.

"Lord's Blessings, old man," he began, leaning against the sword.

*Old man*? "Back at ya," I replied. He looked puzzled. "Same to you, good sir," I rephrased.

"I'm having a small repast and refreshment if you'll care to join me." I noticed a large mug of ale on the windowsill. I had an urge to decline and bolt through the doorway, but thought better of it in light of my situation, and so sat down next to him on the middle windowsill of the tavern.

"Nay, move farther back. I like no man to be so close, lest I succumb to the lures of effeminacy. I'm having my single ale of the day. I drink no mead nor wine nor rarely of the cider, for the sake of my soul. I only drink milk of the cow or goat otherwise, and would drink water, were it safe." I moved away to the far window sill.

"I hear *that*," I replied.

"I'm pleased that you stopped by. It is no doubt the Lord's work, in that we have yet to converse at any length, and I have many questions." He stood back and raising his sword took a couple of whacks at the coatrack, which apparently was a swordsman's dummy, grunting loudly with each swing.

"I see. Go ahead, shoot."

"I beg your pardon?" he asked, taking a huge swing at the rack's head, if that's what you want to call it. The blow glanced off sending a large chip flying.

"I mean feel free to ask."

He fixed me with his stare. "I understand you are of the Devil's faith. I must know why your people killed our Lord, and if you are ready to repent."

Wow. Simply wow. Trying to gather my thoughts, I took a deep breath. "First of all, the Romans killed Josh, I mean Jesus. You *do* know that?"

Actually, the Romans didn't even successfully kill him because I gave Josh the zombie poison to fool them and then helped smuggle him onto a spaceship where he was taken to Mexico and became Quetzalcoatl. As you'll recall. Couldn't say that to Gawain, though.

"Yes, but the merciful Pilate was ready to pardon him. But you people chose the thief Barabbas." He took another swing, this time at an arm, and lopped off a sizeable chunk.

*You people.* I hate it when anyone says that. And actually the jerk Pilate tricked us because he asked the people if they wanted to pardon the "Son of the Father," which in Aramaic translates to *Bar Abba.* Which sounds like the name Barabbas. Couldn't say that either.

I started getting hot, reddening. Jerk. Clenching my fist. I wanted to punch him, slam his head against the wall. But. Can't. Do That.

Plus he has a sword, and all I have on me is a dagger.

Right then, I spotted Timmy returning, and I knew he would tell me to just take a deep breath. Technically, I couldn't start a fight with another armed knight without the King's permission, and Arthur would hardly grant it since Gawain was one of his favorites right after Lanslod and Galahat.

Finally, I just stammered out, "We will discuss this another time, just as we will discuss my repentance another time. Now let us change the subject."

Gawain briefly blanched, noticing how close I came to striking him, then turned it into a sneer and next a sickly sweet smile.

"Very well. How are you adapting to joining our ranks?" he asked mildly.

"Moderately well. But doesn't it seem like the knights are a bit sketchy and that the people don't particularly like them?"

"Not so. It's true that the knights occasionally yield to temptation to sin, as do all, but they are pious and loyal to the king. And our King—Arthur the Jus—is easily the wisest and holiest in Albion, and our Bishop the most righteous. And the people love them for it. You must not ever yield to doubt, for that surely is the work of the Devil, as you must realize even in your benighted state of mind."

Fine. Instead of attacking him, I decided to try to reason with him. Probably dumb of me.

"First of all, do you not see that the knights drink and brawl incessantly and gamble their earnings . . . among other things?"

"It's true that they drink," he conceded, "But the Lord partook of wine, did he not? And as for fighting, perhaps it helps them to stay in shape for war? And gambling. I know some believe that it is bad because the Jews threw lots to divide the Lord's clothes. But we are not Jews, and the King has excepted the knights from his edict against gambling. So in short, we are blessed to be in our kingdom that is ruled by the love and light of God alone."

Okay, he was just nuts. Or blinded by religion. Or both. He took a couple huge swings at the body of the coatrack, sending splinters flying.

"Hear this, my good sir," he began, "The knights of Cantmell have sins, no doubt, but their virtue outweighs them mightily. You must renounce all notions of judgment about us, for the King, the Bishop and the knights are the head, heart, and arms of the Lord. And you must renounce your demonic faith and join us as one."

He paused to take another swing at the tree, a solid blow which whacked off an entire large branch.

"I am pure. I touch no women, I drink but one ale a day, and I flay myself with a chain every night. Would you like to see the scars?" His voice raised in tone to a high pitch, culminating in a weird laugh.

Whoa. I shook my head.

"There is no knight purer than me in all of Albion. Even Lanslod and Galahat," he almost screeched. *That* was a low bar, but he didn't think so.

"Quick question . . ." I wanted to interrupt his rant because it was starting to sound a bit maniacal.

"If the King and Lanslod were to part interests, with whom would you side?"

"It would never happen."

"But if it did."

"After me and the Bishop, Lanslod is most pure, as anyone can see." He took another chop at the tree and hacked off another branch. "Take it from there. But my purity gives me power almost as great as Lanslod himself." He laughed cruelly, but I couldn't tell why. He was thinking of someone or something to slash, was my guess. Maybe me.

Across the street, Timmy was cowering in the doorway. I waved to him and broke from Gawain.

"I must leave you now."

"Repent," he said in parting. "And have a blessed day."

*Screw off,* I thought silently, but responded with fake sincerity. "Why thank you, and have a *damn good day* yourself!"

Probably went over his head, but I was still chortling when I entered the tavern to find Mordred sitting at a front table. He was rolling a couple dice. They were different from ours, oblong not cubical.

"Ah. You are Escobar, a moment to talk?" He rolled a seven. "Practicing," he said.

I sat at his table and Joseph brought ale.

"I see you were collared by that fool Gawain," he began.

I nodded.

"The fanatic hates me," he continued, "because I'm Arthur's bastard son. As if it was *my* fault I was conceived."

"Clearly not," I concurred, sipping the ale which of course was warm. How long till someone invents the icebox, I wondered. Let alone the refrigerator.

"You are new here. But surely you can see the problems."

"I've seen a few."

He rolled another seven. "Ha," he exclaimed. "Arthur is weak and our kingdom weak. One day the island will be a single kingdom. The knights are corrupt because there is no vision to motivate them."

That seemed plausible. I nodded, while taking another swig. I motioned to Joseph to bring several loaves of bread. You know, opening my mouth. Pretending to hold a loaf. Holding up four fingers. Sign language, heh. Joseph nodded.

Mordred continued, "I would like to unite our knights, not through quests or religious follies, but through ambition and self-interest—by forming alliances with the more powerful kingdoms and helping to conquer the weaker ones. That way we can keep united and gain more land. As we gain more, there's further rewards for the knights. You see how the cycle reinforces?" He tapped the dice against the table.

I swigged another mouthful of ale, then wiping my mouth with the back of my hand, raised an objection. "But isn't it quite risky to depend on kingdoms that are strong? For they may betray us at a whim." That was pretty smart of me, I must say.

"True, but the secret to defeating the conniving is . . . To be more conniving oneself," he smirked. "That I intend to do."

He fixed me with a thoughtful stare. Just then Joseph brought my loaves, so I started to rise. "Forgive me, but I must depart, I have a mission involving a lady to attend to."

"Pity that you being detained by the fool Gawain has cut short our time together." He tossed a silver coin onto the table. "Pray use this for tomorrow's ale and a meal, and consider my thoughts." It would've been disrespectful to decline. I nodded and departed.

Gawain's thwacking had stopped, but voices rose, and horses nattered outside. Opening the door, I saw he'd gone, leaving the battered tree behind while our horses had arrived along with Agravain and his squire, a fellow who, if anything, was more squirrelly looking than Timmy - if such were possible. I suppose the requirement to attain the nine agilities weeded out most squires before they applied for knighthood, but if not, this fellow was much more likely to end up as one of the skewered rather than a skeweree. He was thin as most were, short as were many, pale as were all due to the English weather, bad complexioned as were a lot, but singularly goofy-looking mainly due to having crossed eyes. I shot a querulous glance at Agravain, who grimaced and shrugged, as if to say *I know, but what could I afford on the King's commissions?*

Timmy reached out for my loaves of bread and stuck a loaf in each of our saddle bags, then knotted his hands to give me a boost up, saying, "Ready, my liege?" Love it.

They still used Roman style saddles with the four horns and no stirrups, which was a bummer because the horse was large and spirited, snorting and frisking, while Timmy passed me the reins. Despite the lack of stirrups, the boost succeeded at getting me into the saddle and once I got up, the horse quieted. I looked over at Agravain who was mounted on a horse the same size as mine but somehow far more awesome and fierce looking. It seemed to almost emit steam from its flaming eyes. They were both warhorses, or *chargers*, as they were currently known. But his really had spirit. Or something.

Their saddles, though, were not really designed for charging, in that they didn't have a front or back wall for stability, and the lack of stirrups would have made it difficult to swing a sword hard without losing balance. These were clearly still the days of infantry and hand-to-hand combat. Hopefully, which I could avoid. The two squires' horses were much smaller, practically ponies. I also noticed that all the horses were wearing little leather boots, tied on with string. Horseshoes hadn't made it here yet. Okay then.

"Let's set *uff*, Macduff," I said, making the word "off" rhyme, which was my sad attempt at humor. Of course, no one laughed because it was a Shakespeare reference, and the Bard hadn't been born yet—and even if he had, well, it wasn't that funny. Sigh.

Agravain slapped the reins on the neck of his horse, bringing it to the front. I took a last look around, orienting myself. Castle, check. Green hills, check. Stream with bridge, check. Probably looked like a few hundred places in England. Not sure I'd recognize it, if someone turned me around. Agravain led the group forward on his large, impressive charger and I followed, the two squires behind us. I'll bet though that they were the ones who knew the way. We'll see what happens when we get to the first crossroads. Meanwhile, the usual drizzle had stopped which was a relief. Not thrilled about riding in the rain. And we ambled off, not galloping like in the movies.

I can't *tell* you the number of times they show that, the galloping off—but in real life, you don't want to wear out your horses in the first mile . . . Oh, and while we're on the subject, what's up with the night marches in the movies? They're always marching off carrying torches. Never happens. First off, do the dag gone film makers think it's easy lighting fires before matches and lighters? Do they think everybody has big buckets of pitch to dip the torches in just lying around? And then everyone has to waste one arm holding up the torch. And how long do you think a torch lasts? Maybe an hour max. Sorry about that, my mind always wanders when I'm riding.

Speaking of which, you realize that there are 400 billion stars in the galaxy and possibly as many as two trillion galaxies, spanning maybe 46 billion light years? And that a photon traveling from the far side of the universe will never get here because the universe will end before it arrives? But at the same time, to a photon no time has elapsed since it's traveling at the speed of light. In other words, from its own perspective, it's destroyed the instant it's created. Now that's a meaningless existence if you ask me - worse than Doltly's or even mine.

After an hour or so, we got to the first crossroad. Agravain held back until Timmy pointed straight ahead to a river. Ha, I was right. Maybe thirty yards wide, the river lay another hundred yards ahead. Trees, right up to the riverbank except for one spot. There stood an old guy with a raft. To carry us across, he wanted two coppers per horse and one per person, which added up to one silver—a day's eating and drinking at Joe's Tavern. That seemed excessive.

Agravain waved me over to consult. "Too much?" he asked.

"Seems so," I concurred.

"Kill him, then?" Agravain asked.

That seemed excessive too. I winced. "I don't know . . . Let's ask the squires."

He summoned them, and explained the parameters of debate.

"Are we still in Cantmell?" Timmy asked. The other squire nodded. "Probably not a good idea then," Timmy concluded.

"What about threatening to kill him?" asked Agravain. The two squires looked at each other and shrugged. "All right," Agravain stared down the old man and unsheathed his sword.

"Six coppers for the lot then," the old man said hurriedly. Agravain turned to his squire, "Given him six of the most worn." The squire fished around in his pouch and eventually pulled out six suitable coins. The man palmed them, and we climbed aboard the raft. He tugged on the rope that connected to a large tree on the other side, and we commenced to cross. The river wasn't wide, but it was swollen with all the spring rain. And the current buffeted the raft—but we made it across safely.

We remounted, and I started thinking about how I could possibly be having any of Freddie's memories. I wasn't in his body, and it wasn't in the headset. I just looked like him due to slight adjustments in my molecular structure when recomplexifying. My theory last time was that they'd programmed me with a random sample of my host's memory. Or maybe his thoughts were in the ethers of the location, kind of like the Akashic records, and not located in his head at all. I really never studied biology that much, though I did think of the brain as like the motherboard of a computer. But maybe it was more like a switchboard, where the wiring was completely separate from the contents within.

The trail meandered along the riverbank a little way, then started up some gently and lightly-wooded rolling hills. There was light cloud cover—still, it didn't look like it would rain again anytime soon.

A thought came to me. I hollered, "Agravain, if Lanslod is supposed to find the Grail, why is he staying in Cantmell?"

Agravain pulled back on his reins. "Who told you he's supposed to find it?"

Ooops, I probably shouldn't have said anything. "Can't remember, but it's a rumor around . . ."

Agravain pondered for a minute. "What makes you think he is really staying?" Good point. He continued, "If I were him, I would say I was going if I were staying, and that I was staying if I were going." I guess it takes a knight to know a knight.

I looked up and saw two birds crisscrossing in the sky. I've always felt that birds were some kind of messengers, so I considered that for a few minutes. Like an omen maybe. It could mean that Lanslod was double-crossing the knights in some way. It could be the lives of Aelfhere and Elisabet crossing and recrossing my path over the lifetimes. Or it could mean my mission in this period was tangled up. Or all of the above .

Or it could just mean we were about to recross the river. I looked down and could see the river about a half mile away in the valley. Or maybe it was a different river. As we got closer, there was a bridge. Well good, that meant we didn't have to threaten any more peasants to avoid being fleeced on the crossing.

Or not. As we got closer, two men emerged from beneath the bridge. They were big men. Bearded big men. Bearded, burly big men. Closer yet, they had swords. This should be interesting, I thought. In a very bad way, of course. Agravain apparently was not flustered by their appearance, as he didn't hesitate or pause to consult with me as we approached. When we got to the bridge I had a chance to look at them closely. Two brothers probably, healthy from farm work maybe—but then why were they away from their farms? No, they both had a bit of a belly, so that meant they were not farmers. They didn't look intelligent enough to be bridge builders, so they were probably retired bandits who had exchanged highway robbery for, well, highway robbery by adopting this bridge.

Agravain pulled his reins in, and his horse bucked a little as it halted. We reined in our horses as well.

"Stand aside," Agravain demanded of them.

"Nay, pay the toll or turn back," the one on the left replied.

"How much?"

"Two coppers for each horse and one per man."

Same as before. So did they have a union or something?

Agravain turned to his squire. "Are we still in Cantmell?"

The squire turned to Timmy. They consulted for a minute or two, gesturing in different directions. The squire replied, "We think not."

Agravain started to unsheathe his sword. The brothers straightened up, alert, their hands on their own swords.

"Umm, can we not do this?" I blurted out. Maybe it was a good sign that I was not feeling hotheaded. Or maybe I was just losing my edge.

Agravain scowled. "Why not? Death always before dishonor, and to overpay is dishonorable."

"Well, can't we just go around?"

"Nay. There's no other bridges for miles. And to turn aside is also dishonorable."

I looked at the river, and while swollen and rapid, looked narrower and shallower than the previous crossing.

"I mean just cross over there." I pointed at a narrow spot just upriver.

"You mean get our horses and feet wet?" I nodded, yes.

"To get our feet wet when we could avoid it would be dishonorable."

I started to say, *But we are on a mission to protect the Queen's Lady's honor*, but I wasn't sure how much Timmy had told them or how much it would matter, so I just turned my horse away, shaking my head saying, "Fellows, follow me . . . " and galloped toward the river.

After only a second, Agravain kicked his horse and galloped after, now thinking that dishonor was not following me crossing the river.

My horse started gingerly once it was in the water, stepping highly, occasionally stumbling slightly as its hoof hit a loose rock. Agravain's horse was bolder, and he caught up to me mid river. The water was not quite up to the horses trunks, so they were still able to touch bottom. We stumbled up onto the river shore. I wondered whether the horses' booties would shrink because they got wet. I looked back and saw the squires were having a harder time, since their horses were shorter. They were having to swim. And the current was swift enough to make that problematic. Timmy tried to aim somewhat downstream and use the water's momentum to push his horse across at an angle. Agravain's squire tried the opposite approach, angling upstream to counteract the current, which made the horse work harder but might have been a good idea if there were rapids downstream. Did he know something we didn't? It would have worked if he hadn't tried to steer the horse right into a log. I guess being cross-eyed he didn't see it clearly. Surprised, the pony stopped swimming and the current caught him and turned him at an angle, and he started to be swept away.

Agravain shouted, "Shite," and galloped downstream to where the river bent. Timmy and I followed. The squire wasn't as dopey as he looked, and leapt off the pony to lessen its burden and try to lead it across, but the momentum of his leap pushed the horse more sideways which increased its momentum. I felt helpless, as none of my high technology—like my staff that turned into a lightsaber, or my souvenir pen that worked sometimes as a laser—would do any good. A simple rope might have been useful, though.

Agravain hesitated for a moment, then plunged his horse back into the water. He pulled the sword in its buckled scabbard off his belt and extended it as the squire was swept by. The squire caught it, but the pony was still slowly dragging him downstream despite its being able to mostly touch bottom. At this point, it looked like the choice was to tell the squire to let go of the reins or risk losing both of them. But Agravain wasn't the kind of guy to cut his losses. He jumped off his horse into waist deep water, and letting his own horse shield him from the current, grabbed the squire and pulled him close. The squire's feet were able to catch hold of something and between the two of them, they were able to pull the horse back. They stumbled onto the shore and sat on a fallen tree trunk.

"You were useless," he spat out at me. After a moment, he lightened up. "No matter, what's a horse? Or a squire, for that matter."

Agravain and his squire were wet to the waist, and a wind started up from the north, so they must have been cold in the cloudy spring weather, but they paid it no mind, the squire helping Agravain onto the horse, then mounting his pony. Agravain led again as the road wound deeper into the hills and into a forest.

I thought this might be a good place for a bandit attack, but none materialized.

After nearly an hour, we approached a clearing, and behind some boulders one could barely see a small dwelling. For some reason, I was expecting to see some kind of quaint gingerbread house, but as we turned behind the boulders what appeared was a ramshackle, brown dwelling that looked a lot like a hillbilly shack with a thatched roof, shutters dangling loosely, and a fire pit in front. A breeze picked up ominously. Smoke angled sharply from the chimney and fire pit. Several dirty children were playing or fighting with each other next to a stone well.

After a moment, a shapely, raven-haired woman stepped out, holding a ladle and shouting at the children to pipe down. She was disheveled, but through it all shined a pale, sultry sexiness that was startling. In fact, she looked a lot like *Elvira, Mistress of the Dark* who hosted the late afternoon horror movies in LA I used to watch as a pre-teen in the nineties. She was as fair-skinned as a ghost—wearing a dark dress with plunging cleavage set off by a reversed pentacle around her neck. Her eyes—darkened with kohl—sparkled with a tired mischievousness, and she smiled wearily when she saw us. If Queen Gwen looked like an angel from heaven, this woman, who was obviously Mirgan, looked like a pale, sexy demon from the steamiest part of hell. In other words, the penultimate MILF, so to speak. The two squires were totally tongue-tied, and so was I. Agravain, however, dismounted and kissed her hand as if she were a princess. The wind dropped just as she spoke.

"How may I service you?" she asked, or maybe my babelfish was just as much on overload as I. Agravain pointed toward me.

She looked me over from head to foot, which made parts of me stir despite my embarrassment.

"So?" she asked, after I failed to come up with anything other than a few *uhs* and *umms*.

"He wants herbs to end a pregnancy," Agravain replied.

"Who is the fortunate lady?" she asked, looking me up and down again.

"Aelfhere, the Queen's Lady," I finally mumbled.

"I see," she said, pondering something. Then without further explanation, she took Agravain into the house. After a few minutes of loud moaning, they both reappeared, Mirgan looking still more disheveled but even more radiant, and Agravain looking a bit goofy and smiling.

"Your lady is not pregnant, but missed her moon due to nervousness. It will come shortly," she said. "I will give her herbs to relax and others to help if you make another mistake. By the way, I received a message for you while sarding. But do be more careful next time."

"What's the message?"

"The wizard Mirdynn wishes to speak with you. He will be at the tavern in two days, or he'll send a messenger."

"How do you know?"

"I do my best thinking in bed and my best receiving. Judge me not, there are few niches for a bright woman who is not noble in this time. Yet I have amassed enough wealth to buy any inn in Cantmell twice over and birthed enough children to live to support me in my old age."

"I don't judge you," I said meekly. I don't think the squires did either—gape-jawed as they both appeared.

"Then there is one other thing." She leaned over closely, and whispered, "You must make a decision. Which side will you be on—the knights' or Arthur's. The time is coming very soon."

I looked over at Agravain, but he was tending to his horse. The squires no doubt saw her whisper but probably assumed it was an indecent proposal. She smiled and pushed me away, then went inside. After a few minutes, she returned with two pouches. "The one on the left for nervousness, the one on the right for mistakes. Boil for a short time, then steep half a day."

I slipped the pouches into a saddle bag.

Agravain and squire were ready to leave. "We will go back another way," he said. I let them lead and even Timmy go before me, as I pondered her words. I'd thought this all out last night, but was she indicating I'd have to break with the Queen and Aelfhere? I had a moment of doubt. The king was weak. The knights were crooked. On the other hand, Agravain and Balin seemed like decent fellows.

But on the third hand . . . No! I turned my horse around and galloped back to Mirgan's shack. She was still outside, watching us depart.

"Any hints?"

She hesitated, took a breath, then spoke, "Yes, but I doubt if it'll help. When confronted by the evil of two lessers, choose the lesser of two evils." She gave me another big smile, and I swear it seemed like a cloud parted because a light came upon her, and for a moment her sultry steaminess turned into a more transcendental beauty.

# 6

# The Flaggin' Dragon

Taking the longer way back was a good choice, not only to avoid the thugs at the bridge but because in fact it was far prettier. There were green meadows and rolling hills, and deer venturing out from the newly leafed trees. We didn't have bows and arrows to shoot at them with, so hunting was out of the question. Not that I'd enjoy shooting such beautiful creatures. Plus we didn't know which king or earl we'd be poaching from. Also I wasn't much of an archer. I tried for that merit badge in Boy Scouts, but I never really mastered the grip or aiming. I did skin the inside of my wrist quite a bit from the thwack of the bow string. I was definitely better at fencing. Hopefully, we wouldn't need bow skills too much. Or maybe we could use crossbows.

We reached Cantmell in the early afternoon, and as we crossed the bridge into town, we saw a messenger run up. It was a red-haired boy of about twelve. He approached Agravain.

"I've been looking for you," the boy said. "I've been sent to let you know that Sir Lanslod has challenged you to trial by combat tomorrow. He dares you to come to the marketplace to receive his challenge."

I glanced at Agravain. Then back to the messenger. "Wasn't the taint of blood supposed to disqualify a person from the quest?"

"Yes, good sir, but the Queen has obtained a dispensation from the bishop in the matter."

Agravain sighed, shaking his head. "Of course she did. Now he'll be able to slaughter me and still be considered pure enough. But I'm not afraid. Death before dishonor as always."

"How will he challenge you? Will he slap you with a glove?"

"Ha, are you crazy? Gloves are for women and the effeminate. Mittens are much warmer and more manly. Anyway, the tradition is he throws dirt in your face. Maybe I should challenge him first."

"Since he challenged you, doesn't that entitle you to choice of weapons and venues?"

"Verily it does, but he's a monster with a broadsword. He's got that blade Excalimer, supposedly magical but good enough either way. And though I'm better with an axe, he has longer arms which negates my advantage."

Wait, *Excalimer*? Was that actually Excalibur? And wasn't that supposed to be King Arthur's? Well, never mind, but bookmark that.

I thought for a second, then answered. "Verily back at you, but don't you also have choice of venues? Why not make it on horseback? You know he's clumsy there."

"You and your horses. Balin told me. I say it won't catch on."

"Nevertheless, think upon it. And don't give away the advantage by being the first to throw dirt. "

He started to nod in agreement but then shook his head. "We will see." He looked at the messenger boy, "Is he at the market now?" The boy nodded.

Agravain gave the reins of his horse to his squire and told him to take both of their horses to the stables. I grabbed the saddlebag off my horse and instructed Timmy to give our horses to the messenger boy to do the same and gave the boy a copper. I wanted Timmy around as a resource, since it seemed he had good sense.

The three of us turned on foot to the right towards the entrance of the burh. The marketplace was just past it. The area was crowded—probably with people getting last minute provisions for supper or maybe in anticipation of seeing the challenge which might turn into a brawl. They were mostly dressed in drab brown homespun of one kind or another. A couple of knights lolled around at the edges in their mail and surcoats. Aelfhere with her brother Dagen, the jester, were buying some kind of trinkets at a stall nearby. I waved to her, and she smiled as she waved back. She liked my note, I guess.

But that made me think. By being present at the challenge with Agravain, wasn't I taking a side—aligning myself against the Queen's lover, Lanslod? I might even have to be his second. Oy. My head spun as I tried to game out quick solutions to my sudden dilemma. What to do, what to do?

Then there was Lanslod directly ahead of us. He spotted us, straightened his surcoat, and strode in our direction.

Suddenly there was a loud shout, and a commotion followed by the sounds of horses clattering across the bridge behind us. Heads turned. Three men on large horses rode up right into the crowd, which parted in alarm. They rode directly to Lanslod and dismounted and gestured wildly as they talked to him. Then one turned and shouted out, "There has been a dragon sighted near Bumchester!"

Lanslod stepped forward, pronouncing loudly, "We must have a strategy. Tell all knights to come to the palace directly for a planning meeting!"

Dragon? Another planning meeting? Ridiculous. I turned to Agravain. "So much for the challenge. Are you going?"

"Of course, one can't miss a planning meeting."

I replied, "I will catch up with you later," then turned to Timmy. "How big is a dragon usually?"

He pondered and after a moment, said, "Around thirty feet. Maybe forty."

"Do they fly?"

"Oh yes."

"How large are its wings?"

He pondered again. "Maybe five or six feet . . ."

"And do they breathe fire?"

"Oh yes."

"Have you ever seen a dragon?"

He hesitated. "Not personally, but I've talked to them that have."

Hmm. Not convincing. "Timmy, do we have bows and arrows?"

"Yes, both a crossbow and a longbow."

"Perfect. Bring them both, and plenty of arrows, and get fresh horses at the stables. We're not waiting for the meeting."

"Yes, my liege. You are very brave." Love that. The brave part wasn't bad either.

"Tell Agravain's squire I'll have to buy his master dinner another day."

He turned to leave. I glanced up to see Aelfhere.

"You received my note," she acknowledged.

"And you got mine. I have herbs for your condition which help you sleep because you need only that . . . " I handed her a pouch from the saddlebag containing the sleeping herb.

"Then I'm not . . . "

"Nay. And I will be more careful henceforth. I promise. But I will not see you tonight at the meeting because I'm going forth shortly to confront the dragon if that is what it may be."

"Oh Freddie, you are so brave, but . . . " She looked pretty worried.

"There's no need to be afraid. I don't believe this dragon is as fearful as people think."

"But why? People say . . . "

I cut her off. "I don't think this dragon flies or breathes fire . . . "

"But how do you know?"

"Well, which is bigger, a bird's outstretched wings or its length?"

"Its wings?"

"Right, therefore a dragon can't fly. And how can it breathe fire?"

"Oh, I don't know. Perhaps there was fire inside when it hatched? There's so many things we don't know. Please be careful."

"I will. Verily and totally. And I will turn right around if it takes flight or breathes out fire." I certainly would because that would be frickin' nuts. She embraced me tightly which was unusual because we were in public. But then everyone was freaking out about the dragon, so I'm sure no one paid attention.

"Are you taking Timmy? He's good with the longbow, I've heard."

Perfect. I'd forgotten to ask him about that. That was certainly an oversight, haha. She kissed me lightly on the cheek and broke away. I turned around and could see Timmy down the street leading two horses.

As he reached me, he pulled out my helmet.

"You didn't mention it, but I figured you might want it. The crossbow and longbow are sticking out of the saddlebag. I assume you want the longbow as usual"

I took the helmet. "No, you take it, I hear you're getting very good with it. Besides, my wrist is a little sore." It was getting sore just thinking of the longbow.

"My gratitude. I won't let you down."

"But remind me how the crossbow works."

He pulled it off the saddle and held it before me.

"You take this lever and turn it to the left, and it pulls the string tight. Then you place the arrow against the string here. Then the trigger underneath releases it."

It looked simple enough. "How far is Bumchester?"

"Not far, just a few miles."

I nodded, and we mounted the new horses. They were fresh, snorting, and anxious to go—so we took off at a trot. I let Timmy take the lead again. After the bridge, we turned in the other direction from where we'd traveled in the morning. The road was crowded with a number of peasants walking briskly carrying possessions toward Cantmell, apparently fleeing the alleged dragon. No point in talking to them yet. Later peasants would have more recent news. After almost an hour, we approached a village nestled between two large mounds. They looked like someone's bum. Hence the name, right? It looked like it was a prosperous, peaceful place normally, with thin wisps of smoke rising from stone chimneys and a stream flowing beside it.

There were still peasants fleeing, but these ones looked more panicked. The dragon must be nearby. I stopped one and stooped down from my horse.

"Where's the dragon?"

He turned and pointed towards a field maybe half a mile away. There were some blotches, but I couldn't make them out. As we rode closer, I could. It was a large creature, munching on the carcass of a cow. But *what* was it?

Nearer yet, it had neither fur nor feathers. Its skin, or maybe they were fine scales, was shiny and grey. Kind of lizard-like and about ten feet long including its tail. It had two small vestigial wings. It was like nothing I'd ever seen. I was assuming what I'd find would be some large carnivore, maybe a dire wolf, probably with some feature that made it appear like a dragon, who knows what. But this was unworldly.

Then I heard it. A voice inside my head. That hadn't happened much here, but it happened back in Joshua's time a lot. Usually aliens.

*Well, are you going to kill me?*

*Umm . . . maybe . . .*

*Oh, you can hear me?*

*Umm, yes. What are you?*

*You wouldn't believe it.*

*Try me. I came here on a spaceship. Top that!*

*That figures. Me, too!*

*No way! Are you a Reptilian?*

*You mammalians call us that. It's a stereotype.*

*Sorry. Can you fly?* He did have those vestigial wings that I'd noticed.

*Back home I can but not here all complexified.*

*I get it. Do you breathe fire?*

*Hardly. Do I look like I have kerosene in my stomach?*

*I hear you. What are you doing here?*

*A bunch of us hijacked a spaceship a long time ago, and now I'm the last one left.*

*"Bummer. So what're you going to do?*

*Nothing. Live until someone kills me, and I can reincarnate. Would you like to? It'd be doing me a solid.*

*I don't know about that . . .*

*I'd give you a dragon's egg . . . it's not fertile though.*

*Don't need one. You don't happen to have a Grail though, do you?*

*Can't help you. Are you going to kill me, or should I munch on your friend?*

*Hey, don't get all hostile!* He gave me a nasty look. Could have imagined that though.

"Timmy?" He was looking at me funny, like I was talking to myself. Maybe I was.

"Yes, my liege?"

"Would you please shoot this dragon?"

"Certainly. It would be an honor." He lifted his bow and took aim. The dragon made no effort to turn or attack.

*Any last words?*

*Go for it. Goodbye cruel planet. And screw off.*

Timmy shot, and the dragon slumped over giving one last belch, not of fire but of cow breath, though I probably imagined it, since we were still forty yards apart. A few peasants were watching and started to cheer.

Timmy looked all humble. "I can give you the credit, my liege."

"No need. Perhaps this will help get you knighthood." He blushed.

The townspeople started to gather, and one lifted Timmy up on his shoulders.

"To Cantmell. We must tell the King and celebrate," he said.

I figured that might not go over well, what with jumping the gun and all. Let's put it off as long as possible.

"It's getting late. Let's celebrate here and tell the King tomorrow." They carried Timmy all the way into the village.

I followed along leading the two horses, our roles reversed for the moment. A stout merchant matched my strides and started to chat me up.

"You fellows are remarkable. We didn't expect any knights to come for days. They usually don't care much for what happens in outlying lands. Except if they own it, of course. And that young lad, what aim! A single shot right up the dragon's nostril. Don't think we didn't try to take that beast down . . ."

I didn't think they did, as a matter of fact. Certainly a few of the peasants had at least cheap bows, and some had good enough aim to poach deer in the King's forest, even though the penalty for such was death. So from what I'd heard, they actually poached in the twilight which was much harder. My guess was that no one attacked the dragon because they were liking whose livestock got eaten. That might account for why the dragon was having a hard time finding someone to murder it. The villagers and merchants were genuinely terrified, and dragons were bad for business. But they didn't have bows. Not so, the peasants.

As we entered Bumchester, the people made for the town's tavern. Contrasting with the general quaintness of the village, it was a small dingy place fronted with a sign of a raven. There were brown spots where the whitewash had worn off. By the time I squeezed in, ale was already being brought out and people were drinking freely. The place was completely packed, so I sat on the windowsill. There was no cheesecloth, so I didn't have to worry about letting flies in, haha. Timmy had a mug in each hand, and two village wenches had their arms around him. They were dirty and a bit scrawny but spirited, and my guess was that Timmy hadn't ever had any female attention, so it was probably a big boost to his self-esteem.

As I sat with one leg hanging out the window, who should I see but Mirgan, leading her children like a column of ducklings, except they were all holding hands. She still had a small smudge of dirt on her cheek as did her children, but she looked as sexy as ever. She came up to me.

"So you fellows killed my dragon, yes?"

"What? *Your* dragon? I thought . . . " Wasn't sure how to finish the sentence.

" . . . It was from the sky?" She said, completing my thought. Good enough. She pursed her lips seriously for a moment, staring me in the eyes, then laughed. "Don't worry, I was just japing you." That was a relief, I didn't need a witch as an enemy. I wouldn't know whether her spells worked, but I guessed her poisons might be top notch.

"Although we did work together once or twice," she said, referring to the creature. "It came in handy to scare people. I'll miss talking to it when I'm around here."

So it "talked" to her too. Well, that was also a relief—to know for sure I wasn't making it all up. I looked her up and down, and noticed the intelligence in her eyes and the pride in the way she carried herself. She was a witch, but what did that mean? She made potions, cast spells and . . . talked to dragons. She probably would have been a workshop leader in modern times and a social media influencer with thousands of followers. There wasn't anything sinister or weird about her vibe. Sinister just means left-handed in Latin, so there's *that*. In fact, she seemed kind of wholesome in a chaotic Middle Ages sort of way.

"What brought you here?" I asked. Seemed strange that our paths should cross twice in the same day.

"After you left, I foresaw your meeting the dragon and its outcome. And a couple other things I wanted to tell you about. But first there's something I want to do." She let go of her children's hands and told them to circle up. They did, holding hands with each other. It was very cute. Then she reached over and put her hand behind my neck and kissed me hard. Lights literally flashed in my head, sparks flew, if you will, and my temperature felt like it went up ten degrees. After a moment, she pulled back, still holding my hair.

"I know you're betrothed, and I mean no disrespect to the Queen's lady, but I know no other way of convincing you of the sincerity of what I'm about to tell you."

I was barely able to tell her to go ahead.

"First, have you thought about what I said this morning?"

"About the choice between the knights and the King? I managed to get out, "Not really. I mean the King is weak, but he does have good intentions. And the knights are crooked, but they're not all bad." I was thinking of Agravain and Balin.

"I understand. Here is what I have to tell you: I foresaw that your particular choice will have the greatest of consequences. And that the knights' true nature will be fully revealed to you very shortly."

"Alright, I hear you."

"Oh, and one other thing. There's a certain kind of kiss that a witch can bestow. I have bestowed it on you. And it has more power than sarding or fighting or coin."

She again looked me in the eye. My head was still reeling, so I guess that was proof of what she said.

She added, "I will help you, so believe in yourself and your mission. You must not fail."

"My mission?" I stuttered. What did she know about it?

"Don't think upon it now, just let the kiss take its effect." She let go of my hair and looked down at her children who were still silently holding hands. She took one of theirs, turned away, and the column of ducklings followed. She didn't look back.

I watched as they walked away. My mind started churning. How did they get here? They must have left right after we did, but I didn't see any wagons or horses. And being human, the kiss made me reflect on Aelfhere. And Elisabet. It suddenly struck me that far from being the sophisticated woman that she was as Delphine, Aelfhere was currently very much like Elisabet when I met her in Galilee. A little more elegant maybe, but with the same simple virtues of goodness and kindness.

By contrast, back in France, Aelfhere as Delphine told this joke to Casanova, Robespierre, and me:

"Mr. Isaac Newton invites John Locke and Monsieur Descartes to go into a salon-bar. The waiter asks for their drink orders. Mr. Newton orders apple brandy for himself and a cognac for M. Descartes. Mr. Locke ponders, but then says, 'I don't know, my mind is a blank slate.' Newton mentions his niece recently had a child. 'Was it a boy or girl?' asks Descartes. Newton replies, 'Yes,' and laughs. Descartes rolls his eyes and downs his drink, and the waiter asks if he would like another. Descartes replies, 'I think not!' and disappears."

Now that was quite a sophisticated jest, far over the heads of any of the current 600 AD crew and only understandable to someone versed in philosophy. On the other hand, none of those personages would be even alive for a millennium, so . . .

Anyway, did the similarities between Aelfhere and Elisabet mean that everyone was the same inside, but that circumstances brought out different qualities? Or was it simply that I was attracted to a certain type as a love interest? There were too many variables between the time periods and the ages, with Aelfhere and Elisabet being much younger—both less than twenty—and Delphine older and more experienced. But then, wait—like I'd noticed—the Venusian dudes had never specified that Freddie was a previous incarnation of me the way they did with Matthew, so maybe all of this is just synchronicity, or coincidence. And what about Mirgan? She'd made clear the kiss was an energy transmission, but what would it be like to be with someone like that? I scotched the thought. She was, if anything, a mentor.

Then it hit me. She was Rebecca, Joshua's girlfriend in her past life. Did she remember me? Did she remember that life? Well, she was certainly a force to be reckoned with then. And a good ally if I don't screw it up.

Turning back to the pub, the party was getting even livelier. And then Timmy made a point of acknowledging me. All heads turned and the partyers pressed towards me, until I nearly fell off the windowsill. One of the wenches leaned against me and breathed against my neck. She smelled like beer and stale dirt. And parsnips. She whispered that she was ready for some serious sarding. Fortunately at that moment, the mayor, or whatever he was, of the town walked up to the window, and leaned in to speak. A chubby, jovial fellow, he shook my hand vigorously and loudly announced that the two heroes—us—were to be named patrons of the town and be presented with a reward, and that we would be his guests.

He exited beckoning for us all to come with him, and I climbed out the window after him, followed by Timmy and the rest of the crowd.

7 |

# Bringing The Thingie

It was a pleasant night of feasting at the mayor's home. The town's notables were there—all eight of them.

Small town. Plus their wives. The villagers had their own party outside. It looked like they were roasting some rodents on an open fire. We ate pheasant and drank some mead, and were presented with an award of a gold coin each. Then the mayor noticed Timmy was starting to nod off, so he dismissed his guests and ushered us into a bedroom. We slept well. It'd been a long day.

In the morning, the party started up again as the villagers gathered outside. The mayor woke us to tell us that they'd decided to cut up the dragon carcass and feast for a couple days. That didn't sit well with me, having never previously eaten anyone I'd conversed with the day before. I told the mayor we needed to get back to Cantmell. He consented and told us he would send some men along to accompany us and if needed, corroborate our story. It took a while to gather the men, but after a bit we got under way. We were accompanied by six men including a couple of the notables. Timmy and I led, followed by the six. A dozen more of the villagers followed on foot just to get in on the excitement. The skies were gray, but it didn't look like it would rain.

About a half an hour along the road, we saw dust rising ahead and soon made out about a dozen men riding toward us in a trot, carrying banners.

"This will be interesting," I said quietly to Timmy as I pulled close to him. He turned to me, puzzled.

"What do you mean? . . . it's probably just the knights."

"Yes, that *is* what I mean."

Sir Kay was leading the group which contained all of the knights of the Oval Table except Lanslod and Mordred, who, while a knight, had never actually sat at the Table. A second group trailed behind, likely their squires.

As they came up to us, Sir Kay immediately rode forward. He eyed us head to foot suspiciously.

"And what are you doing here?" Before I had a chance to answer, he continued, "You weren't at the planning meeting. You realize they are mandatory . . . ?"

I interrupted, "My squire has killed the dragon."

His eyebrows raised and his face reddened. "Impossible."

A member of our company murmured, "It's true." We sat there glaring at each other while our horses nodded restlessly. He reddened, clearly fuming inside.

After a moment Galahat rode up to us, "What's going on?"

Kay turned, "They claim Escobar's squire killed the dragon."

Galahat looked us over for a long moment then raised an eyebrow and said, "That's untrue. My father, Lanslod, killed the dragon last night."

"What?" Stunned and dumbfounded. Expected some kind of blowback but this was preposterous. "He wasn't even here. Nor were you."

Galahat said, "Do I hear you say I am a liar?" This was a challenge, for if I said those words, trial by combat was next. A purple rage started to boil up inside, but Timmy leaned his arm across my chest, restraining me and spoke up, "Nay, we simply assert that you may be mistaken. My liege and I confronted the dragon, and the town is currently cooking its carcass."

Sir Kay turned and waved the rest of the knights forward. "Escobar claims his squire has killed the dragon, but I and Galahat claim it was killed by Lanslod last night. Does anyone contradict me?"

The knights all shook their heads or said no. Those stinking rats. Just as Mirgan predicted. They had no shame. Except for Agravain, Balin and Bedivere who just kept their heads lowered. But they didn't speak up. I looked back at our company, and they were all looking around nervously. They were unarmed. Finally one of the notables turned his horse around and galloped off. Then a few seconds later another, and then the rest. The villagers all turned around too. It was just me and Timmy. He winced, then shrugged. "Perhaps it is as you say," he conceded. I was furious but managed to hold it in. Hooray for me. A few more lifetimes like this and I'd end up being the repressed loser I was in modern day.

Satisfied, the knights reined their horses around to head back to Cantmell. How they were going to explain their claim and their therefore needless journey forth, I did not know. But maybe they didn't need to explain, everyone would just say okay that's the way it's going to go down. Timmy and I sat stunned on our horses for a few minutes watching them, then I told him we might as well head back too. We fell in silently at the back of the column behind the squires.

When we crossed the bridge to town, Sir Kay and Galahat started shouting that the dragon had been slain. A few townspeople cheered. The knights didn't mention that the alleged slayer wasn't even present, but I guess it wasn't necessary because everyone expected that it would happen just that way. It would be pretty funny to be a fly on the wall when Galahat informed his father that he had killed the dragon in his sleep, or while sarding or whatever. But then Lanslod would just accept it as his due, no doubt. I did wonder why he hadn't bothered to sally forth in the morning with the rest of them to fight the dragon. That was weird—what was up with that? Maybe he slept in or was enjoying a morning sard with the Queen.

The knights rode on to the palace, but I signaled to Timmy that we'd split off and head back to the stables. We dropped off the horses and were walking back to the inn when we came across Dagen, Aelfhere's brother the jester, who told us the knights were planning a celebration in the evening. Of slaying the dragon plus the commencement of the quest to find the Grail, the next day.

"It's funny because the knights are saying Lanslod killed the dragon, but I know I was entertaining him and the Queen last night, and my sister told me you left afternoon last to confront it."

"Leave it alone," I said, because the reminder was starting to tick me off again.

"Well, I have some news that may cheer you up. There's a fellow at Joseph's Sign of the Pig who says he has something important to tell you."

"Who?"

"A peasant fellow."

Hmm, Mirgan told me that the wizard Mirdynn would meet me in the tavern. Maybe it was him. I could use some ale to quench this resentment that kept bubbling up. Also I knew that Kay would be watching to see whether I'd boycott the celebration. He'd then know whether I'd try to make trouble, so maybe go and put a good face on, or things could get worse. Better get there already happy, if you know what I mean. Dagen squinted at me trying to discern how I was feeling.

"Do you want me to do the wide-mouthed frog?"

"Nay, I'm good." We were at the tavern, so I bid them both good afternoon and walked in.

The smell of stale spilt ale hit my nostrils. Hadn't noticed it as much before for some reason. I sat again by the window and gestured to Joseph to bring me ale and bread.

After my order had been brought, the mangy fellow who I'd met my first day started to come over and sit.

"Be gone. I'm. Meeting. Someone," I said tersely.

He shook his head, "Aye . . . But I'm the clod you're seeking."

"Ha, don't think so."

"But I do. Remember . . . I'm Berthulf, who knows many secrets."

"But forget most of them." Couldn't help saying.

He laughed, "Most truly, I have not forgotten this: that I know what you seek and where to find it."

"Hmm? Then speak it, before I throw the ale in your face." I knew that was being unnecessarily rude, but I couldn't keep things in forever.

"I know you seek a cup of sorts. And I know it to be in Salisburh by the ancient ruins."

Ok, check and check. "But how do I know you tell the truth?"

"I have this . . . " He fumbled in his shirt. I leaned forward. I expected the gem from the grail, but what he came up with was even more intriguing. He placed it in my hand. It looked like an integrated circuit—about the size of a thumbnail.

"Where did you get this?" I literally grabbed his collar.

"I took it off of a messenger last night. From Wessex. He told me his tale and got drunk, so I palmed it."

"Who was he bringing the message to?"

"Queen Gwen. But she wouldn't see him, as she was disposed otherwise." With Lanslod, no doubt.

"Did he tell anyone else?"

"Couldn't say, but he seemed as not. He was all frustrated like."

"Let me have this thing, and I will give you a silver now and a gold solidus when I gain the cup."

"Ay, but you're a knight."

"I pledge on the cross." Easy for me to say, but I wasn't going to cheat him. And here is the coin which I will give." And showed the coin I'd just been given in Bumchester, then put it back in my pouch.

"I believe you then. Here is that thing. And may I have the silver?"

I placed the silver on the table but put my hand over it. "And say nothing until I return." He nodded and I lifted my hand. Berthulf wandered to the back of the inn and showed his silver to a ginger-haired wench who was lounging at the back. She gave him a big smile and grabbed his arm.

Suddenly I felt a spark of optimism. This thingie was clearly something significant and somehow related to the Grail, which meant the Grail had something to do with space or time travel. I also felt buoyed by the fact of knowing where the Grail was—more or less.

"Joseph, send a message to Timmy to prepare some horses for departure tomorrow!" I hollered and headed down the street to my room to get ready for the false celebration of Lanslod.

Felt a little drunk, but not so much that entering, I wasn't surprised at a weird dim glow in my room. I placed a poker into the hearth and once the end lit, used it to light a candle. The glow still radiated. I turned around and was surprised to see a hazy figure kind of shimmering behind me, like Hamlet's ghost. Well, like Hamlet's dad's ghost to be precise.

"What the heck?"

"Good eventide," the apparition said.

"Yikes, you talk!" He nodded in an apparition type way. I thought for a second. "Are you a friend of Jesus?" Think that was the right protocol. Especially since I myself was a friend or at least acquaintance of the fellow. Of course, I called him Josh personally, but I didn't want to confuse things.

"Verily so. In fact I've talked to him recently."

"Oh really? Then who are you?"

"My name be Mirdynn. I believe you've been told I would contact you."

"Yes. But tomorrow. And in the tavern. And I assumed in person."

"Ah, but why travel when one can astral project? I came tonight because I foresaw you were about to leave."

That was true, I'd actually forgotten that I was supposed to wait for Mirdynn.

"Okay, so why did you want to see me?"

"To aid you in your mission . . ."

"Great. How so?"

"Remember this phrase: *When the hurly-burly's done, when the battle is lost and won . . .* " Okay, that was right out of Macbeth.

"And . . . ?"

"That'll be time to eat a bun!"

Seriously?

Apparently, I said that out loud, or maybe he read my mind because he said, "Ay, verily so."  A few seconds later he added, "It will make sense at the right time."

I hoped so, but it seemed unlikely. "At least tell me if I'm on the right track going to Salisburh?"

"Very well . . . Yes. And no. And yes again."  Okay, that was clear as mud. The apparition started to fade.

" . . . And keep close care of that little thingie . . . " was the last thing he said.

After he faded out, I tried to make sense of things. Hamlet and Macbeth both had in common the killing of a king, so maybe it referred to the death of Arthur. In Hamlet, the murderer was the king's brother and his wife's lover and in Macbeth it was the King's trusted liege. Mordred was the King's son and obvious threat, but Lanslod was both the Kings wife's lover and his liege. There was likely war brewing between those who followed Arthur and those following Mordred. But the bun? The lowest form of wheat? Puzzling.

After a bit, I shrugged it off. Mirgan the witch was on my side, apparently Mirdynn the wizard as well, plus I had a thingie and directions to the Grail. Probably in like Flynn. Whoever *he* was. Plus got bestowed with a witch's special kiss, which had to count for something. Had to go to this BS party tonight celebrating Lanslod's fake killing of the dragon, but why not enjoy it?

After all, things were looking up. Still might not know exactly what my mission was, but one by one, pieces were seemingly falling into place.

I was digesting that satisfying thought when there was a knock at the door.

Puzzled, I opened it. Timmy, along with—of all people—Mordred.

Mordred stared at me pointedly for a moment, then gave a slight nod. He was maybe expecting me to bow, but I didn't know the correct protocol for the King's bastard son. I gestured for them to enter, but Timmy excused himself, saying only, "He asked for you."

There was a long awkward silence, and then he sat on the stool by the table while I sat on the bed.

"Ahem, I wanted to catch you. We don't know each other well, but we have something in common."

"Pray tell," I said, trying to keep sarcasm out of my voice.

"You and I are both outcasts in Cantmell. I, because of the circumstances of my birth, and you, because of your heritage. And neither gets the respect we deserve."

"True. And so . . . ?"

"I propose an alliance . . ." He paused, fixing me in his gaze.

"But why? Only one person can find the Grail. Or do you suggest we agree to share credit? And that I trust you to keep your word, and you trust me?"

Mordred was quiet, and then: "What if I were to tell you that another relic is available to be found, far more powerful perhaps than the Grail? Do you believe it possible?"

"Surely, why not? 'There are more things on Heaven and Earth than dreamt of in your philosophy, Horatio.'"

Mordred stared at me blankly. "Are you drunk?"

Ooops, got caught up in Shakespeare again, thanks to Mirdynn.

"My apologies, Mordred, I did just return from the tavern."

"Well, then listen more carefully. I have just been told by a usually reliable source of another and better relic of our Lord."

"Namely?"

"The Lance of Longinus!" His eyes shone with palpable glee. It sounded familiar, but I couldn't quite place it.

"Of *whom*?"

"Longinus. The centurion who pierced the side of our Lord on the cross."

Okay, now I remembered it. Not from real life, even though I was there—but from some books I'd read on, of all things, the Third Reich. Also known as the Spear of Destiny. Hitler collected occult items and one of them was the lance of Longinus, who allegedly pierced the side of Joshua H. Christ on the cross. Supposedly blood and water spilt forth, blood signifying his humanity and water, his divinity, yada, yada.. Typical religion stuff. In WW2, Hitler had stolen the lance from a museum in Austria, I think. It was supposed to secure his victory. Worked out well, haha. Of course, like most relics there were multiple claimants to relic-hood, seven, or so I recollected to have later found out. Anyway, I recalled that in actuality the centurion had poked and not pierced Joshua's side, so it was probably BS just like the Grail. But if Mordred was going to pursue it, then better tag along. Or risk being blind-sided if it did show up.

"Who was your source, if I may ask?"

"A fine fellow from Dolwyn's Sign of the Ram." That was the tavern the opposite direction from Joseph's. I'd never gotten around to checking it out. "His name is Rodrick. He has his ear out for many things." Rodrick sounded like the counterpart of Berthulf.

"He is trustworthy?"

"Certainly. So long as he is properly paid." That also sounded like Berthulf.

"And where does he say we might find this treasure?"

"Right here in this town. It is apparently on its way to Glastonburh, but we may be able to intercept it. By force or by price."

"I have no money," I pointed out. Except for the gold solidus already promised to Berthulf.

"I do, but I need a companion, as it's in a rough part of the burh. The tanner's section."

That *was* a rough part of town. I'd in fact never been there either as myself or Freddie.

"Why me? Surely you have supporters—as the King's son—you could muster?" I lit a candle from the hearth fire as the afternoon was getting late and shadows were deepening.

"I do," he answered. "But I fear the King has spies among them." That indicated that the aim of his plan was ultimately not on the up and up so far as the King was concerned, but I was now committed to following what the Queen decided, whenever she got around to it.

"So you will give me at least a small part credit if you obtain it? That I assisted you?" I was trying to let him know that should it pan out, I would be happy to receive only a fraction of the credit, so as not to incentivize him to betray me. Of course, since it was going to be fake, it wouldn't pan out . . . unless he had some tricks up his sleeve. He nodded.

"When shall we go, then?" I further asked.

"Immediately, while the knights are gathering for the celebration."

I nodded and picked up my sword. He shook his head, "Nay, take this," he said, handing me a short sword, a blade that looked like a long dagger. I placed it under my tunic. Surreptitiously, I hid the gold solidus under a blanket, while on a hunch, I grabbed my staff as well. He nodded in acceptance and pulled a cloth from his bag. "Swath yourself in this. We are not going as knights."

I draped the cloth over my mail, and he did the same with another. The two were dirty and spotted and made us look like ordinary townspeople. Well, except for our footwear.

"Boots," I said, pointing down.

"Rats' tits!" he exclaimed. "I didn't think of that."

"Do you have more cloth?" He nodded. "Shroud them with the cloth then."

He pulled his short sword out and cut large swathes that we wrapped around our boots. Having done so, we left my annex turning left instead of my usual right. At the front of the Sign of the Ram, we were joined by a mangy character, no doubt Rodrick. He mumbled something unintelligible and without looking up took the lead as we ventured through the growing darkness. There was a low moon, but the streets were increasingly narrow, the buildings older, and the further we walked the more foreboding I felt. Maybe this wasn't such a good idea. Though I couldn't say I'd mind missing the party. Just so long as I didn't die in the process.

Finally we reached a darkened doorway. Mordred stood back as Rodrick knocked three times and after the third, a man emerged holding a candle. He beckoned us in and we followed him up some stairs and up to a room lit only by another candle. Two large men stepped out and demanded our swords.

"Let's turn around," I whispered to Mordred. He hesitated, deciding.

"Stay or go, I must have your swords," the nearest man said, brandishing his which had been hidden in the shadows. I looked around and there was little room to maneuver, though our short swords might mitigate our disadvantage. And suddenly the man behind us brought out a sword, though I could barely make out its glint in the dim candlelight. I offered up my shorts word. Mordred did the same.

"We shall see this through to the end," he whispered. I wasn't sure if that was supposed to be reassuring. I looked around and noticed Rodrick had disappeared. *That* was definitely not reassuring.

We stepped into the room which was also lit by a single candle. There were four men in it, their features mostly indistinguishable in the minimal light.

The closest spoke. "Pray to show us the money."

Mordred lifted a money bag from his tunic and held some gold coins to the candle. The man nodded. "Bring the lance," he declared. The furthest man rose and entered an even darker room to the right and emerged with a lance. He handed it to Mordred, who extended it to the candle trying to get a good look.

"It's so dark, very difficult to tell anything."

I bent over the candle too—it was hard to see anything, but it did look familiar. Could it be?

Then I remembered. No. It was not from Joshua's time but in fact from the bishop's guard. I remembered them leaning lazily while the bishop was ranting on about the effeminate. Bored as I then was, I was letting my attention wander freely. There was a notch on the lance at shoulder height to help the guards wield it more easily. I wasn't positive that no Roman lances had that feature, but I was inclined to be skeptical, and even in the dark the lance we were looking at didn't give any indication of being six centuries old, despite being stained with dark oils to make it look more ancient.

Mordred leaned in and whispered, "What do you think?"

"Fake."

"But good enough to pass it off?"

"Doubtful." The bishop's guards had ones just like this, and someone is likely to notice."

Mordred straightened up. "We will pass on it, at least until daylight when we can look again and more closely."

The nearest man shrugged, "Buy or don't buy, your money shall remain." He reached and grabbed the bag from Mordred who gasped in outrage.

"How dare you! Do you know who I am? I'm the King's son!"

"Bastard son, no?" the man noted.

"Nevertheless, I have followers who will persecute you to the ends of the kingdom."

The man laughed, "Do you think I care? I'm already a wanted man in five kingdoms. All I care about is coin." He turned to the others and said, "Escort him downstairs. And then let him find his way back to the palace in the dark. If he doesn't get mugged first." He laughed again.

After Mordred was pushed out of the room, the man turned to me, his face in a bemused grin.

"And you? What do you have in the way of currency?"

"Verily nothing. I'm a knight but a poor one who has yet to receive any revenues." I clutched my staff tightly.

"Then take his clothes and we can sell them in the morning. And send him to find his way home naked." The other two men snickered and approached.

Okay, that was it.  No way.

"Well, do you know *who I am?*" I started to twist the handle of the staff.

"As you said, a poor knight awaiting some revenue . . ."

"Nay!" I shouted as I twisted the handle, turning it into a lightsaber.  It hummed and glowed brightly as I shouted, "I'm the bastard son of Mirdynn, you fools!" That wasn't true of course but sounded great. Their eyes widened in shock.

I started to swing it, and in reflex, he raised the lance of Loginus to ward it off, but I sliced through the blade like warm butter, and it clattered to the floor. He cringed and the others cowered in the corner. *So much for that bogus relic*, I laughed to myself.  I grabbed the money bag and pointed the throbbing lightsaber at them.

"Into the back room!" I commanded. They fearfully obeyed, and I propped the table and chairs against the door. They'd get out after a bit, but I'd be long gone, with the light of the saber to help me find my way back to my annex.

And I did, after a few wrong turns and amazed stares by some tanners, and turned the lightsaber off just in time to see the knights passing by on the way to the celebration.

Ah well, at least I was in a better mood to face the party.

# 8

# A Questionable Quest

The party was a blow out, I suppose. In addition to Dagen, Arthur had engaged three jugglers and several musicians playing instruments: a *shawm*, a *rebec*, and a *tof*, which looked, respectively, like a kind of lute, flute, and tambourine. The shawm drowned out the other instruments, so they played it sparingly. Mead was being served, and a stuffed pig and several stuffed pheasants as well. There was dancing, a roaring fire and pretty maidens, most of them the knights' mistresses, sitting at a separate table away from the fire. Lucky for them because a lot of the smoke--as usual--wasn't going up the chimney. I rubbed my eyes and blinked a couple times.

King Arthur set off the proceedings with a prayer and said that in fact the quest would not start until two days' time. But tomorrow he would make an important announcement about the future of the kingdom. That set off some speculation, but after a bit everyone settled into drinking and celebrating. The knights pretty much ignored me as someone who was contradicting the dominant narrative, but the word had gotten out about what had really happened, so several people made their way over to whisper a thanks or congratulations for killing the dragon, mostly the ladies and servants. Not one of the knights did, however. I made a point to acknowledge to each of them who'd really shot it, though I suppose I deserved some credit for actually making it happen. In fact, I was starting to think I might be less of a screw up than I thought—back in modern times, that is. I'd pulled off the emerald tablets caper—against all odds—for Joshua H. Christ, hopefully preventing some possible Armageddon scenario and helped him escape to Mexico, helped slay a dragon—well, a suicidal Reptilian—and was on my way to finding the Holy Grail. Adonai willing, and the creek don't rise!

Then a page approached me. He told me the King wanted to see me privately. An audience! My first since I'd been hired. This was the Big Time! I nodded, and the page pointed to a curtained area behind the head of the room. I followed him.

Behind the curtain, the King sat stiffly at a small table, in front of a candle, holding some mead. In that moment, with the shadows flickering across his face, he looked years older than the forty or less I believed him to be. I bowed, and he nodded back, acknowledging.

"I wanted to thank you for your role in slaying the dragon . . . " he began. That was good, the word had gotten to him.

"I'm sorry I can't acknowledge you publicly. Sir Kay and Lanslod are too important to upset. Any day now, Kent or Wessex may move against us, so we can't afford to look divided."

"Then why launch a quest if the time is so inopportune?"

"It's not my idea. Anyway, I rely on the rural knights more—I just created the Oval Table to be able to keep an eye on at least *some* of them. Although it would've been nice if more knights had come to join. Which is another reason I am grateful. By the way, how is the land I bequeathed you working out?"

Oh, I have land? I should have guessed. Apparently it wasn't working out well, given the pittance that I had in my room. "It's alright, I guess."

"Well, I'm sorry that it's all the way in Scotland, but the Thane's man is due any week now with some revenues." The Thane was a Scottish Lord if my memory of MacBeth wasn't faulty.

"Say, might I ask for a favor?"

"Of course."

"Could I exchange it for something closer? Even if it is a little smaller. I don't believe in taxation without representation."

"What do you *mean* 'without representation'? *You* represent them. Because you own them."

"Ay, right? But anyway?"

"Do you have a parcel in mind?"

"Yes, I was thinking maybe you could switch mine with Agravain's by the river?" That would put a crimp in Lanslod's plans to win it from Agravain..

"The river plot is smaller for certain. Agravain'll be pleased. Granted. And by the way, you have permission from me to marry Aelfhere. Though really, it's the Queen who decides." He sighed and rolled his eyes.

"Anything else, your Highness?"

"Yes, if possible make sure neither Lanslod nor Kay gets the Grail, nor Mordred, for that matter."

"Why?" I asked, though I could guess the reason.

"I can't let them gain the prestige, because . . . " he trailed off, not wanting to put into words the possible coming power struggle. Denial, it's a *bi-otch*.

I nodded, bowed and took my leave. He waved me off, preoccupied.

As I came out from the curtain, Aelfhere approached me.

"You've seen the King, then?" I nodded. She continued, "I told him you'd been courageous and faced the dragon alone with your squire." I performed a fancy 18th century bow in appreciation and asked her if she wanted to join the dancing.

"No, I must be ready to attend to the Queen." I scanned the room. The Queen was sitting on a throne-like chair with Lanslod on a tall stool next to her—both of them looking like the real rulers of the kingdom. The Queen was watching us.

"I'm very glad you have chosen our side, and the Queen is, too." But what side was it? Had the Queen actually chosen or was she still watching how it'd play out? Or was she looking for a loophole to avoid the fatal choice? And was that even a possibility?

"There are, of course, some ripples from you having really killed the dragon, but . . . "

"Timmy killed the dragon, but Galahat made up a story. So the ripples are from that."

"Freddie, you must forget that. The story is set now and cannot change."

"I understand. At least I made a gold solidus from the endeavor. And when I find the Grail, we will be rich enough to build a castle. Or burh. Or whatever."

Aelfhere blanched. "No Freddie, you must let Galahat or Lanslod find it, there's too much resentment of you already."

"We will see. A rich man has many friends, while a poor man next to none." That sounded wise, if I say so myself.

"Well, it's in God's hands most truly. But be careful and don't confront them."

"I will try not to. And I'm off in two mornings like everyone else."

"Where first? Glastonburh and Salisburh are opposite directions." No wonder the knights laughed so hard. I guess I didn't notice because of the shadows on the map.

"Salisburh." She seemed to think it over, but then shrugged.

"Have a safe journey." She leaned over and kissed my cheek. Behind her, Queen Gwen frowned.

I was woken up the next morning by Timmy who had a message. The knights were being summoned to the meeting with the King at the Oval table. I looked at him groggily.

"Do you know what it's about?" He shook his head. I sort of remembered something about an important announcement. Future of the kingdom. Maybe he *was* getting divorced. Or abdicating. Probably not. I've noticed that leaders think everything they do is important, while the rest of us don't care unless it affects us directly. Timmy brought over my tunic, pants, surcoat, mail and boots. The shirt was marginally cleaner than the one I'd been sleeping in, so I put it on. He helped me with my pants and then wrapped cloth round my feet and pulled my boots over them. It was a little harder than last time—apparently my feet had swollen a little, though it was hard to tell.

"Do I have time for breakfast at the tavern?" He nodded. He was being a little quiet today for some reason, but I didn't want to embarrass him by asking. I'd probably find out if it was important.

The morning was moist and foggy. I looked both ways before crossing the street, trying to make sure I wasn't run down by a horse coming out of the fog. I also looked up to see if I was in danger of being doused with someone's chamber pot. But the fog seemed thicker farther from the ground, so I realized I'd have to take it on faith.

When I got to Joseph's, the place was nearly empty, except for Berthulf and Joseph who was behind the bar. I guess most people weren't chancing the hazards of the fog. Berthulf smiled at me, expecting an ale and some conversation but I was not in the mood. I waved to Joseph, and he asked, "Bread and ale?" I nodded. I took my usual place by the window. Joseph brought my breakfast. Sure would be nice if I could have some coffee, I thought pointlessly. After a few minutes, Berthulf came over to the table.

"Scat, gnat!" I hissed at him. He was nonplussed. In fact, he smirked a little. Smug little jerk.

"Perhaps you'd like to know the purpose of your meeting today?" He raised his eyebrows expectantly.

"And how would you know?"

"Spend all day and night in a tavern, and find out many things," he replied. He had a point. I surrendered.

"Okay, fine. Sit and have an ale . . . " I waved to Joseph to bring one. He did. No reason to go to a meeting unprepared.

"Fine. And now tell me what you know."

"Aye, it seems the knights are to receive a comeuppance, indeed, indeed."

"How so?"

"It seems that the knights, excepting you of course, esteemed sir, are a motley crowd of scurrilous varlets. And someone who was wronged managed to catch the ear of our holy Bishop. Who knows how. But the Bishop has gone to the King and demanded justice, and the King has listened. Who knows why. So there is to be a meeting where the King will do something, but who knows what."

"And that's it?"

"More than that I don't know," he shrugged.

"Well, it's worth an ale, but certainly no more."

"Oh, one more thing."

"Yes?"

"Mirgan and Mirdynn are in town, but I don't know why," he stated indifferently.

"Your knowledge, though wide as the sea, is deep as a puddle," I muttered loud enough for him to hear between swigs of ale.

He laughed, self-consciously. "Be that as it may, it's certainly worth the pittance you pay."

That made me angry. "Begone then, until occurs your next brilliant tidbit." He got up with the remainder of his ale and pissily headed to the back of the Tavern.

After I finished, I decided it was time to head to the palace. I stepped out into the gray soup. Just before I passed the gryphon, Mirdynn and Mirgan emerged from the fog, surprising me.

"Ah, we thought we might find you here . . . " Mirgan said. In the fog? Peculiar. And why not wait till we met in the Palace? If that were where they were heading, which was most likely.

"Are you going to the Palace? For the meeting?"

"Yea, to the Palace but not for the meeting," she replied.

"Then what?"

"A private matter. But we wished to talk to you too."

"Then go ahead."

"You are entering a time of great danger." That was reassuring, haha.

"So what should I do?"

"Be loyal and true. And do those words. The ones Kasper and Mateno told of to you."

The mantras. I had to admit I'd been a bit lackadaisical about them. "Anything else?"

Mirdynn responded, "Hold to the light."  Hmm. That was all pretty vague, certainly not something I would think required a special meeting. In the fog. That last was what Saint Germain told all of us back or forward, just before the French Revolution, though. Not that I knew what it meant. But before I could ask for further explanation, the two of them stepped back into the fog and disappeared. Through it, I heard the voice of Mirdynn faintly, "And fear not."

Okay then.


The two guards lolling at the entrance of the palace looked at me skeptically. Or maybe it was derisively. What rumors were being spread about me, I wondered. Or maybe they just didn't like their jobs. As I entered, Bors was climbing the stairway with Kay and Bedivere. Bors, of course, was gabbing away, and Kay looked annoyed, while Bedivere pretended to listen. Following them, I was the last of the knights to enter and ended seated at the Oval Table—next to Bors, of course. A fire was burning full on in the fireplace.

Arthur started right in. "It has come to my attention that several of you are behaving in ways that have given cause for complaint. As nobles, we are called to act nobly, are we not?" There were grumbles heard around the room. Queen Gwen was not in the room, however. Perhaps that was whom Mirgan and Mirdynn were going to see. "Therefore, I have decided to codify expectations I have for my knights' behavior." More grumbles ensued. Galahat stood, then walked over to the fireplace and stirred the wood, sending the flames higher. Lanslod made a point of stretching to indicate his discomfort with Arthur's direction. A couple of the other knights followed suit. However, Arthur plunged ahead.

"I have decided to make a *Code of Habitus* to guide us. It is written on this skin." He pointed to a lettered skin nailed to the wall behind him. Of course, most of the knights couldn't read. After a moment Arthur remembered that, and looked around the room for someone who could. His eyes briefly alighted on Lanslod and Galahat, but then he chucked that as a bad idea, and then on me. Which he also disregarded. Then he shrugged. "I will read them."

He pointed as he read:

"First, you must be fit. You must not engage in activities which weaken you, for your duty may be called upon in battle."

That was in contradiction to the knight's tendency towards drinking and gluttony, but whatever. A few knights sighed.

"Second, you must be loyal. You have all taken oaths, and you must fulfill them on pain of death." This one got general assent. Like I've said they liked loyalty. Especially from others towards them, but again whatever.

"Third, forbearance. You must have self-control, especially towards your fellow knights." This generated a couple groans, especially from the other knight next to Bors.

"Fourth, Largesse. You must be kind and respectful to the less fortunate. To women and peasants." This got a loud gasp from a couple knights, and Sir Kay almost got up. I guess he didn't like the idea of abandoning fun and rewarding activities such as rape and plunder.

"Finally, honor. You must consider honor to be like courage. For they are akin." This elicited general agreement.

"Is there any discussion?" He looked around the room.

Sir Kay stood and cleared his throat, then spoke. "Some of these are common sense. But there are others that infringe upon our rights as knights."

Most of the other knights nodded and several applauded. Arthur scanned the room again, then asked for a show of hands from those who objected. All of the Knights did, except me and Bedivere. Though Agravain and Balin raised their hands half-heartedly.

"Nevertheless," Arthur continued, "You will follow these if you are to remain at this Table."

"I thought we were all equals here?" Kay protested.

"We are. So you may remain. But if I find you in violation, I still may withdraw the lands I have given you."

This elicited yelps of protest. Arthur raised his hand to silence them. "The matter is settled. Does anyone else wish to raise any other issue while we are convened?"

Lanslod stood. "There are, of course, times when these rules may conflict. For example, you say forbearance, but sometimes one's honor is involved. For example, I'm aggrieved by offenses by Agravain who has refused to pay a debt. And I have dispensation by Bishop Wulfric that I am not tainted from the quest if I shed his blood. Surely, you will not deny my chance to regain my honor?"

Arthur considered. "I am respectful of your honor and the dispensation granted. But I can't afford to lose any knight with Wessex and Kent harrying our borders."

Lanslod reddened, "Then you require me to fight alongside a man who's dishonored me?" The knights murmured their discontent—loudly.

Arthur raised his hand. The room quieted a bit. "I understand your dilemma. But under the present circumstances, I'm at a loss for any solution."

I pulled myself up to speak. "I have an idea. Instead of trial by combat, how about a trial by horseback? Each man shall try to de-horse the other by means of a dulled lance. Who falls first from his mount shall be laughed at, thus restoring the honor of the victor. But both will be fit and available for a battle, should they be needed."

Balin snickered and nudged Agravain in the ribs. "He never gives up."

Agravain poked him right back, shaking his head. "I tell you again, it will never catch on."

Lanslod sputtered, but couldn't think of any objection. Other than that he was a weak horseman, of course. Which he would never admit. Arthur looked me over and remembered that I was one of the only ones who hadn't objected to his code. So he stated, "Then it shall be. Let the contest occur tomorrow noon in front of the city gate. And we will postpone the quest one more day. So unless there is another matter, we will end the meeting."

No one spoke. Agravain and Balin came alongside me and started jabbing me in the ribs. "Where do you get these crazy ideas? Are they all this mad in Galilee?"

I glanced back into the room. None of the other knights had left. They were engaged in a whispered but heated conversation, amidst broad gesturing and striking adamant poses. If I didn't know better, I would say maybe they were starting to plot. And if I *did* know better, I would say certainly they were. In fact, when Sir Kay noticed me looking in, he turned his back to me and made a gesture to the knights to speak more quietly and discreetly. Then someone shut the door.

I turned to the Agravain and Balin. "Aren't you afraid of being left out of the conversation?"

They looked at each other then, turned around and went back into the room. The door was closed promptly behind them.

The next morning, Agravain showed up at the annex, asking if I was willing to be his second. I questioned him about the little meeting behind closed doors. He said, "You don't want to know." I did want to know, but knew better than to push him. I declined his request and suggested Balin. He nodded. I felt bad, so said I'd help by advising him. And he accepted the offer. There were a few hours before the joust, so I figured I'd cross the street to Joseph's. The weather was nice for a change, which probably meant the joust would be well attended. Also, I had less chance of being run down in the street while crossing or having slop dropped on my head from a chamber pot. The combination brightened my mood.

Entering the tavern, I was not surprised to see Berthulf, but I *was* to see Mirgan, of all people, talking with him. At closer glance, I was able to see she was reading his palm. After a couple minutes, she rose, and he bowed to her. I didn't see her children around, which seemed strange until I remembered she hadn't had them with her the day before either.

She came to where I was sitting. "Don't mind him," she allowed, "He is harmless and indeed useful at times."

"And what do his palms tell you?"

"That he won't live long, but I didn't tell him that."

"What did you tell him?"

"To drink a less and to take care whom he befriends."

"So what will kill him? Drink or his friends?"

"One or the other, or the combination."

I nodded. "Did you have more you wanted to tell me?"

"Yes, caution will harm you, but loyalty will not." That was surprising because Freddie seemed to me to be more than a bit under-cautious, as the attempt at fording the river clearly demonstrated.

"Anything else?"

"One more thing, though I don't know what it means: Avoid hitting the snooze button. That's just training you to oversleep."

Wow, she nailed me. I can't tell you how many times I was late to work because of that. Not that it was a problem here, but if I ever made it home. I guess that meant I would, though the prospect didn't soothe me the way it might've on my first journey. I was getting acclimated to being a stranger in a strange land and time.

Since it was getting close to time for the joust, I waved to Joseph to bring me some bread and ale. And some for Mirgan too. She brought out a strange sense of familiarity as if I'd known her before. Or would know her again. She was wise. I could relax in her presence.

I toasted to Mirdynn. Something she could get behind. She raised her mug, and we tapped them together. Which made me think to ask, "Oh, and where is he today?"

"Busy," she said tersely, and her face closed. Oh well. We were mostly silent the rest of our meal, but strangely it didn't make me uncomfortable. After we finished, she rose and fixed me in her gaze. "Remember what I tell you. Always." I nodded. Seemed like the thing to do.

I went back to my annex for a few minutes and then headed out to the gate. People were starting to gather outside for the joust, but it wasn't going to be anything like in the movies. No arena, no lanes for the match, just people sitting mostly on rocks or stools that they'd brought. There were several dozen people already there and more coming. The only thing in common with the movies was the sunniness of the day. Maybe they cancelled jousts if it was rainy. Made sense 'cause the horses could trip in the mud.

After a little bit, palace guards and servants showed up, the servants carrying chairs and a canopy. Then a little later, the King and Queen, accompanied by Galahat and Gawain. Gawain of course, had his hands folded across his chest in a reverent fashion. Lanslod and Kay followed with their squires. Lanslod naturally sneered when he saw me, but Galahat ignored me with his nose up, guess where . . . in the air.

I supposed Kay was Lanslod's second because he waved to a stable boy to bring forward Lanslod's horse, a beautiful white mare. I thought it looked like the equine version of Queen Gwen, though probably a lot more docile if his reputation as a weak horseman was true. Not necessarily the best horse in a fight. At the last minute, a similar realization must have crossed his mind because he shook his head and signaled the stable boy to go back. After a few minutes, he returned with a frisky brown stallion, who snorted and reared before calming down. The King sat in his chair next to the Queen under her canopy and engaged in animated but quiet conversations.

Then Agravain appeared with Balin leading his horse, their two squires following. It was the same one he used the day we crossed the river to visit Mirgan. I again was impressed by the horse. Advantage: Agravain. But then, Agravain seemed a bit too loose and carefree. Okay, he was drunk and so was Balin. Advantage: Lanslod.

Arthur rose and pointed out the starting place for each rider. A servant came forward with two blunted lances and handed Kay one, and then the other to Balin. The two sides retreated to their bases where their squires helped them mount their horses. The seconds handed them up the blunt lances. All in all, it didn't look much like the jousts you see in the movies. Like I said. Not even real armor, just the usual suit of mail. They were not even wearing helmets. It kind of reminded me more of a picnic with a couple horses. Neither side went to a fair maid to get her scarf either. But then there were a few centuries ahead to firm up the details.

Finally, the squires led the horses to their starting points. Arthur signaled for them to approach. But Lanslod's mount immediately bucked, and he slid right off the horse's butt, almost landing right on his own rear. He looked around embarrassed, but nobody said anything, although some of the younger people snickered. They were quickly shushed by their elders. Technically, I thought that it should have counted as a fall, but the King gave him a mulligan. He remounted and they approached the King. Arthur had them touch lances and explained it would be best of three falls, unless someone had to forfeit. They both bowed and then headed back to the starting point. But Agravain's horse turned around early and started his charge. When Lanslod's horse saw the large beast charging straight at him, it took off at an angle, and it took a hundred yards for Lanslod to get him under control. By the time he got back to the starting point, Agravain was downing a mug of ale with Balin. Arthur conferred with Gwen and decided to give him another mulligan.

They started again, and this time Lanslod turned early and managed to keep his horse trotting straight. He held his lance forward with his shield on his forearm. I've mentioned that the saddles didn't yet have the wooden front arch that allowed a knight to lean forward against it while aiming the lance. So unfortunately, with one hand on the reins and the other holding his lance, Lanslod started to slip forward. That was lucky in a way, though, because Agravain was right upon him and would have hit him in the head. Instead, Agravain, bracing for impact, started to slide backwards. After missing Lanslod, while trying to regain balance, Agravain dropped his lance. A squire chortled. Lanslod was in no position to capitalize as his saddle started to come loose. Arthur signaled for them to return to their starting positions. Agravain's squire brought him his lance. I decided this was a good time to share some advice.

I sauntered up to Balin and him and shared, "Don't even try to strike him. He will fall off on his own. Whereas if you try, you're likely to fall instead." Agravain and Balin pondered this for a moment. "Hell's knells. Where's the glory in that? I'll topple him easily." He slugged down some more ale.

Lanslod finished resecuring his saddle and then remounted with the aid of his squire. They faced off again. Agravain's horse snorted fiercely. Lanslod's whinnied and reared a little, but he was able to maintain. Then they both charged. At the last moment, Agravain ducked and sent his lance under Lanslod's shield, and Lanslod tried to writhe away but the blow glanced against his side, and he fell sideways. A couple people gasped, and a couple others cheered. Agravain raised his lance in drunken triumph but leaned too far back and started to slide. He waved his lance in the air like a trapeze artist trying to balance but it didn't work, and he fell too. More cheers. More laughter.

Arthur looked impatient. He scowled at those laughing and they shut up. Agravain and Lanslod both struggled to their feet

Arthur exclaimed loudly, "I declare the match a draw," and shook his head. "Bring on Dagen!" He gestured behind, and Dag appeared, juggling and making faces. The crowd cheered. Arthur shot me a dirty look, and I shrugged. I overheard Balin telling Agravain, "I said it'd never catch on," and he left for the pub. The rest of the audience slunk off bit by bit, mostly ending up at one tavern or another. Probably you think the proper way to have spent the evening before a quest to find the Holy Grail would be in solemn prayer, but apparently you'd be wrong, or at least the knights thought so. I didn't join them.

9

# Rocks Of The Ages

You might also think that I set off the next morning bright and early with Timmy on my quest, but I didn't. Or you might think I hesitated, feeling that something was wrong, but that's not right either. You might even think I stayed in bed, suddenly doubting myself. All those things were reasonable guesses. Nope, I stayed in bed because my allergies were bothering me. They were bad even indoors, so I guessed they would be much worse outside. Sadly, the day was beautiful and sunny, which must have brought the pollen out. You won't be surprised to know that Cantmell did not have much in the way of facial tissue to blow one's nose. Instead, I had to use a piece of cloth which quickly got saturated. Gross. Anyway I wasn't going to go anywhere under the circumstances. I had planned to meet Timmy at the stables early, but I suppose he figured he could let me sleep in a little, and around mid-morning he knocked on the door.

"Hewwo, cumb in," I muttered. He entered.

"My liege?" He bowed a little. Didn't do a thing for me. Too miserable.

"Get me some bewwadonna, pwonto!"

"What's bewwadonna pwonto?"

I blew my nose. That's better. Trying again, "Belladonna, you dope. Right away." That was harsh, but I was never a good patient when sick. "Sorry," I said as an afterthought. He bowed again and ran out. Belladonna's active ingredient is atropine, a decongestant of sorts. It's also an antidote for blowfish poison. I got some of both for Joshua H. Christ in order to fake his death. Also good as a poison itself. Got to be careful of the dose.

Timmy returned a little later with a small pouch of the herb.

"How do I take it and how much?"

"You didn't tell me to ask . . . " He bowed and ran out, expecting another harsh comment from me.

When he came back, he showed me how to brew it into a tea and how much to drink. I brewed and drank, and sure enough soon started feeling better. No runny nose, no sneezing. A bit of a fast heartbeat. The stuff is strong.

"Hey, let's get moving." Heartbeat definitely elevated. A little like doing coke. Not that I would ever try that. Wink, wink. Timmy nodded, and we gathered my gear and headed to the stables.

"Give me a fast one," I told the Stablemaster. I didn't currently have a regular horse, just paid a fee to have one when needed.

"That's extra."

"Naturally. Actually, give him a fast one too." Nodding toward Timmy. That was probably unusual because squires typically travelled second class, so to speak. But I wanted him to keep up with me in case we were pursued. Or maybe it was drug talking, heh. The Stablemaster threw the saddles on, and tightened them. We threw on saddlebags with our swords, one longbow, blankets, and a few loaves of bread.

"Let's jet!" I exclaimed. Not sure how that translated. I climbed on and was out the gate before Timmy even mounted. I had to stop and wait by the bridge because I didn't know which way to turn. Timmy pointed, and I set off at a half-gallop. This stuff is a kick.

We made really good time, thanks to the belladonna, although we nearly did in the horses. By sunset, we'd gotten far enough into Salisburh plain to spot the spooky forms of some giant rocks jutting out of the grasslands. OMG, it was Stonehenge. I knew there was a reason why the name Salisburh was familiar.

As you probably know, Stonehenge was constructed by aliens to help the ancients keep their calendars straight. It aligned with the sunrise on equinox days. Considering that nearly all ancient calendars used the moon and were thus poorly attuned to the solar calendar, this was a singular achievement. There's thirteen months of twenty-eight days with a day and change left over, or twelve months of thirty with five intercalary days. The Jews had an extra month every seven years or so.

The monoliths were a huge achievement too, having come all the way from Wales, being rolled on logs, and somehow being levered upright? No, it wasn't done that way at all, mainly because those Druids were blessed with some interplanetary friends who did the heavy lifting, just like with the pyramids. Maybe this was before the Prime Directive, or maybe there was another exception—creating things that helped spiritually inspire the puny humans into dreaming big and progressing.

Anyway, it seemed like the perfect place to find the Grail. We spread our blankets, and I gathered twigs for a fire. Timmy had a fire kit, which was two pieces of wood, one with a string that you twirl to create a spark. Hard work. They didn't even make us do that in Boy Scouts. We got three matches. But he was able to do it. It took a while for the fire to build and boil, and then Timmy soaked some jerky in the boiling water to soften it, and we ate that with the bread. The belladonna was wearing off, and I was tired, so I laid out and climbed into my blankets and started to snooze.

Maybe it was the belladonna, but I went right into a crazy dream. Timmy and I were in front of this big gray government building. We entered and were directed to the second floor—the bureau of Cosmic Affairs. They asked us what we wanted, and we told them we were applying for a Holy Grail.

"Next door to the right . . . " a squirrely-looking dude said.

We went to the right and inside there was a Reptilian wearing glasses and sitting at a desk behind a glass, bank-type window. This wasn't going to be good.

"You can't have the Grail," he said before we had a chance to open our mouths.

"You speak English?" I asked.

"Tuesdays and Fridays. You shouldn't call us Reptilians. We've been here longer than the Saxons, you know."

"What do you prefer to be called then?"

"Anglo-Reptilians, if you please. You can't have the Grail because you're not pure of heart."

"Timmy is though," I asserted.

"Ha, not so. He killed Swarg."

"Swarg? The other Reptilian?"

"Anglo-Reptilian." He slammed the window shut to signify the interview was over, and I woke up.

I looked around to see Timmy had dozed off and the fire was almost out. That was a weird dream. It did remind me of something. I'd forgotten that in the legend of the Grail, it could only be found by the pure of heart. Supposedly, that was Gawain, if I remembered his epithet correctly – The Pure. But he was a fanatic and friends with Galahat, so it was unlikely. Plus, he sat still while Kay and Galahat lied about killing the dragon. So no way. In fact, none of the knights were even close. King Arthur wasn't too bad, but he was a king, and that meant he'd probably done a ton of bad things on the way to the top. Aelfhere was pretty pure, but maybe only because she was so sheltered. Anyway they'd never let her out of the burh. Joshua H. Christ. He could do it, but he wasn't available in this time slot. What about Talmo and Lamo? Hmm. Maybe. There was a bit of light from the moon and the fire. I started rummaging through my gear. Did I have my souvenir pen? Were they even around? Ah, there's my pouch. I got the pen out and turned the top to maximum power.

"Come in, dudes, I need you. Over." I always said "over," 'cause I'd seen too many war movies with walkie -talkies. Well. They'd get a laugh out of it, if they heard. They didn't. No response. I tried again. This time it went to voicemail.

"Hi, you've reached the message box of Kasper and Mateno. Or maybe Smith and Brown. Or maybe Hall and Oates . . . We're not currently in this time period, but leave a message and we will get back to you in this lifetime or the next." There was a beep.

I said, "Hall and Oates? Seriously? Hey. It's Freddie in Cantmell. Need your help. Over." Something told me to leave the pen turned on. Nothing more I could do.  I fell asleep.

I woke up right at dawn from the familiar screech of the pen. It was them. I picked up the pen.

"Hullo," I said dully, still sluggish.

"What's wrong with Hall and Oates?"

"What? Oh. Um, it's from the seventies . . . "

"Yeah, we were there recently. Liked the music."

"Seriously? Well, it's kind of dated."

"Well, all dates are dated to us. Anyway, we're down at Rockhenge."

"What? No you mean Stonehenge . . . "

"I thought rocks are bigger stones. So Rockhenge. Anyway, we're here. Come down and meet us."

"Copy that."

"Come down and meet us."

"No copy that means I got it."

"Got what?" This was getting absurd.

"I mean we will be there. Soon."

"Okay. Your communications. Try to be more precise"

"Copy that. I mean right."

I roused Timmy, and we started the trek across Salisburh Plain, which was deserted at the moment. Closer up, the ship showed behind one of the monoliths. As we dismounted, Talmo greeted me.

"Howdy partner."

"Huh, what?"

"Sorry, we were also recently in the American West. Your horses reminded me. We were just passing through this century to touch in with Emperor Constantine when we got your message."

"No problem. Say, we need to find the Holy Grail. Do you know about it? Also, I had a dream that it could only be found by someone pure of heart. Anything to that?"

"Sure. I remember a Holy Grail. We did it after we dropped you off. Cleanup. Can't remember precisely. The pure of heart sounds right. We've been experimenting with security parameters to make sure things are done for good, not evil."

"Alright, I'm assuming I'm not pure of heart, but what about Timmy?"

"Umm, no." Right, killed the Reptilian. Maybe I could pay off a Bishop though, haha.

"What about you guys?"

"Hardly. You get a little cynical in this line of work," Lamo piped in.

"Who then?"

"First of all, let me straighten you out on something," Talmo continued. "Purity and innocence isn't something you start with. Because you've had past lives for one thing."

"Okay, then who *is* pure of heart?"

"Good question. Let me think." He stood there for a while.

"It occurs to me," I said, "that perhaps your security parameter is a bit too stringent?"

"Could be. It's beta. Needs tweaking probably."

"Wait, I know," Lamo interjected. We both turned to him.

"Doltly is pure of heart!"

"How so? Does he even have a heart?" I had to ask.

"No, but that's the point. The null value is pure of heart. So the program searches for impurities. Since he doesn't have a heart he has no impurities. Doltly, come here!"

Doltly emerged from the ship. He faced Lamo.

"Yes, Boss?" Lamo looked embarrassed.

"I get a kick out of hearing him say that," he said.

"No problem. I feel that way about 'my liege'."

"Doltly, can you find the Holy Grail?"

"Right away, boss." Lamo snickered guiltily at that.

Doltly made a beeline to the far side of the monoliths and returned after a few minutes with a clay goblet that had a ruby in the side. He gave it to Lamo.

Okay, the Holy Grail! That wasn't hard at all. "How the heck did he do that?"

"He's programmed to note every object that he comes in contact with and its exact chemical composition. Which, in fact, he did note at one point, though *when*, I can't quite remember. Then he just does a scan of the area—radius of ten miles."

"Pretty impressive."

"Yes, he was very popular in the seventies for his ability to find car keys. We're thinking we could start a side business. You know—remotes, cell phones, wallets . . ." Lamo handed it to me. I turned it over and over in my hands.

"Hey, what does this thing actually do?"

Lamo thought for a moment, then turned to Talmo. "Do *you* remember?"

"Something important."

"Or was it something magical?" Lamo considered.

"Something magical *and* important!" replied Talmo.

"Like what?" That was me.

"Umm, maybe it Holy-ifies?"

"Or Grail-ifies."

"Or holy-ifies *and* grail-ifies."

They both laughed goofily. Clearly I wasn't going to get an answer from them.

I remembered the thingie in my pouch. "I think it might need this . . . " I brought it out.

"Oh, right. Put it in the bottom . . . there." I placed the thingie in the base, and it snapped into place. "Be careful. It can get stuck." I nodded.

"Now I remember," Talmo said. "It turns wine into blood."

"That's disgusting."

"You should see what happens when you put a matzo into it."

"Flesh?" I guessed.

"Yeah, really gross. Religion. So silly. Anything else you need?"

"Can't think of anything right now, but anyway you usually can't tell me."

"You're learning. Any message for Constantine? Not that we'd transmit it."

"Yeah, tell him to can it with the boiling his wives deal."

"Can it?"

"I meant stop."

"Right, canning them would be gross, too." He gave me back the Grail.

Lamo and Talmo turned away and headed towards the ship. I suddenly remembered Timmy. He was standing next to the horses frozen in place. Was it the shock of seeing the ship or had they hypnotized him? Just to be sure, I waited until the ship disappeared, then said, "You will remember nothing that happened today." Then I snapped my fingers.

That actually worked. Timmy opened his eyes.

"My liege. Where are we?"

"Salisburh plain. Some ruins called Stonehenge."

"I've heard of it. Uther Pendragon sent 15,000 men to fetch the rocks, but they were too heavy, so Mirdynn brought the rocks from Ireland by magic." Yeah maybe. If spaceships are magic.

"Do you remember? We have the Grail."

"We have the Grail?" He dropped to his knees. He raised his hands in prayer and looked skyward.

"Thank you, Jesus and Mary. I can't believe it. And thank you my liege, I owe you so much. You took me in and gave me a chance to see miracles."

"No biggie. Want to see it?"

"Oh yes, may I?"

I held it up. "Doesn't look like much, right?"

Timmy shook his head. "But it means so much. It means that Jesus is real. The communion. Everything the church teaches . . . "

"Yes, Jesus was real. But his name was Joshua. Actually, Yashua. The rest, not so much . . . "

Timmy looked confused. "I don't understand." I instantly felt guilty.

"Don't worry about it, leave that to others."

He looked relieved. "Yes, that's what the Church teaches us."

I started to shake my head, but caught myself and pretended to swat away a fly.

"We should start to head back. You carry it in your saddlebag. But we won't show it to anyone until we get back to Cantmell. He nodded.

I put the Grail in Timmy's saddlebag, and we started off for home. There would be no stops along the way because I wasn't about to lose this item before we got back. That had already happened to me back in Joshua's time when I spent 50 gold aureii on some emerald tablets, only to have them lifted from me by a band of Zealots. It turned out they were fake though, so except for the financial loss, I had the last laugh.

Kind of like *Mrs. Lincoln, aside from the assassination, how was the play?* Criminy. Of course, the Grail was fake too, but you could say it was a *real* fake, and could turn wine and wafers into blood and flesh. Not sure what the market was for something like that, but maybe I could unload it for a crapton of gold before everyone realized how pointless it was. Or its batteries ran out. Or maybe it was important for some undisclosed reason, and I'd find out how.

We mounted our horses and started to head back. With no stops and a little luck we could make it by nightfall.

After about an hour or so, we came to a river. Up a ways ahead, a stone bridge. I didn't really remember it from the way back, but then I was hyped up, speeding on belladonna, so maybe I wasn't paying good attention. Well, if needed, I'd, of course, pay the toll and not fight, threaten, or try to ford. Timmy turned to me and noted, "Bridge," and started to fumble through his pouch for some coppers.

"I'll get it," I started to fumble through mine. Sure enough, as we approached the bridge four men emerged from underneath. They were wearing hoods and looking down but otherwise didn't look out of the ordinary. I had a strong urge to turn around, but I ignored it. As we got close, one shouted, "Two coppers to cross." Okay, nothing to worry about then. We slowed as we got to the bridge and one of the men leapt and grabbed the reins of Timmy's horse. His hood fell off. It was Galahat. The other pulled a sword and stood in front of me. I had a sinking feeling. To say the least. He pulled down his hood. It was Lanslod. That figured. Like Agravain said, if he said he was staying, it meant he was going. I could have turned and fled, but I couldn't abandon Timmy. Or the Grail. Even though it was really worthless.

"What ho? Have you bought this bridge?" I asked. I still don't know what it means, but I guess it's rubbing off on me.

"No, I won it in dice," Lanslod smirked. Naturally.

"Fine, we will pay you the toll."

"We don't need your coppers, just the item you found." Oh no. Not again.

"What makes you think we found anything?" I bluffed.

"Search their bags," Lanslod sneered.

Probably the drunk in the pub sold me out. Or maybe the messenger from Wessex told Queen Gwen and she told Lanslod, and he figured it out. Although he probably wasn't that smart. Well, I guess smarter than me, because the same thing keeps happening. Crap! I had a surge of hot anger and was ready to pull my sword and lash out despite the odds. But I glanced over at Timmy and saw the look in his eyes, and I knew I'd at minimum be sacrificing his life for my pride. I fought down the bile rising in my throat. It surged a second time, and again I managed to swallow it. The only thing I could think of was to silently rain down a curse from the heavens. Which was probably bad karma for me, but I had to do something. *May you be eaten by a Reptilian and have your bones turned into toothpicks!* It made me feel better. Almost.

The two others, their squires, saw me steam and drew their swords. Then Lanslod came up to my horse and at sword point rummaged through the saddlebags.

"Go through the squire's," he said when he failed to find anything. Timmy gasped.

"Ah, ha." Lanslod smirked again. Timmy dived from his horse and knelt before him.

"Please good sir, we have been divinely gifted with a miracle. Do not thwart God's will, for it was destined for my blessed master . . ."

"Escobar—pure of heart? Ha!" He had a point. But then he was no better and likely worse.

The two squires grabbed Timmy's arms, while Galahat went through the saddlebag. He lifted the goblet into the air. The two squires cheered.

"I can't wait to drink wine from this cup," Lanslod said. He'd be in for a rude awakening, I thought. Hmm. Maybe I could play it to my advantage.

"You cannot. All manner of vileness will issue forth if the wrong person drinks from it and without the proper protocol."

"Is that so?" Lanslod glared skeptically.

"Most certainly. Do you dare tempt the Lord?" I was going out on a limb here, maybe even tempting the Lord myself. But hopefully, the Lord's son would remember the little favor I did him back in Judaea. Or maybe the whole thing was BS anyway. I thought of telling them that anyone else who touched the Grail would die, but knowing Lanslod, he'd just order one of the squires to do it. Not such a smart move for me. But with a little luck, I could maybe bluff this through.

Lanslod beckoned Galahat over. They huddled for quite a while. Finally Galahat turned to us.

"You will return now. Follow behind shortly. We will not announce finding the Grail. If you do not reveal the secret to mastering the Grail in three days, Lanslod will kill you in trial by combat. And no getting out of it by a joust, or whatever you call it. Then, the Grail will apparently go unfound."

That was pretty clever. Because killing us without the King's permission was a capital offense. But in a "fair" fight? No problem. Okay, that would give me a little time to figure out a way to get it back, especially since Arthur might delay the fight until after any attack by Wessex or Kent. As for getting it back, I currently couldn't imagine how. I nodded, still fighting down the impulse to punch him or worse. Galahat placed the Grail in his own saddle bag. Timmy looked downcast, almost in tears. I patted him on the back.

"It's just a test." I told him. "All will work out in the end." I didn't really believe it.

The four of them turned around and headed back towards Cantmell. The two of us stood on the bridge and watched. I was in no hurry to get back now. At least last time, there were a few who knew the truth. This time, no one. Plus, in three days I would have to fess up to Lanslod about the Grail or face him in combat. Maybe Agravain would end up fighting first, and slay him. Though he didn't seem very confident. I wasn't either, though my fencing was greatly improved. Not with the heavy swords they used this time period. And even if Agravain or I did best him, there was no way it would help us retrieve the Grail.

"Is there a town nearby?" I asked Timmy.

"Yes, a few miles ahead there's a crossroad, and to the left a village another couple of miles or so further."

"And is there an inn where we can stay?"

He nodded.

"Then let us spend the night there and return to Cantmell tomorrow."

We mounted up and plodded toward the crossroad. I let Timmy lead because I wanted his mind to be occupied instead of filled with doubts and remorse. Like mine was. The sky was graying, and a light spray of rain commenced. It started and stopped intermittently as we approached the crossroads, which was pretty much in the middle of nowhere, with just small hills on three sides. There was no sign marking directions, but in the distance a small village was nestled between a hill and a stream with a grove of trees, a bit of smoke rising thinly from a dwelling or two.

"There it is," said Timmy, pointing. "It's called Shrew Towne."

"Really? That's its name? How odd." Not really, I thought since we were recently in Bumchester, but I wanted to keep Timmy's mind occupied, lest it take a dark turn.

"Nay, its real name given by Thane of Wiltshire is *Scrifrm*, because it is the sheriff's farm."

"Obviously there must be a lot of shrews living in the ground nearby?"

"Yea, indeed, but also the villagers much dislike the sheriff's wife," he chortled to himself.

It was great to see Timmy cheering up, but now *my* mood was darkening. Couldn't Talmo and Lamo have warned me about what was about to happen? Or were they prevented by the stupid Prime Directive? Or were they too stupid themselves? If it was the first, this whole thing was just some Kabuki theatre—pointless and difficult to understand. If the second, well, my life was kind of in their hands, which sucked. Maybe worse, *everything* was nonsense, from Mirgan's kiss to the Grail, to my mission—if I even had one, and it wasn't just made up in my own stupid brain as a rationalization for bopping around in time when there were better things to do. What better things? Who knows. But something.

I hollered to Timmy to stop and dismount. I climbed down and gave him my reins, and told him I needed a few minutes to figure out something, then started walking through the chalky fields, even as the rain quickened. The clouds continued to blacken, and a bit of wind whipped up, lashing my face.

Why, why, why, why, *why*? I thought. Why what? Not just this. Everything. I don't even know . . . just why. Why-the-heck everything. Why must we suffer and die and make up reasons for suffering and dying? Why are there wars and poverty and sickness and deceit and treachery? Why does everything eat everything else? Asking for a friend, haha.

The rain let up for a minute, and I took a moment away from my existential crisis to glance back to Timmy, who was waiting patiently for me to do whatever he thought I was doing. The poor sap. Had no idea. Just a pawn in the game. Followed the rules and was a good dude, and believed in the right things. He would probably be a good knight if he made it, otherwise he'd just be a servant his whole life and die a pointless death having never stepped out of line. If he did become a knight, he could step out of line as he wished but would die a pointless death for honor or King or something. And not that it matters, he'd never even know there was a time traveler in his midst.

Which reminds me, what about me? I'm zipping around eternity allegedly trying to make things better, but the only thing that does anything for you personally is doing your mantra, according to the Venusian dudes. But no one does mantra here, or even anything close to any kind of spiritual practice. They just mumble prayers in Latin, a language they don't even understand. What good is that? And who am I to be trying to fix the world when I couldn't even—back home—fix my own life?

On the other hand, why not? Who says there *shouldn't* be death, wars, disease, famine and all kinds of shite? Where was anything *better* promised to us? Why not even worse? I mean it could be . . . right?

I know people ask how could God allow to happen this tragedy or that travesty. But maybe tragedy or travesty—it was irrelevant to God, who only cared if you did your mantra or maybe not even that. Maybe He was just hanging out in heaven, waiting for us to show up and party. Or maybe He was a She. Or a Reptilian.

Or maybe He was doing His dangest and succeeding at removing 99.9 percent of the mess, and we were complaining about the lousy 0.1 percent He hadn't gotten to.

Or maybe He'd delegated the job to folks like Talmo and Lamo. Who'd delegated a small part to me. Yikes, that meant I needed to get my act together.

Somehow the thought that things could be worse, and that I had my part to play, was bracing to me. I did need to get my act together. And stop whining like Bishop Wulfric did about the effeminate. He was certainly a role model, haha.

But I. Had to. Get it. Together. I *did* have to. I *really* did have to. I slapped myself in the face a few times. Get it together, man. Get it together. Only way out is forward.

Okay. I sighed, straightened up, and turned around. Then walked back through the drizzle to the horses. But I didn't really believe it.

# 10

# Get Your War On, Warren

Despite failing to buck myself up, I felt a little better as I walked back to the horses but noticed that Timmy's mood had started to sag again. And why wouldn't it? He'd slain a dragon and had the glory stolen, and now witnessed a miraculous finding of the Holy Grail, only to have it robbed as well. It was certainly an adequate reason for loss of faith in any normal circumstances. Still bummed *me* out too, even though I knew neither of them—the dragon and the Grail—were what they appeared to be. I patted him on the back, and he boosted me into the saddle, then struggled up onto his own.

"Let's go into the town," I suggested, and he nodded.

Shrews Town was nothing much to speak of size-wise, even less than Bumchester, which wasn't much. And it was a lot less prosperous. The wood looked older, many of the houses had a decided lean, and the thatching on the roofs looked thinner. As our horses ambled in, we passed a blacksmith, a rickety store, an even more rickety stable, and a small inn, signified by a sign of a bear. The bear was crudely painted though and could have been a cow on its hind legs trying to box.

I dismounted, deciding to handle things myself since Timmy was in a mood. Inside was a small front room, walls darkened by smoke stains, with a couple tables and a keg on the counter and a stairway up to some rooms.

"Any room for myself and my squire?" I asked a fat lady who was cleaning up.

"I happen to have an empty room," she replied. "Will your squire be wanting a place in stables?"

"No, tonight he will stay with me." I felt bad for Timmy, so why not treat him to a night in a bed? "But no others please." She raised her eyebrows. "I mean it."

She nodded. "Well, unlikely there be others in this rain."

"Food and drink soon?"

"Yes, shortly. Room is on your right whereafter you get up the stairs."

I fetched Timmy and we carried our saddles and saddlebags upstairs. After we settled our gear and tried to dry off a bit with the blankets on the straw mattress, I checked the sheet for evidence of bedbugs, but it looked clear. Timmy asked if he could lay down, and when I nodded, he plopped down and promptly fell asleep. I figured a nap might be good too, so I followed suit.

I awoke after an hour or so when it was starting to get dark. Timmy looked peaceful, so I decided to let him sleep and bring him back some food while I had supper and some ale.

Downstairs, a few villagers were at the tables. One was sitting alone, so I joined him.

He had a low brow and dark hair but a pleasant face under graying whiskers. He was well dressed in a simple country way.

"Good Even, stranger," he smiled as I approached and motioned me to make myself comfortable. "It's a decent stew they have here, and passable brew." I motioned to the fat lady, and she ladled my stew and poured my ale.

"I'm the warren of this town, meaning I do nothing and get paid nothing to keep my people and animals in line. But I get to hunt freely of the beasts and vermin for my own. And you, good Sir, appear to be a knight. Is that so?"

I nodded.

"And where be you heading, Sir, and from where if I may be bold?"

"You are bold, but I'm heading back to Cantmell." I smiled.

"Ah, then we two be at war today, do you know that?"

My jaw dropped. "No. What? How so?" That was fast, although Arthur knew well enough that sending the knights on the quest right now was asking for trouble.

"A messenger just came through mayhaps an hour ago."

I tensed up. My sword was up in our room. He noticed.

"Worry none. It matters not to me, war and peace, and who rules. Though I prefer peace to having my home burned, as you might guess. But we get so little of it, no use in expecting it."

"But what started it?"

"A heinous crime. Our Holy Bishop was caught in unnatural acts with a stable boy. He said he'd been bewitched by the effeminate while in Cantmell."

"And you believe that?"

He shrugged. "He is the Bishop. And it would be a sin to lie. Surely it is a great victory for Satan to conquer such an ardent foe of the effeminate."

"Do you want to know what I think?" The fat lady brought over my stew and my brew.

He thought for a moment and then nodded, indicating for me to eat, drink, or speak as I saw fit.

"I think a man obsessed with the effeminate as much as he, must be fighting strong inner urges to sin all on his own," I said before taking a large quaff of ale.

He pondered that for a moment, "Aye, I never thought of it that way, but it could well be."

"So Wessex is about to attack Cantmell? What about Kent?"

"To be sure, they will join in. Whether to join the winning side, or defeat them if they are weakened enough, remains to be seen."

"So what's the state of play? When do you think Wessex will attack?"

"Who knows, but if the messenger went out today, they could depart early tomorrow—at least the knights could. Or perhaps the messenger started before today. We are off the main road, so usually near the last to hear."

I had the thought to try to rush off to warn Cantmell but it was too dark. Also I suspected that Arthur had spies, like every-one else, and would know soon enough.

We sat there nursing our brews for a while mostly silently. There was a fire going, so watching the flames bristle and flare seemed good enough. Occasionally, the warren stroked his whiskers and remarked under his breath, "The Bishop and the ef-feminate. Who would think? It couldn't be, but maybe it could."

In the morning, Timmy and I saddled up and made it back to Cantmell by a bit past midday. News of the invasion had travelled quickly, and with the knights of the table gone, Arthur had sent messengers to the rural knights to meet him on the field to intercept the forces from Wessex. Perhaps battle had already been joined. Word had also been sent out to the questing knights to immediately return, but it might be a day or two for them to begin straggling in. Lanslod and Galahat had left for battle with Arthur, which meant now I was practically the only knight in town.

Not wanting to be in that position, I headed straight to my annex and sent Timmy to Joseph's to get bread, plus sausage and ale. I stayed there until perhaps an hour before nightfall when I heard a commotion. It was the rural knights returning. I loosened the door to see Arthur leading a forlorn group, many of whom were bloodied. Not so Lanslod and Galahat, who were right behind him, and clean as a robin's whistle with their noses—as always—in the air. The squires led their horses, and they too were unbloodied and not dirty. Arthur looked grim and, glancing up, acknowledged me.

"Ah, Escobar, find the palace guards and bring them atop the walls of the burh to keep watch. Wessex follows closely, and I fear we may be in for a siege."

I nodded and proceeded past the gryphon toward the palace entrance, and collared a couple of guards and sent them to the escarpment to keep watch. I had the thought that the reason Lanslod and Galahat looked untouched by the battle was that they'd not probably made it there in time. They'd gotten back last night, but I was willing to bet they hadn't stirred when the

King and his men left early in the morning for the battle. In fact, I'd be willing to bet that Lanslod spent the night with Queen Gwen and Arthur had been too embarrassed to fetch him in the morning. Sad.

I reached the door of the palace and there were two more guards lolling around inside the entrance. I wasn't sure why Arthur wanted me to summon them, since presumably he was coming here soon himself, but either he wanted to stop off for a brew or three before returning to face Queen Gwen, or maybe he didn't even want to face the guards at all.

"Good fellows, can you round up your colleagues and bring them out? We must move to reinforce the walls."

"Says who?" the thinner of the two said, without changing position.

"The King!" I retorted.

"Says who?" he repeated.

"I said, 'the King.'"

"I mean, how do I know what the King said . . . " That was a fair point, I guess. I didn't have a good answer.

"Fine. Stay where you are but, when the King comes and sees you here, he'll be mighty angry." I leered at him. In an hour or three if he's at the tavern.

"Hmm. Mayhaps." He thought for a moment and turned to his fellow, "Roust up the guards and bring them here!" The other guard looked at him skeptically, and I thought he might say *Says Who*, but after a moment he shrugged and went into the palace. The first guard looked at me and smirked, and then resumed his reclining position.

After a few minutes, the second guard returned with eight of his colleagues. They all looked a bit threadbare and slovenly. I recalled that I rarely saw many guards around the palace, so perhaps they were all just a bunch of slackers.

"Is this all of them?" I asked the second guard.

"There's six more that come on duty for the night."

"Well, stay here and send four of them to the wall when they arrive." He shrugged, which I guess was an agreement. "The rest of you come with me. Are you all armed?" They showed me what they had. A few had swords, the rest had daggers. Good enough. Maybe. I turned around saying, "Follow me." They did, I thought a bit unenthusiastically. But whatever.

We came to a ladder leading up to a parapet. I pointed to the first three. "Go up and spread out. If you see any knights coming, holler loud." They climbed up lazily. We continued around the inner edge of the wall. Cantmell is kind of a small place actually. A third of the way, there was another ladder. I sent up the next trio and continued on. Then we came to the last ladder, and I motioned the rest to start climbing and then followed them up. I hoped Arthur was bringing out bows and arrows because if the enemy made it onto the walls, these guys wouldn't cut it. Literally. But they probably weren't good with bows either. When I got to the top, the wall appeared well stocked with bricks and rocks, so at least we had something that didn't require close defense.

I looked over the wall and as the sun set, surveyed the countryside, shielding my eyes from a gentle rain that'd just started. Rolling hills on all sides meant we wouldn't see attackers until they topped the hillsides, which didn't give us much time to respond. Would any of the questing knights be able to return before we were surrounded? Fortunately, the quest had barely gotten underway when news of the attack had come. Presumably, fast riders could have intercepted them before they'd gotten far. Some might even be back tonight or early in the morning—hopefully before Wessex surrounded us. Wessex would proceed slowly, fearing an ambush. Otherwise, they would have pursued Arthur in his retreat, I reasoned.

As I looked, a solitary knight on horseback approached, followed by a smaller figure on a smaller horse, undoubtedly his squire. That was promising. He had only one arm which meant it was Bedivere. Well, a one-armed knight who was present was better than a two-armed one that wasn't. Actually, it might be a good sign, in that Bedivere was liked by all the knights which gave Arthur a reason to put him in command instead of Lanslod. Then a second pair on horseback appeared coming from the opposite direction. I strained to see who it was. After a while, I could make out his surcoat. A black cross on a red field. That would be Mordred. Interesting. I might have thought he'd have sided with Wessex in an attempt to gain the throne. Or maybe he was planning to undermine Arthur from within. Or perhaps he wasn't on good terms with Wessex.

I looked down at the revetments below us. Someone should be digging a channel from the river to flood the pit and make a moat. Maybe they were waiting for more knights to join in. Or maybe nobody thought of it. I'd better find Arthur.

I scurried down the ladder and made my way to Joseph's Sign of the Pig. I didn't know for sure he would be there, but it was a reasonable choice given that it was on the way to the palace from the main gate. It was starting to get dark, and the usual drizzle seemed to be picking up. I'm surprised people don't just molder away in this climate. I'd probably need to spend a week by the Dead Sea, just to dry out.

As I approached Joseph's, Bedivere entered the gate, so I waited for him.

"What ho?" I hollered him as he neared, even though I *still* didn't know exactly what it meant or how it should be answered. And I didn't find out. Bedivere nodded at me, and motioned to me to wait up. He dismounted and turned to his squire, directing him to take the horses to stable. He nodded at me again and approached.

"What ho, Escobar?" He said as he got up to me. *Wait, I said it first.*

"I'm looking for the King, I think he might be in here." Bedivere gave me a querulous look as if thinking - *You must be nuts.* But he didn't know of the King's defeat or the likely possibility that the Queen had spent the night before battle with a knight—Lanslod.

"Wait outside, I'll look within." That was fine, Arthur might be less embarrassed if discovered by Bedivere. I stood on the street, and occupied my mind trying to solve the riddle of *What, ho.*

There was *Tally ho*, which was what the fox hunters said when they spied their quarry, and sometimes now meant goodbye. There was *Heigh ho*, which the seven dwarves sing in *Snow White* when off to work they go. *Land ho*, sailors say when they spy the coast. Seems like it means "over there," in land sighting. And then there's *Yo ho ho, and a bottle of rum* from Treasure

Island. Who knows WTF *that* means? In fact, *maybe* it means that—the WTF, I mean.

In Shakespeare's *Romeo and Juliet*, Prince Escalus ends the brawl in the first scene with a speech: *What, ho! You men, you beasts/ That quench the fire of your pernicious rage/ With purple fountains issuing from your veins.* Which clearly meant *WTF, you frickin' a-holes.* Had to memorize a paragraph of that speech for English class in 9th grade. Tenth grade was a Hamlet speech. Eleventh was *Julius Caesar.* Still remember snippets. *What ho—that* was certainly old school. Hey, it was Santa Monica High. Everybody there is going to be an actor. But only a paragraph. Memorizing the whole thing would have been *really* old school.

Bedivere came out just then and nodded for me to come in. The familiar scent of stale spilt brew hit my nose right away, but I was getting used to it. I guess. Arthur was at a back table with a couple of the rural knights, no one I recognized though. They were grimly getting wasted in a methodical way. Arthur looked up as we approached, and one of the knights kicked a bench a few inches so we could sit down.

"Escobar, here are Cynric and Derwin." They nodded at me. I nodded back. End of introductions. Arthur contemplated for a moment and decided to get back to reality. He straightened up.

"Bedivere, you will be in charge of the defense. Escobar, have you had a chance to survey our situation?"

"I've been on the parapet. I have stationed a half dozen guards as lookouts. There are plenty of rocks up there, but I think we need to get bows there, dig a ditch from the river to flood the revetment ditch, and fortify the main gate against ramming—if Bedivere is in agreement."

Bedivere replied, "All of that. Cynric and Derwin, finish your ales, then make a torch and press into service all knights and townspeople you can find. But the problem will be getting enough shovels for the flood ditch." He thought for a moment. "And visit the stables, the gravediggers, the manure collector and the builder. Any other ideas?"

"It's too risky now to collect them from the farms. But I think shields might be used to shovel soft soil," I suggested, "And maybe the swords could be used to soften it."

"It will dull the swords, but it may be worth sacrificing a few of them," he stipulated.

"Oh, and one other thing I interjected. "Go to the butcher's shop and see if he has any cow shoulder blades. Those can be used too." Bedivere looked impressed. I learned that in archaeology. I'm telling you, a college education is extremely useful.

"Escobar, see to the shovels, and I will inspect the outside. Cynric, make sure that everyone who has a second sword brings it as well."

That meant making a torch, a subject of which I was unfamiliar because they never show that in movies despite them being used all the time. And too modern for Archaeology. Oh well. Fortunately, Cynric rose and found Joseph who obtained three torches and handed one to me. They were staffs wrapped in waxed cloth. Smelled like there was some sulfur mixed in, as well. We rose and dipped them into the fireplace to light them, and left Arthur sitting there, still looking morose. Joseph patted him on the shoulder and then sat with him.

Amazingly, I was able to find a half dozen shovels. Plus one shoulder blade. Not sure what happened to the other because I believe cows are normally equipped with two, haha. I headed out the gate and saw a dozen men, half of them trying to dig with their shields and half standing around. I passed out the shovels to the men digging on the theory that they were the most motivated and told them to give their shields to the others. There was some protest, but they did it. I tried out the shoulder blade. It wasn't terrible. We made some progress but after an hour the torches were dying, and some fires blazed on the hillside. Wessex was here. It wasn't safe to continue outside the gate, but what was the alternative? I told the men to keep digging even in the darkness. The results would likely be a mess, but we'd find out one way or another in the morning. We took breaks every hour and at one of them we all fell asleep.

I woke up at dawn, in a panic. Many sleeping bodies were huddled together for warmth and our ditch lay unfinished. I was freezing. I shook each one awake and told them to get back to work. And then I approached and pounded on the gate to let me in. After a long time, it opened, and I marched straight to a ladder and climbed the nearest parapet.

In the distance, Wessex had formed ranks and was heading downhill toward us. A column of knights in single file—to their right, a small company of archers and to their left, a group of peasants probably pressed into service, carrying axes and swords. Not a huge group . . . Maybe one hundred in all, but far more than we had. The watch on the parapet was also asleep, so I woke them too and told them to pass it on. Then I climbed down.

At the bottom, Bedivere was standing, waiting.

"They are coming now?"

I nodded.

"How is the ditch? Is it completed or nearly so?"

I shook my head. He winced, "Supplies are low, too. The granary has been pilfered, it seems."

"I thought it was a duty of the knights to guard it?"

"Indeed."

"Lanslod?"

"I'm sure he was hardly the only one."

"Speaking of knights, did any more make it back? I didn't see any."

"Gawain and two others. They came in through a back portal, but it is secured now. How many in the attacking force?"

"I would say at least a hundred, but it might just be part of their force."

"Verily so. I would not be surprised if they kept a guard back in case of a rear attack by Kent."

"How long can we hold out?"

"A week fed, and another hungry."

"Not good, but more immediate is the need to finish digging."

Bedivere nodded, "Suggestions?"

"Every available person digging, except one on watch. Knights can use their helmets. Or their gloves. Even barehanded."

"You mean their mittens? Gloves are unmanly."

I resisted the temptation to say something sarcastic, just replying, "Of course, but the women and effeminate can use their gloves."

He nodded again and left to spread the word. I had the gate opened and returned to the channel being dug. Sure enough, one at a time, men and women joined us, some with garden spades, others with mittens and gloves or with their hands wrapped in rags.

I was directing everyone and scooping out dirt with my cow shoulder blade when I suddenly felt hot breath on the back on my neck.

It was Galahat.

"Who put you in charge?" he sneered. I glared back.

"No one, but ask Bedivere if he objects. Or anyone."

"*I* object," he said, poking me in the chest.

Okay, that was it. I saw red. I'd had it. I sucker punched him right in the stomach. Galahat staggered away, fighting to get his air back. For a moment, he looked like he would puke, but he managed to straighten up. Pure rage crossed his face. I heard a voice in my ear, an echo of some other place: *Don't ever fight angry. That's not what the game's about.*

No one had ever told me this. Actually, someone did. My martial arts teacher before I dropped out. Also my fencing teacher. Okay then, take a deep breath. Two. I waited.

He charged me, fists flailing. But I was ready. His guard was not up. A quick feint with my left and then a fast straight punch to his unprotected jaw and his head whipped back, his body arched backward, all of his momentum snapping back on him like a broken rubber band. He lifted up almost off his toes, practically clearing the ground. For one long milli-second, it seemed his body hung in the air. Then he landed with a thud. Wow, I don't remember being that good a fighter. Maybe that was Freddie coming through. Seemed like Galahat was out for a second or two, but then he shook his head, clearing it. He reached for a knife in his belt.

Just then a boot came down on his arm. I looked up. It was Joseph from the tavern. He'd been shoveling with a pan from his kitchen, which he still held in one hand. Good thinking about using a pan. And good timing. Again.

He looked at me and sighed. "Knights. And their fights." He shook his head. "Let's finish this," he said. He meant digging, not the fight. I went back to it, and so did everyone else, except Galahat, who skulked off. I was definitely headed for combat with him. Or Lanslod. But I couldn't hold things in any longer.

We were almost done when the columns from Wessex arrived. A shout from the lookout warned us. Enemy archers were preparing to shoot. We would probably have fled to the gates, had not the lookout shouted a moment later that the rest of our knights were approaching. From the other direction.

Bedivere shouted from the parapet, "Stand fast. Shields above your heads."

A few of the women fled but most stayed, trying to huddle under the shields that'd so recently been used for digging. The first volley fell short, and only a few arrows fell among us. The next would be more accurate.

At that moment there was a cry from the other side. I peered up. Two figures were crossing the middle ground. The archers lowered their bows. As I squinted, I realized that the pair were Mirdynn and Mirgan. The Wessians were afraid to shoot over them. I looked again, and noticed a line of children behind her, so maybe it was that as well.

The line of archers stood down, but just then the company of knights attacked. Then they too stopped short at the sight of Mirdynn and Mirgan. That is, the knights did, but suddenly four large hounds bounded out from among them, heading straight for the children. People gasped.

Mirgan turned, pulled a short sword from her belt and swinging it, ran towards them. One hound in the rear turned back but the rest continued. At the last moment she stopped. And kicked. The toe of her boot connected with the first hound's muzzle and sent it flying with a sharp bark. Paws hit her back, driving her to the ground. The second hound had split off and come around. She somehow twisted her arm up, wedged it between her body and its furry neck. Pushed. With a grunt, she flipped it onto its back, her forearm braced against its throat. She snarled at it, mirroring its own rage. The third hound leapt at her.

In mid-air it vanished. Another gasp. Mirdynn had his arm outstretched. A spell? The last hound, deprived of its pack, growled and ran back, but its owner, infuriated, charged his horse forward.

And it, too, disappeared along with its rider. A third gasp from the crowd, and a whelp of surprise from the hound. Something made me look upwards. There was an unusual dark cloud directly above us. Was it the ship? Probably. Though how this squared with the Prime Directive would be interesting to hear.

Mirdynn raised his hand. All eyes moved to him. He waved two fingers at the Wessians, motioning for a couple of them to come forward. Then he did likewise to us. I looked back at the parapet and saw Bedivere looking down. He signaled I should go and take someone along. I looked around. Joseph was the only one imposing enough to make much of an impression, so I called out to him. He started walking, still carrying his pan. It wasn't quite the proper look, so I grabbed a sword that someone had been softening the ground with and handed it to him. He accepted it but kept the pan in his other hand.

"Maybe you should leave that," I suggested.

"Someone might steal it," he objected.

"No, the knights are here now . . ."

"That's who I'm worried about," he pointed out.

"Fine," I said in compromise. "Carry it and put it down halfway." He nodded.

We approached Mirdynn and Mirgan. The wizard was a small fellow, thin and almost frail. He had a small, floppy, flat cap on, not at all like wizards are usually portrayed, and wore pants and a thick vest but not robes. A knight in mail approached on foot hesitant and alone from the Wessian ranks. He looked back and waved for another to join him. That started a bit of a commotion, but no one stepped forward. Maybe they were afraid of Mirdynn. Probably. He *did* just disappear a knight on horseback. Or the space dudes did.

Finally, a second person emerged from the ranks. He seemed more commonly dressed. As he got closer, I recognized him. It was the warren of Shrews Town.

When we got up to Mirdynn, we hung back, so that we could all approach him at the same time. I didn't want it to seem to Wessex that we had an inside deal. And maybe we didn't. Mirgan also stepped away, still flushed from her encounter with the hounds. She shepherded her children into a circle and talked to them in low tones.

While we waited, Wessex unfurled a large banner with a two-legged dragon on a red field. It was called a *wyvern*, I recalled. Kind of reminded me of the poor Reptilian we had killed. I felt a brief pang of regret until I reminded myself he'd asked for it. Literally.

When the two Wessians got close, we stepped forward to meet Mirdynn simultaneously. He nodded at both pairs, but made no acknowledgement that he'd met me before. Well, met me astrally, actually.

"We foresaw you being here," he said, turning his head to indicate all of us. "But what is this all about?" His voice was higher than I remembered.

The Wessian knight, a tall fellow in mail with a blond beard, harrumphed. "Surely, you have heard that Cantmell has bewitched our Bishop and turned him effeminate?" The warren looked pained, remembering our conversation but also not betraying our previous acquaintance.

"Come, come . . ." Mirdynn interrupted. "True or untrue, wars are only worth fighting for land or money, isn't that so?"

"But the Bishop's honor . . ." he protested.

"Is his affair. Wars cost much—in gold and blood and loss of harvest, isn't that true?"

The knight looked down at the ground. "Indeed," he said after a moment.

"And isn't it so that Kent breathes down both kingdoms' necks?"

"It is."

"Then the best war would be one that gains treasure enough to repay its costs, and strengthens you against Kent, true?"

The knight started tracing circles in the dirt with his boot, and mumbled something.

"Speak up!" Mirdynn's voice was suddenly commanding.

"That is true."

"So what is the point of this war?"

The knight mumbled something.

"Louder!"

"It's the Grail." Right, the messenger who'd told us about the Grail had *come* from Wessex. But why had he wanted to tell Queen Gwen? As an excuse to start the war? Then why use Wulfric?

"Ah," Mirdynn exclaimed. He turned to me, "Do you know where the Grail is?"

"Not exactly."

"And where is the person who is pure of heart?"

"I don't know." That was technically true, but there was a strong possibility he or it, rather, was inside the ship, which just might be hovering overhead behind a cloud.

Mirdynn glowered sternly at me then turned to the knight, "Tell your King there must be no war!"

"I will try, but . . ."

Glances were exchanged between me and Mirgan, and between the warren and Joseph, while Mirdynn stared down the knight. But he never finished the sentence, finally turning on his heel and heading back to his men. The warren shrugged and followed, giving me a look that said *we're all pretty much screwed*. But for some reason, I felt optimistic.

# 11

# She Sells Siege Shells

Mirdynn's appearance probably wasn't going to stop the war, but it did buy us some time. Wessex deciding whether to fight us gave us more time to prepare.

The channel was almost ready to flood the trench next to the revetment, creating an erstwhile moat. That would prevent Wessex from easily scaling the walls, either with ladders or with a siege tower. The only problem was our bridge wasn't a drawbridge, and I didn't have explosives to blow it up. But I looked at the burh walls, and they towered over the gate pretty menacingly, so that any attempt to crash through with a battering ram would likely be costly indeed. So most probably they would try to starve us out. But that would only work if Kent didn't attack their rear. And one thing I figured about armies is they don't like to sit around. So either Kent would attack Wessex, or Wessex would attack Kent. Either way, the siege would be lifted. Probably before we started to starve. Hopefully. Or maybe Wessex would say *Screw it* and attack us anyway.

As I entered the gate, townspeople were stacking up furniture and other wooden stuff, and bricks to reinforce the gate. Others were carrying bricks and rocks up the ladder to the ramparts. I pitched in wherever I could for the rest of the day and went home to the annex exhausted.

The next couple days were much the same for me, working on our defenses, up on the parapet mainly. The gate wasn't blocked yet because knights coming to our support were occasionally sneaking through the Wessians' lines, and a rope from the nearest tower was strung to silently let the Gate Watch know when to open it. The King spread the word that the taverns were to be closed two days out of three to save food, and the rest of the days a ration would be given.

On the third day, I was eager for a break, so I headed out to Joseph's for some ale. I expected everyone else to have the same idea, but I was wrong. The townspeople apparently were expecting a long siege and were hoarding their money as they assumed they wouldn't be accumulating any for the duration of the siege.

Just before I got to the tavern, I came across Arthur along with Queen Gwen and Aelfhere, talking with Bedivere. He motioned me to join them. They were preparing to confer with Mirdynn. Bedivere complimented me to the King for my role in the preparations, and Arthur clasped my forearm, looked me in the eye, and vouchsafed his appreciation. Aelfhere beamed. Gwen looked away though, clearly thinking about something, God knows what. After a moment, Bedivere excused himself and the King to meet with some of the other knights to discuss possible strategies to break the siege. The Queen and Aelfhere pivoted to return to the palace, and I headed by myself toward the tavern to take a quick break and a bite. Maybe thirty steps later, I heard Aelfhere call out to me. I turned and saw her scampering toward me, holding up the hem of her dress to avoid it being muddied, her blonde hair flowing.

"Freddie, you can come see me tonight in the palace," she exclaimed excitedly. "The Queen has given me permission that we may get married. So we can celebrate. She and the King will be gone to sup with Lanslod and Galahat, so she says we can even use her chamber."

Well, that was a weird change of heart, though perhaps consistent with my sudden transformation from goat to lion in their eyes. She gave me a quick kiss on the cheek and whispered, "And you may caress me as much as you like." Then she blushed and turned away to scamper back to the Queen.

As I entered Joseph's pub, I was surprised to see Kasper and Mateno sitting at a table in the back. In their medieval dress of course, which is why I didn't think of them by their Venusian names. Surprised to see them in the first place, and second that they were in the back, where you couldn't tell if you were imbibing flies with your ale or grubs with your stew.

They motioned me over and had me sit. And pushed a mug in front of me.

"Last of the hard cider. Enjoy it while you can." I pressed the mug to my lips. Dang was that good!

"What's up, fellows?"

They looked down and then at each other as if they were reluctant to speak. Finally Kasper spoke up. "We need the Grail back," he said and winced.

"What, why?"

"Well, we need the thingie you put in it . . . " He looked embarrassed.

"Seriously? How come?"

"When we were last in your future, we forgot to stock a certain spare part . . . " He winced again.

"I get it. So now you can't replicate things. But why can't you just go back to the future and pick one up?"

"Umm, the thingie is a little more important than that. We need it to go anywhere, timewise."

"Well, that's a serious problem. Kind of an omnishambles. If you ask me, that is, which you won't."

Mateno jumped in, "No, you're right. Major screw-up. Anyway, once we get the thingie, Doltly can jerry-rig the rest enough to get us back to the parts store."

"Only one hang up, though. I don't know where the Grail is."

"Not good. What happened?"

"Lanslod and Galahat took it off of us, not long after we left you. Which reminds me, why couldn't you have warned me?"

"Umm, we're macro, not micro. You know, centuries and millennia, not days and hours. Mirdynn and Mirgan are better at that stuff."

"Fine, but anyway I don't know where it is."

"That's not a problem. It's probably somewhere in Cantmell. Doltly can find it again."

"Well, I am invited into the palace tonight. So he needs to find it by then."

"Well, he's right here." Mateno gestured at a cowled figure huddled over a mug. The figure lowered his hood, and yep, it was him.

Doltly rose and came up to the table. "Yes, boss?" He said. Kasper smirked.

"Tell us where the Grail is located now."

Doltly raised his head, and his eyes went back and forth as if he was scanning. He looked down then back up and repeated the process.

"It's that way," he said, pointing to the palace. "Upstairs in a large room."

"Can you tell us anything about the room?"

"Composition indicates a wooden frame above a large woolen cushion."

"A bedroom probably. But the King's or the Queen's?"

"It's got to be the Queen's," I jumped in.

"Does it have frilly things?" Kasper asked. I glowered at him.

"Hey, just want to confirm . . ."

"It has numerous frilly things."

"Good, we are in business then. Can you sense where in the room?"

"Above the large woolen cushion, below a small feather cushion." Under a pillow. They didn't even bother to hide it well.

"Okay, I'll try to get it. Have Doltly stand below the window after dark, and I'll toss it down at some point."

They nodded.

"Meanwhile you might want to get out of here. Wessex is about to besiege us. I'm assuming, though, that Doltly is pretty much indestructible."

"Yes, certainly at the current level of technology." Kasper slugged down the remains of his cider, and they made ready to go, instructing Doltly to stay hidden in the corner of the tavern until nightfall and then to stand below the window where the Grail was hidden and bring it back to them. It was like watching someone explain to a child, making sure nothing would be misunderstood. First law of robotics: Computers are dumb.

I ordered some bread and sausage, and ate it while they departed. A nice break from the rations, although the bread was fairly stale. As I finished, I heard a commotion from the doorway. I looked up to see Lanslod and Galahat pushing through and scanning the room.

"Escobar, are you in here?"

I stood. "I am," I said, defiantly, I hoped.

Galahat remained at the doorway. I stepped forward to meet Lanslod.

"So you struck my son . . . " he began, hostile. Galahat was probably reluctant to have mentioned his humiliation which accounted for the delay in Lanslod's response.

"I did indeed. And would again under the same circumstances."

"He would meet you in combat, were it not for the siege, which precludes the King granting permission."

"Tough luck, then."

He raised his eyebrows. "Perhaps not. Because I will instead challenge you now to a game of chance, which you will not again refuse or else be revealed as a coward."

Crap. That was tough luck for me. But wait, that makes me think. He was crooked, but maybe I could think of a way to negate at least some of his advantage.

"I accept. But as the challenged, I believe I retain the right to choose the game . . . "

"That's so, but it is traditional that knights play hazard." A more complicated precursor to craps.

"Nevertheless, I choose *Tanto en uno como en dos*." Something from Freddie's memory banks.

"What in God's blood is that?"

"It's a simple game played in Spain, but it's considered the Grail of gambling." I stared at him pointedly.

"Fine, but that's one thing we shall not gamble for. How do you play?"

"It requires three dice. Each player takes turns rolling up until two dice combined match the third." Which meant that if the dice were loaded or shaved to favor a particular number, it wouldn't matter.

"But I have only two dice," he replied. Even better, I thought, one more thing he couldn't control.

"I'll get another." I scrambled quickly to the window and climbed out, avoiding Galahat at the doorway.

Ah, fortune was already smiling. Agravain was across the street. He had returned.

"Have you dice?" I hollered. His head turned and eyebrows raised when he recognized me.

"I do, but are you playing Lanslod?" he grimaced.

Then I added, "I am, but don't worry. Toss them to me."

He fumbled in his pouch for a bit, then came up with the dice. Crossing the street, he placed them in my palm. They were a bit lopsided. I also noticed the one was opposite-sided to the two instead of to the six. And the five opposite the six instead of the two, as with modern dice. But that would not affect anything.

"Are they crooked?"

"Only a tad. Much less than Lanslod's, though." I laughed and clapped him on the back.

"Wish me luck," I said and re-entered the pub, this time through the door. Galahat glared at me resentfully as I pushed by.

Back at the table I offered Lanslod a look at the dice.

"Pick one to add to yours."

He picked up both of the two new dice and placed his dice on the table for me to examine. I felt them in my hand. They weren't noticeably loaded, but they were lopsided as well, and, looking carefully, there was a difference in the surface area which though slight, favored the five and six, and which, like Agravain's, were on opposite sides. But that would hurt him and not help him in this game.

I handed them back. He turned them over and over, lost in thought.

Finally, he looked up and spoke. "As a kindness, we will use both of your dice and only one of mine." Ha, he figured it same as me. So *kind*, haha. So I looked at his dice and picked the most lopsided of the two. Then I spoke.

"Let me give you the rest of the rules. Both players roll one die to see who goes first. Then the higher rolls all three, and if any two dice add up to the third die, he wins—if the second player doesn't match. If it doesn't add up, he may roll all three again or only one. If it still doesn't add, then the dice go to the other player who tries his luck. If neither one wins, or both, another round begins as before. If one person wins, the other begins a new round. Do you understand it?"

He nodded. I continued, "Shall we just play for ale, since you are new to the game?

He shook his head, "I have no fear of a new game. Let us play for higher stakes."

"But I am not as wealthy as you and indeed await any currency to be remitted to me from taxes on my meager estates, once the siege is lifted."

"No matter, should you lose you may owe me." That of course, was his real intention—to get me indebted to him like most all the other knights and win my allegiance, hopefully. But there was no way to refuse again, so I nodded.

"Let each game be one silver, then," he announced. I nodded again.

We each took one die and rolled. He had his own and rolled a six. I threw a two. No matter, there was no advantage in going first.

A few townspeople stood by the table watching. Going first, he rolled again, and a six, five, and three came up. Since he couldn't throw away two but only one, he could either throw away the six and hope for a two on next roll, or throw all three. He threw away the six but rolled another five. He handed the dice to me.

I rolled a two, three and five—a clear win, the first two adding up to the third. The bystanders gasped. Since there was no knowledge of probability, it was believed these games were decided by God. Which was one reason the poor were not allowed to play, in that it was well known that God didn't care about them. That wasn't anything that Joshua H. Christ actually taught, but it was certainly their daily experience. And the knights' perspective as well. So it all implied that Lanslod had to win. Which meant if he were to start to lose, he had to cheat or accuse me of cheating. Great. So win or lose, I would be screwed. I rolled again for the next game: a one, two, and six. I threw away the six but then rolled a four instead of the needed three. I handed the dice back to him.

He crossed himself and rolled two fives and a six. No way forward except to roll all three. He rolled and got a one, three, and five. I rolled two, four, and six, and got another gasp from the peanut gallery.

"Enough. The game bores me. Let's raise the stakes to five silvers." I had to agree, since he was fronting me the money. A few more folks drifted up to the table to gawk.

Seemingly, God was on my side because overall, I kept winning. Or maybe not, because Lanslod's response kept being to raise the stakes, first to ten then to twenty, which was the equivalent to a gold solidus. The bystanders started placing side bets on me and then taking odds. That wasn't making Lanslod happy either. And this wasn't going to end well. Really, the only way out was to somehow lose enough to break even and then find an excuse.

Wait, I thought of something.

"Good sir, I will give you a chance to break even, but I must depart forthwith for I have an engagement with my lady. If you like, we may play a round of thimble-rig for double or nothing. You may place the thimbles, and I will try to guess."

This was the gambling equivalent of suicide, as it was a scam. You know it as "the shell game." Literally one of the oldest tricks in the book. There are three thimbles and one peppercorn. The dealer places the peppercorn under one of the thimbles and moves the three around while the player tries to keep up with the movement, and then guess which one has the peppercorn. Of course, at some point the thimble goes near the edge of the table, and the corn is palmed, so that all the thimbles are empty, and whatever is guessed is wrong.

Lanslod's eyes lit up, then darkened as he got suspicious of my motives, not realizing that not everybody was as greedy as him. But after a moment, he agreed. A search was launched to obtain the thimbles, and more ale was brought.

Lanslod studied my face. "Do you think God favors you suddenly?" he said after a moment.

"No, I'm sure He favors you . . . after a fashion."

"What do you mean, after a fashion?" Hmm, I guess I should've left those last three words out, but I couldn't help myself. Okay, let's see if I can dig myself out . . . or if I'll dig myself deeper.

"I see you have the love of a Queen, the friendship of a King, and the respect of a kingdom. Yet, our Savior said, 'Beware, for the last shall be first, and the first shall be last.'" I didn't grow up with a born-again mom for nothing. Plus, there was the small fact of me having been there when he actually said it.

Lanslod started to boil. At least, that was my conjecture as his ears were starting to redden. He wrestled for control of himself because he was just about to win all his money back—so long as he didn't topple the table now and storm out.

"So you think you will be first soon?"

"No, I just quoted scripture."

"And what would you know of that, being a greasy Jew?"

Oy, not that again. Well, he was friends with Sir Kay so maybe no surprise.  But like I said, I would happen to know a *lot*.

"I have accepted him in my heart," I said mildly. Along with Krishna, Buddha, and St. Germain. Allah, too . . . why not? But that wasn't for him to know.

Lanslod untensed a bit. Right then, the man returned with the thimbles. Lanslod made a show of placing the peppercorn under one, then slowly moving them around giving me chance to follow it with my eyes. Then faster. I pretended to try to follow it but didn't really care. I did notice one of the thimbles went dangerously close to the table edge, so that was where he probably palmed it. Finally, he stopped, and I pretended to ponder. After a moment, I picked the middle thimble. He turned it over and it was empty. *Surprise, surprise.* I feigned consternation, saying over and over how I was sure it had been under the middle one. Lanslod smiled, gloating.

"One more for equal stakes?" Oh no, that couldn't happen. Absolutely not. I'd lose and become indebted again. I shook my head.

"Why not? I'll even let you play with just the two remaining thimbles. Only a blind man could fail to find it." The bystanders murmured in agreement. But of course, neither of the two thimbles actually had the peppercorn either.

"Nay, as I said, I have an engagement. But I will play you tomorrow whatever game you choose at whatever stakes."

His eyes lit up. It worked. But with any luck, by then I will have made love to Aelfhere, stolen back the Grail, and be headed out of Dodge. See you later, sucker. I stood up, and pushed away my stool. Lanslod briefly tensed again, as if he had a premonition I was escaping his clutches, but then it passed.

"'Til the morrow then," I said and walked out into the usual drizzle.

As I stepped out, I suddenly heard shouts and screams. I looked around to see the beginning of pandemonium. People running away. Others rushing forward. Knights on horseback swinging swords by the gate. Had the gate been breached? If so, the battle was already lost! We hadn't time to set up any last ditch inner defenses.

I pulled on my helmet, reached for my sword, and slid it out to hold forward as I ran through the fleeing townspeople. Then the fight reached me, with fighters on all sides of me in a free for all. I swung my sword at one, two, and then three men rushing by. All were thwarted by shields. I kept swinging and dodging as Wessian knights swung back at me. Our palace guard surged forward to engage them. Sweat stung my eyes like horseflies, creeping down from my forehead. All around me, a whirlwind of disorder and violence, a blur of color and vicious motion. I was swinging my sword wildly without even aiming as the Wessians surged around me. I kept feeling my sword glancing off of shields, other swords and even helmets, never knowing if my blows struck home. Miraculously, none of their blows struck flesh either, mostly thwarted by my own sword. My mouth suddenly dried from tension, my parched, panting tongue tasted like sand mixed with the bitter taste of metal. Deafening me, blood pounded in my ears, drumming to a ferocious beat inside my helmet. The sound was almost enough to obscure the cries of men, the whinnying of injured horses, and the clash of steel striking steel. Above the wild scent of sweat was the acidic smell of pervasive fear, carried along from the clashing, howling bodies amidst streams of scarlet liquid which drained from friend and foe alike into the mud of the streets. Then there was a crazy cheer and the battle moved away from me. There were bodies in the street, mostly townspeople. What had happened? Who had let the Wessians in and what had pushed them back?

People pointed to the parapets, and I followed their gaze to see Mordred, his hands skyward in triumph.

I asked everyone what had happened. Most didn't know, but those who thought they did said conflicting things. Mordred opened the gates. Mordred turned the tide. How? Someone claimed that Mordred had signaled the Gates Men to open. Another said that Mordred dropped a brick on the helmet of the prince leading the Wessians, knocking him cold, ending the attack. Who knows? Probably only Mordred. The palace guards led away a couple prisoners who'd been left behind. A few family members were crouching over their wounded or dead loved ones. At that moment, the sun broke through the clouds giving a false cheeriness to the scene.

After the surge of adrenaline and fear faded, I was suddenly and inappropriately hungry. *Let me grab another quick bite back at Joseph's,* I thought. For a moment, I worried that Lanslod might still be there, but then I realized he would have come out for the fighting. Ha, hopefully he got slashed. Squelch that, probably bad karma, and I'm already way behind in my mantras. I wonder how much extra you had to do if you killed someone. Probably depends on the circumstances, I suppose. Fortunately, as far as I knew I hadn't. Yet.

I clambered into the tavern which had mostly cleared out. Joseph was behind the bar and Berthulf was alone at a table drinking some ale. His eyes lit up as he was expecting a gold solidus for telling me where the Grail was. He stood.

"Not so fast, *Bert*," I said in as derogatory a tone as I could. "I don't have the Grail, and I'm wondering who else you told about it."

Berthulf looked genuinely surprised, "I swear by the nails of the cross, no one!" That was a pretty severe oath, and while the townspeople were no more superstitious than the knights, they weren't any less. Maybe a little more cynical, though. For good reason. "Couldn't you find it?"

"I found it, and then Lanslod found me. But you would not know anything about that?"

"I swear on the Lord's crown of thorns!"

Hmm, what ever happened to *Let your No be no, and your Yes be yes*? Pretty sure I recollect Joshua saying that back in Kfar Nahum. Something about don't swear on holy things, I believe.

After a moment Joseph came to the table. "Quite the fight, eh?" he said. "I clubbed a couple Wessians from the window. Didn't do as much damage as I'd hoped, though. Some more ale?" he continued, "And I have a couple of crossed buns left. Have one and take the other home."

I nodded. He brought the ale, and I snarfed both of the buns, practically in two mouthfuls. Then I downed a couple ales. Finally, the edge wore off, and I was ready to leave.

Joseph came to clear away the dish, and looked at me querulously. "So, where's the second bun?" he asked.

"I was hungry, so I ate it."

"But I don't have any more, and now you won't have any to take with you . . ."

"You are kind, but I'm fine." He shook his head as if he was very disappointed. That was weird.

"You really should have taken one home," he said again as he turned away. What the heck was that about? Who knows. People are weird.

I repaired back to my annex to briefly rest and to change clothes. Timmy had thoughtfully placed a bucket of water and a cloth by the bed, so I was able to give myself a kind of sponge bath, so I didn't smell too terrible. I lay down for a moment and must have dozed because next thing I knew it was almost dark. I lit a lamp with the poker from the hearth which somehow hadn't gone out. Then dressed in the flickering shadows. I was tired from the fight but excited to see Aelfhere. But suddenly nervous about the Grail. Would it still be there? Would Doltly be ready when I found it? Would I really be done once I retrieved the thingie? If not, I still didn't know what I was supposed to do. But if so, the mission seemed a little pointless. They should have just gotten Doltly to find it, and kept the Grail and not given it to me. Well, the good thing was I got to see Delphine again as Aelfhere in an interim incarnation, and to meet Mirgan and Mirdynn, who were certainly interesting characters. Not to mention King Arthur and Queen Gwen. Too bad I couldn't post it to Instagram. Although, from a broader perspective, I wasn't really making too much progress on my 72,000 mantra repetitions, so there was that.

Fortunately, my thoughts were interrupted by the arrival of Timmy before they took another doubtful turn. It was also perfect timing to help me on with my boots. But then I thought, if I'm going to bed Aelfhere, maybe these clumsy boots are a bad idea.

"Timmy, what else can I wear besides boots?"

He pointed to a pair of moccasins in the far corner. Perfect.

I dressed in my cleanest clothes and stepped out. It was twilight. As I walked by Joseph's for at least the third time today, I had an impulse to take a quick nip. For courage. About Aelfhere? Or about the Grail. Maybe both. Suddenly I had a worry. What if it was a trap? No that couldn't be. Aelfhere was good. And pure. And we were engaged. Officially, now that the Queen had acknowledged it. As I stepped past the gryphon glaring down from the edge of the roof, I reached up to the top of the doorway and rubbed its beak. For luck. Just in case. Might need it.

There were the usual two guards at the door to the palace, lounging indolently. As if nothing had happened and the kingdom hadn't almost fallen. You'd have thought otherwise, but you'd have been wrong. They eyed me resentfully, probably remembering how I rode them at the beginning of the siege. Whatever, dudes. But they let me through. I nodded to them and headed up the main stairs to the Queen's chambers which I recalled were near the front of the palace. The King's were near the back, or so I'd heard, giving them plenty of space.

"Freddie?" Aelfhere called out from the top of the stairs. I looked up and saw her shyly smiling. She waved a finger, then touched her lip nervously. I waved back and she smiled again. When I got to the top, she took me by the hand and led me to the door of the Queen's rooms. There were no additional guards. I pushed the heavy door open and looked around the room. There was a large, canopied bed in front of the window, a fireplace, wardrobe, lounge and table and chair set arranged around a large reddish carpet. A dressing screen was in the right corner, next to a chamber pot. The fire was blazing warmly casting shadows that flickered darkly. A small doorway was in the left corner.

"Is that the doorway to your room?" I asked.

"Yes, Freddie." She sat down on the bed and patted it. "Come sit with me . . ."

I sat between her and the pillows, and as we kissed, I ran my hand under the nearest one. Nothing there.

"Let's stretch out," I said lying backwards and using the opportunity to probe under the next pillow. Nothing there either. Hmm.

"Wait, I'm not comfortable," I said, standing up, pretending to stretch, then pretending to look around the room. "Maybe I pulled a muscle during the battle." I plopped down on the opposite side of the bed.

"Oh, you were in it? Was it terrible?" I nodded.

"Yes, but mercifully brief, and successful somehow." I ran my farther hand under the last pillow. Nothing. What the heck? Could it have been moved in the last few hours? I glanced over at the lounge. There was a pillow on it as well. Maybe there? Aelfhere rejoined me and started kissing me.

"Can we sit on the lounge?" I asked.

"Freddie!"

"Just for a minute."

"Don't be odd!"

"Fine, never mind. May I caress your bosom?" I'd look later. She blushed.

"Yes, Freddie, you may." I kissed her and rubbed her but over her clothes. Fortunately the corset hadn't been invented, or it would have been not very exciting. After a few minutes she started sighing.

"I will undress now," she announced, and getting up vanished behind the dressing screen. Perfect. I quickly rose and ran to the lounge. Nothing under that pillow either. I sighed and started to undress, and then spotted it. The Grail had rolled under the bed. I ran over, grabbed it quickly, and headed to the window.

"Doltly . . . " I half-shouted, half whispered.

He emerged from a shadow below.

"Yes, Boss?" It *was* fun to hear. Although I still prefer *my liege*.

"Catch!"

I tossed it out, and it tumbled end over end in mid-air, almost seeming in slow motion, but that was certainly my nerves. He reached out his hands to catch when suddenly a drunk stumbled out of the shadows behind him and fell against his shoulder. Doltly made a valiant effort to grab the Grail one-handed but bobbled it for a moment and lost control. And then it fell, hitting the stone wall and shattering.

I stared, stunned for a moment, then shout-whispered, "Save the thingie! . . . and then run!"

He nodded and groped around until he found the fractured base, took the thingie out, and then ran off, a bit clumsily, I thought, but that's how robots run I guess.

At that moment, Aelfhere emerged. "Freddie, you still have your clothes on!" I looked back, and she was wearing a sheer nightie, practically something out of Victoria's Secret.

"I was thinking, can we caress in *your* bed?" Something made me say that.

"What? Actually, no. The Queen and Lanslod are in there."

"Huh? I thought that they were dining with the King?"

"They were going to, but the King cancelled because of the battle."

"Very well. This bed is much larger, I'm sure."

"Oh yes, they were kind enough not to make me change our plans."

I sighed, well business is taken care of, now time for fun. I pulled off my top shirt and started on my pants. Aelfhere pulled her nightie over her head. We kissed fully naked.

Then there was a crash from the right. Behind the screen. It was at the back entrance that I'd climbed up to when I overheard the King and Queen arguing. Palace guards started hacking through the doorway with axes, or so it sounded. Aelfhere screamed and ran to her own room. Then just as the guards grabbed me, the Queen came out of Aelfhere's room, half undressed. The King came up the stairs with Sir Kay, and they entered to find me and Gwen.

"The infidel has defiled the Queen," Kay said flatly. The King looked at me astonished, as no doubt he was expecting to catch Lanslod and not me.

The Queen stepped forward saying, "Yes, I fear I've betrayed you with Freddie." She shot me a look saying, *Keep quiet if you know what's good for you.*

I didn't know what to say anyway so just stood there dumb-founded.

# 12

# Jail To The Thief

I guess I was set up. More precisely, it's likely I was set up by the Queen who figured out that *she* was being set up by Arthur. The only questions were was it an improvised setup or a long planned one, and was Aelfhere part of it? In other words, was the Queen's permission to marry part of the scheme, or was the plan just hatched when the King cancelled the dinner? Or it could have been a combination, in that she agreed to the marriage and was just waiting for an opportunity to spring the trap. And did Aelfhere know? I recalled someone telling me not to trust the Queen's ladies as she used them in her plots.

Well, I'd likely have some time to figure it out. Maybe a lot. The guards dressed me, except for my moccasins, bound my wrists with rope behind my back, and frog-marched me out the main door of the chamber into the hallway. The rope chafed my wrist. I wasn't going to say anything though, because I always hated it in the cop dramas when the suspect complained about the handcuffs being too tight. Of course, they were too tight. That was a feature not a bug. The cops liked it. You could call it a pre-trial punishment, haha. I wasn't gonna give the guards that pleasure.

They marched me down the stairs to the ground floor and then turned a couple times to the stairway I'd never noticed that went farther down. Not all the way underground but a bit. Maybe the ceiling was a foot above ground, which is what provided the light in the daytime. Saves on torches, I guess.

Fortunately, they threw me into a cell by myself. We'd passed a few other cells crowded with mangy-looking prisoners, who were probably sick with all kinds of communicable diseases. They didn't isolate me as a favor of course—undoubtedly more to prevent me from telling anyone my side of the story to anyone, even another prisoner. In the cell there was a stool, a bucket, and a ratty blanket. The blanket was to sleep on or under, the bucket was to defecate in, and the stool clearly a sign of the King's favor. Or maybe it was just left over from the previous occupant.

I tried to look on the bright side. I'm not dead yet. That's good. Anything else? Not really. After a few minutes, I thought of something. I could catch up on my mantras. Ha. Well, better than nothing. I decided to give it a try. Nothing else to do after all. I sat on the floor and leaned against the wall. After a moment I grabbed the blanket. If it was under my butt that would be easier to sit, and I wouldn't be on the cold floor. But then, it seemed that the wall was hard on my back, so I rolled up the blanket and used it for lumbar support. That's important for spinal health, you know? And it felt better.

The next question was what mantra to use. The space bros had mentioned *Om* and "One," and of course there was *Nam Myoho Renge Kyo*. I spent a few minutes debating which one, but then decided what the heck, just try them all. So I did. I think you're supposed to just pick one and focus on that, but that's if you're not indecisive. Which I was, not Freddie, but the original me. Was I starting to disengage? Was that a sign of imminent death? Who knows. Anyway, the thought passed. As did many others. On all kinds of subjects. I would get engrossed in some thought or some fantasy, and it would play out, and then I'd remember the mantra and go back to it, or maybe a different one would start. I did notice myself start to get more peaceful after a bit, and then, after a longer time, I started feeling space starting to clear around my head. I was really starting to get into it when I heard someone approach.

I opened my eyes, and weirdly it was darker in the cell then it was with my eyes closed. Does the brain have interior lighting? I looked up and saw two people peering in the small window of the wooden door. One was probably the jailer, and the other definitely was Lanslod.

The jailer opened the door and they entered. Lanslod sat on the stool and the jailer stood.

"It's a good thing we ended up even, because if we'd kept playing, you'd owe me money which you wouldn't be able to pay," he allowed himself to chortle, then cut it short.

"I wouldn't want to be indebted to you," I replied truthfully.

"Well, you may not be, but it's worse now because you're under my complete control here," he helpfully pointed out.

"Fine, what do you want?"

"The Grail. It's missing." He scowled.

"I don't know where it is." That wasn't completely true. I knew where *parts* of it were.

"You must, it's never been taken out of the Queen's chamber."

"How do you know? Maybe a chambermaid took it or one of the Queen's ladies?"

He thought for a moment. "Impossible."

"But is it really? Did you search everyone each and every time they entered and left the room?"

That's good. Keep asking questions. The more you ask, the less you'll have to answer.

"Nay, but I saw it only yesterday," he replied

"Then you've narrowed it a bit. But did you strip them naked? I was that way when you found me."

"Yea, but you could have thrown it out the window."

"And could not have anyone?"

He pondered for a long minute. Then tried a different tack.

"If you see that it's returned, then you will be pardoned and indeed acclaimed as the finder of the Grail." Hmm, that was interesting. Perhaps he was desperate for some reason. But it was an impossible deal to make.

"Did you try to drink from it?" I hazarded.

He grimaced, "I did, and it was as you said. A foul, bloody taste indeed. Which is why I may spare you if you return it." I shook my head.

"If you do not, I'll see you killed."

"I don't doubt you . . ."

He snorted, frustrated. After a moment he turned to the jailer. "Let's go," he said.

I went back to meditating.

After a long time, I sensed someone or something in the cell. Not in a creepy way, though. Or maybe I was just peaced out. I opened my eyes. In front of me was Mirdynn. Not the actual physical Mirdynn but the virtual one, imbued with the same bluish light. Astral projection, again. He looked more impressive than in real life, actually. Blue auras do a lot for one's image.

"Mirdynn?"

"It is I. And it appears you've gotten yourself into a fix difficult to extricate yourself from."

"Well, you could have warned me. Nobody tells me anything!" I complained. He looked at me skeptically.

"Nay, I did . . . " he said.  I shook my head, disagreeing.

"Yea, recall what I told you in the tavern?"

"Namely?"

"When the hurly-burly's done . . . " Oh *that*?

I bit my lip, then continued the line, which, like I'd said, was straight out of First Scene, Macbeth. "Right . . . when the battle is lost and won . . . "

"That'll be time to eat a bun," he finished. Which wasn't. In Shakespeare, that is.

"Well, as a matter of fact, I ate two. Not that it makes any sense."

"Aye, right there is the problem. You were only supposed to eat one. Had you taken the other with you, you could have pressed the Grail into the second bun, which would have protected it from shattering, when the drunk stumbled into your friend." Doltly, that is. Or maybe I'm the doltly one.

"And . . . ?"

"Then you could've returned the Grail minus the thingie to Lanslod and he would have released you.

I did a wide-mouthed frog. "Oh."

After a long embarrassed silence, I asked, "So can you get me out of here?"

He shook his head. He seemed to be dissipating though.

"Then I'll be executed!"

He shook his head again. "Nay," he said. I was going to ask him to explain, but then he slowly vanished into nothingness.

# 13

## Burning Man

So that pretty much brings me back to where you found me. Though there were a few days where they let me stew and ponder the error of my ways. Which were many. Or none. Depends on how you look at things, really. If it's all predetermined, then everything happens as it must. So in that case, no blame.

I've been meditating a lot. So maybe I'm feeling kind of chill. Or maybe Mirdynn's denial of my execution made me optimistic. If I can just get the refill to my pen/communication device, then I can call the Space Guys. If they are in the time zone. By which I mean time period. And if my rescue doesn't violate the Prime Directive. Seems like a lot of ifs, though. Particularly, the prime directive—a UFO showing up, blasting a hole into the dungeon. That's probably how the first Joshua won the battle of Jericho. You guessed as much? It sure wasn't a bunch of trumpets that made the walls collapse. Not sure why this would be any different. It's also not that it necessarily would have any direct impact, because this kingdom is clearly doomed. And there's no way it would affect the future technology since the gap is so great. But maybe what it *would* do is influence the myths and legends just like with Jericho, and over the centuries maybe somebody, somewhere would do things differently.

So I don't know how it'll work. My rescue. If it does. And I don't know how time adjustment by the Venusians and that Prime Directive even jibe in the first place. But maybe that's why the Directive is so important because the interface is incredibly delicate.

Early on, Dagen was able to take up a collection. In order to bribe the jailer to feed me better, which he occasionally does, and not to torture me which he generally doesn't. Well, occasionally he mentally tortures me, but that's not a big deal. Aelfhere has come a couple times, but they generally only let her wave to me through the window. It's hard under those circumstances to tell if she feels guilty for betraying me or if she even knew. I assume she probably did. But in terms of the contemporary values, maybe she did the "right" thing—supporting her liege over her personal interests. Not that it makes me feel better . . .

None of the knights that were semi-friendly to me came by, which confirmed what I long knew, that they were essentially scum, though perhaps with a few redeeming qualities. Some of them. There was one day when my hopes were briefly lifted because I was told that Queen Gwen might come by. They even washed me up so I wouldn't smell too bad. But she never showed. They did start cleaning me up every few days after that so when she and Aelfhere finally did make it, I wasn't a total stink pot.

Then one afternoon, there was a big commotion. I was washed and an extra guard was posted. The jailer came by and informed me to give him my toilet bucket so the place wouldn't smell because the King was coming to see me. Although why all the ruckus, I don't know because he was literally visiting his basement.

King Arthur came striding up to the window of my door—flanked by Bors and Gawain. Kind of an unlikely combination, but not one that gave away any particular bias. When he got to my door, he waved them away, and the jailer let him in. He sat on the stool while I stood, and he tut-tutted over my predicament for a moment. He let me know that there wasn't anything he could do. If he let me go, he'd be seen as a cuckold, which of course everyone already believed because of Lanslod, but then Lanslod wasn't the one caught naked with witnesses in the Queen's chambers.

"Are you willing to let me die for a false reason, then?" I asked, trying to minimize the peevishness of my unreasonable request. I was being sarcastic. In case you missed it. He did. In fact, I *felt* like I was being peevish.

He looked up, and sighed compassionately. "I know you must be worried, but Mirdynn has assured me that he has the matter under control."

"How so?" Seemed like a fair question to ask.

"I don't know." Fair answer, too, I suppose. Did it mean that Mirdynn planned to intervene, or that he foresaw my survival? I didn't bother to ask out loud because Arthur wouldn't know. We looked at each other silently for a moment.

"You have been a trustworthy vassal in the time I've known you, though it be short."

"I think gratefully of that remark," I said, remembering that the phrase *Thank you* was not yet a thing. "I am appreciative of your willingness to employ me and to allow my marriage to Aelfhere," I continued. He nodded.

"I have a question to ask, though, if it be not impertinent . . . " He nodded again.

"My apologies for asking but why do you let Lanslod get away with so much?"

He pursed his lips and remained silent. I shifted uncomfortably from one foot to the other. The silence stretched on for quite a while, before he took a deep inhalation, getting ready to speak.

"There is a secret I have from all except the Queen and Lanslod." He paused again for a long minute or more. Then he blurted, "I fear I am one of the effeminate." He winced and looked up at me piteously.

"But why do you think so?"

"Because the Queen and I are childless. And . . . " He stopped and bit his lip. " . . . because Lanslod and I . . . " He couldn't finish.

"A lot? Or just once or twice?" I had to ask, not sure why.

"In between."

"And with anyone else?" Unsure why I kept probing. He shook his head. I wasn't sure what to say. Finally I said, "I don't think you're effeminate. First of all, you seem very manly. If you weren't, you could hardly have pulled Excalimer out of the stone." I guessed that he did, but who knows. "Second, it has nothing to do with bearing children—maybe that's the Queen's fault." I was possibly on shaky medical ground, I think, so I quickly moved on, "And I think effeminate is a label and not a good one. We don't call them that where I come from."

"What do you call them?" I couldn't think of what they were called in Spain or in Galilee, so I said, "Gay."

"Gay?" He looked at me incredulously. "Really? Meaning they are happy?"

"I guess . . . " I said, cautiously. "Maybe it means that they are happy being who they are, I suppose." I was possibly on shaky ground again, but it seemed plausible.

"That's very interesting. But won't I go to Hell?" I had to resist the temptation to tell him about that room on Saturn, so I just answered, "I don't think so."

"Well, if I do go, I'll have the Bishop to keep me company." He sighed, relaxed finally, laughed then rose, and I bowed.

The next day was when Dag and the Queen, Aelfhere and Mordred all visited, as I related at the beginning.

After Mordred left, things got pretty interesting. First, the jailer informed me that he was being reassigned.

"Got a new job," he laughed, holding up a pouch to the opening in the door and jingling some coins. "Going to work for Sir Lanslod. New clod takes over in the morrow. Suspect you won't like him so much. Maybe he won't even take a bribe, could be so."

That wasn't good. I might even get tortured for real. What if that happened? I needed a strategy. I cast around my memory for any tidbits. The only thing I could think of was to lie and keep at it. But the lies had to be hard to disprove and take time to do so. I started pondering. And I couldn't start too easily if it was to be believable.

There was a sudden racket as guards brought in some other prisoners. I rushed up to the opening. They looked to be towns-people. About four of them. One protested, "We are not traitors. We love our King." The others murmured concurrences. The guards shoved them sharply into the cell across from me. I leaned forward against the wooden door, trying to get a better view of them through the narrow opening. The guards mostly blocked my view, but after a few minutes they hustled off.

"What are you in for?" I asked. One of them came to the opening and shook his head dolefully. "Treason," he said, quietly.

"How so?" He looked both ways to try to see if there were others that could hear.

"The King is ill. Probably poisoned. They arrested us because we brought him food that he ate last."

"What kind?"

"Turnips." As you know, not my favorite. I grimaced. Not sure if he noticed.

"But they were perfectly fine. Delicious in fact. We ate some ourselves."

I guess our tastes differed. "Sorry to hear," I said, then stepped back and sat down. From their cell I could hear sobbing from time to time as they bemoaned their fates. I wondered who did it and why. Well, the why part wasn't that hard. There was about to be a thrust for power. The King needed to be removed for it to play out. But was it Mordred or Lanslod? And did it matter?

I sat for the longest time listening to them moan. After a while they became silent. There was a commotion outside though. I went to my "window" and could see lots of boots and hooves. I heard shouting. An army? Whose? Then boots coming from the opposite direction. And more hooves. I heard the clash of steel against steel. And their thwacks against shields. There was another sound when it hit home, but hard to describe. The yelp of pain that went along with it was obvious though. Then some bodies, wounded and dead. One right next to my window, his leg obscuring much of my view. Seemed like the battle was moving toward my left, the palace entrance.

After a few moments, I could hear cries from the stairway up to the main floor. And curses. Directed at Mordred. It was he who was making his move. The clatter of steel and the cries moved closer, down the stairwell, and though I couldn't see it, the echoes magnified the racket. The guards moved from the cells toward the stairs. Now the shouting was loud. The guards stepped back fighting a foe that was just around the corner. A hand, probably of an attacker, reached around the corner but then slid to the floor, either gravely wounded or dead. Then the guard moved forward out of sight. The attack had been repelled. At least for now.

I moved toward the window, and looked through the bars. The body that had obscured the view had either been dragged off -or not actually dead -had risen on its own accord. Now boots were shuffling forward from the left and other boots were retreating to the right. The attack was definitely being pushed back. Then the defenders continued their advance, and some bodies fell as the fighters moved out of sight from my narrow viewpoint. The commotion gradually faded. Eventually, normal activity started, and carts and horses began to move. Bodies were being loaded on one cart, pulled by a horse. An arm dropped loosely over the side. I shuddered. The battle was over. Mordred was defeated. Which meant I was not going to be rescued. At least by him.

I sat huddled in the corner. What if I couldn't get my pouch with the refill for my pen and couldn't contact the space dudes? Would Talmo and Lamo leave me here? Would they even care? They had a very detached view of things. Aelfhere would probably be crushed, even if she were partially responsible. Maybe more so because of it. Aside from that, probably no one, either here, the past, or the future. Amanda back in modern times would never know, and I'd written a note to Elisabet in Josh's era saying I was leaving for parts unknown, and she was probably caught up in whatever events followed the crucifixion, recorded or unrecorded. I sat there thinking for hours, but nothing worthy of note.

Finally, there were sounds of men climbing down the stairs. One of them sounded like Lanslod. After a moment, the jailer opened the door. He was carrying a tall stool. With him were Lanslod, Galahat, and a third man. The third fellow had a grim delighted smile on his face. Actually, so did Lanslod and Galahat. But his was worse, and it punctuated his grizzled, mean face like a scar. They sat me on the tall stool, and Lanslod sat on the other.

"We are going to ask you a few questions," Lanslod said, "and we hope you will be cooperative."

"Of course," I replied. No reason to assume that this would be torture yet.

The grizzled man punched me in the face. Okay, I guess now I could assume.

*That was rude,* I started to say, but then thought better of it.

"What?" Lanslod said.

"Nothing."

"Well, you had better say something." The grizzled man brandished a knife and smirked in a self-conscious way. Maybe he was embarrassed about how much he got off on this.

"What do you want me to say?"

"Tell us that you sarded the Queen to disrespect the Kingdom!"

"What? That's stupid. First of all, you know I was with Aelfhere, and second of all . . . " I was going to say anyone who *didn't* want to bed the Queen was blind. Or gay, I suppose. But probably not a good idea. To say either thing.

"Finish your sentence!"

" . . . I was there to steal back the Grail." They were going to get to that eventually, I figured.

"Ha, so you admit it."

"Why not?"

"Ha, you are a coward." Probably, but I needed to play this smart. Just cowardly enough to be believable, and not a smidge more. Not sure how big a smidge actually is, though.

"Where is it now?" Okay, here was the time to be brave.

"I don't know." He smacked me in the face. I could taste blood.

"Of course you do!" And of course I did—part of it was in fragments in a gutter and the important part back in the ship. But the truth would not set me free. Josh was wrong about that—in this case. He placed my hand on the high stool, and pulled the knife out again.

"What are you going to do?" I asked shakily.

"I'm going to cut off your fingers one by one until you tell me. And then I'm going to do your toes . . ."

"And then what?"

"Why, then I'll do your nuggins and your prod," he said. My babelfish didn't translate it, but I could figure it out. I shuddered, wondering how many members I'd have to sacrifice before my lie became believable.

"And if I tell you, you won't cut off any?" Best be sure my bluff would help.

"I'll cut off a few fingers just to make it worth the trip . . ." he said, smiling.

But Lanslod interjected, "Indeed, but we *are* pressed for time, given that Kent is massing and will probably attack tomorrow."

"Really, so they beat Wessex already?" I asked.

"Oh yes, quite handily," the grizzled man answered. "We could see it from the parapet. Of course, *we* deserve some of the credit for taking out the Wessian prince. I heard he still gazes cross-eyed. But stop distracting me—are you going to talk, or am I going to slice?"

"If I talk, will you let me go?"

"Haha, hardly. But if you don't, you'll have the worst of it."

"I'll tell you where the Grail is, but you will have to act fast if you want to get it." Creating a little urgency seemed like it might help make the sale. Lanslod's eyes perked up. He glanced at Galahat who nodded.

"And you won't lie?" Galahat asked.

"Cross my heart."

"Swear on the blood of the Lord?"

"Yes and on his tears as well." That seemed like a good icing on the cake. Probably wouldn't cost me more than a few hours of extra mantras.

"Ah well, then pray tell . . . " Galahat responded.  I thought of saying that I'd sent  Berthulf to Glastonburh to give it to a knight to take to Ireland. He was doomed anyway, or so Mirgan foretold. Hey, maybe I was even part of the bad crowd she said he fell in with. But then I realized he'd probably still be in the tavern. So maybe just leave out the first part. And I would've felt guilty even though I didn't much like the guy.

"There's this knight errant that I had met in France, who was on his way to Glastonburh, and he said they'd pay a high price for it in Ireland."

Lanslod asked, "When will he sail?"

"I'd assume on the next high tide, winds permitting."

"Was he riding a fast horse?"

"Perhaps, but he was with his squire whose horse was likely not." That of course was all fiction, but presumably believable.

"Did anyone see you with him?"

"He was at Joseph's, so perhaps Berthulf noticed him." Ha, that was inspired. If anyone came to the tavern asking questions, Berthulf would be glad to provide answers for money, even if he had to make them up. Of course, if his answers caused him harm—well, that was on him, not me.

"What was this knight's name?" I almost said Sir Fenturf, but then chose differently.

"Sir Rhosis."

"An odd name."

"French." I nodded sagely, man of the world that I am. They nodded back.

"Shall I trim a couple fingers now?" the grizzled man asked.

"Nay, prepare him for the stake," Lanslod stated. "And make yourself ready for the parapet." Uh, oh. I was too worried about the torture to remember I needed time to be rescued.

"Umm, maybe you could just take a finger or two and leave the burning until tomorrow as planned?" I suggested hopefully.

"Don't be a coward. We will send in a priest to hear your confession if you want one." I nodded. Confession isn't part of Judaism of course, but nothing to lose, and I needed time.

After an hour or so, a bent elderly priest came up to the door followed by the jailer, who almost seemed to be pushing him. The jailer unlocked the door and shoved him in. I offered him the higher stool since I was afraid he might not be able to get up from the other.

He nodded and smiled benignly, or maybe senilely. "How long since your last confession?" he asked.

"Years," I lied since I'd never been confessed at all. He looked confused then nodded sternly. I decided to tell him everything since I arrived no matter how crazy it might sound, why not? And if I had time, I'd tell him about Joshua, St Germain, and modern times.

It was kind of therapeutic to get all of this off my chest. I looked up at him from time to time to see his reaction, but there was never anything but "*Go on my son.*" After a while, he dozed off, so I started reciting the high school Shakespearean speeches I'd memorized so as not to waste any material. He snorted and woke up briefly a couple times but didn't notice the change in subject.

Finally after almost an hour, the jailer became impatient. He stormed in. "That's plenty enough, I think."

The priest who was nodding drowsily came to life in an angry fashion. "He must confess *all* his sins that they may all be forgiven."

The jailer tensed. "No, we must finish now," he insisted.

Frowning, the priest summoned a hidden energy, "Preventing a confession will endanger your *own* soul!" The jailer stepped back and cringed. Typical superstitiousness, but, hey, I'm not complaining.

"Fine, I will give you a little longer, but make sure he's done the next time I come in."

The priest sat back on the stool, and I restarted my recitation. After a few minutes, he started to yawn again and nod. I was afraid he'd fall off the chair, but then there were sounds from outside the cell, people approaching and then conversing with the jailer. The door opened, and the jailer appeared with Berthulf and two veiled women. For some reason, Berthulf was carrying a staff. It kind of looked like mine, not that it was easy to tell one from another.

"Begone priest," the jailer said gruffly. "This fine fellow has brought a couple harlots to give this poor sod some last comfort and me as well."

"What?" the priest sputtered and reddened. "You will have him commit a final sin now of all times? That will endanger your soul as well, you know."

"This'll be worth it. Besides, you can finish his confession and hear mine as well. After we are done." He looked at Berthulf. "Stand outside the door with him, keep watch, and make sure he doesn't wander off." Berthulf grabbed the priest's wrist and led him out.

The petite woman came up to me and lifted a corner of her veil. Well, his veil. Because it was Timmy.

"What the heck?" I whispered.

"Dag and I paid Berthulf to help us enter dressed up as harlots. He is drinking friends with the outer guards who let us through."

"But how is this going to work?"

"Watch but pretend to embrace me. By the way, I had Berthulf bring your staff. I would've brought your sword if I'd thought we could get away with it," he giggled.

I looked over Timmy's shoulder. Dag was undoing the jailer's belt and pulling down his pants. [nm1] [MR2] The jailer had his eyes closed in expectation. [nm3] Dag got hithe guy's pants down to his ankles, then turned to us and nodded. Timmy broke away and dived behind the jailer just as Dag gave him a push. The jailer tumbled backwards over Timmy, and, legs bound by pants, his arms sprawled out seeking balance. Once he'd hit the floor, Dag pulled the jailer's tunic over his head to trap his arms but was having trouble with the left arm. I jumped up and tugged the tunic over. The jailer was fairly well trussed between that and his legs being trapped in his pulled down pants, but that didn't keep him from shouting. Dag grabbed his scarf and stuffed it in his mouth, narrowly avoiding being bitten. We scampered to the door and opened it. Berthulf was still holding on to the priest.

"Umm, wait—how's this going to work? I asked. "We can't just walk me out of here, right?"

"Oh right," Timmy winced, "We didn't think of that." Frickin' amateurs.

"Well, I guess I can put on the priest's robe. Maybe that'll work." Probably not, but it might be my last shot. Dag and Berthulf pulled off the priest's clothes, ignoring his weak whimpers and bound him with mine as I undressed and exchanged clothes. Laughing to myself, I grabbed my staff, which—you remember—was a lightsaber in disguise, and we hustled out of the cell and lowered the bar behind us, past guards in the hall and more guards on the stairs. Being a priest, I stayed a few steps behind them, so as not to be too closely associated, and nodded every few seconds benignly with my cowl pulled onto my head to minimize the chance of blowing my cover. As we reached the main hallway, the townspeople outside were scrambling to man the parapets against Kent, but when we got to the entrance, we were confronted by Lanslod and Galahat. They recognized Berthulf.

"What ho, you tavern toad! Bringing tarts to the palace?" Still don't exactly know what it means. Everyone but me started running, Timmy and Dag holding up their dresses as they ran. I lagged back a bit. The last guards parted for them but closed ranks for Berthulf. Whoa. I bet he stiffed them. He struggled against them, but Lanslod calmly plunged his sword into Berthulf's back. "An end to you, and your antics."

Berthulf gasped then swayed his head and looked at me. "I venture I'll see you soon Freddie," he whispered, staring me in the face, then his eyes glazed, and he fell. I shuddered. Poor doomed dude. I didn't think much of the guy, but it is a whole other thing to watch someone snuffed right in front of you.

Lanslod pivoted and tipped off now, recognized me under the cowl. "Ha, Escobar, you've saved us the trouble of fetching you." He waved to the guards who pulled swords. I grabbed my staff and twisted the end to make it turn into the light saber, but it just flickered and then flickered out. Out of juice again. I guess I was supposed to recharge it, but who knows how. Two of the guards took my arms. I looked at Lanslod and realized that as I suspected, he'd been Judas back in his previous life. But what I realized for the first time was that Galahat was Simon Pedro. You know who I mean, the Apostle. Other people called him Simon Peter. They were bitter rivals then, him and Judas, , but now father and son. Reincarnation. It's got a sense of humor. I could use one right now, 'cause time was getting short before they fried me. The guards yanked off my priestly garb, leaving me shivering in my medieval underwear. At least not as bad as being in tighty-whities. Then they bound me with a rough rope.

As they frog-marched me to the market square, the streets were fairly empty. All the men of fighting age were on the parapets awaiting the attack by Kent. Old men and kids and women watched me from their doorways and windows. A few started following us. Apparently, I was going to go out in a minimal blaze of glory so far as audience was concerned. I kept scanning the doorways for any friendly faces and the skies for a friendly UFO, but saw nothing to encourage me. Mirdynn had claimed I wouldn't die. Could he be wrong? Inconceivable! Umm, no - it was conceivable, all right. In fact, for the first time I did start to conceive it right at that moment. I remembered as a kid in junior high we debated which was worse: death by drowning or by burning. Can't remember which won. I do remember cringing when studying how Joan of Arc got BBQed. Was that reaction some kind of a past life flashback?  But again, I never did figure whether Freddie was my previous incarnation or just some random dude. I felt a little sad as I had just started to get used to being him. Then it really hit me: I. Was. Going. To. Be. Burned. At the frickin' stake!

"Let go of me!" I started struggling. I did manage to get one hand loose but was rewarded with a smack in the face by my own staff. It flickered as if taunting me.

"Don't be a coward," one of the guards hissed, as he grabbed my arm again. "This'll just be a small taste of what you have in store . . . forever, in Hell,"

That quieted me down. Because I realized that burning, while extremely unpleasant, was not going to be for too long. Then it would be some additional unpleasant moments in the Hall of Judgement on Saturn, but the one thing it *wasn't* going to be was eternal fire and brimstone. So relatively speaking, haha—things could've been worse.

We were at the market by the stake. The guards were walking me to the post while another dipped a torch into a fire that had been started in a kind of pot. As I neared the stake, I felt this weight on me, as if I weighed a million pounds. Lanslod approached me. I managed to hear him offering to make it quick by slicing off my noggin if I denounced Arthur. Screw that. Arthur was a good dude at heart. He meant well. In fact, I suddenly had a lot of respect for what he had to deal with, I thought dizzily. Something was wrong with me. Everything was weird. I tried to scan the small crowd of women, children, and old men, but they were kind of a blur. There was to be no flying saucer to rescue me, I barely managed to realize.

I summoned up all my strength and managed to weakly shout, "Long live King Arthur the Just!" I don't know if anyone much heard me, but Lanslod did, and he slapped me in the face. Two guards tied me to the stake, and I woozily saw another one lighting the wood at my feet with a torch. I felt the fire's fierce heat as it came closer, then I passed out.

# 14

# Witch Do You Choose?

I passed out. And in. And up and down. And sideways. And backwards. And loopity loop. Was this death? No. It seemed strangely familiar. I was Schrödinger's cat--both existing and nonexistent. Like in the quantum thought experiment. Where was Wigner and his friend? Who were they, and why did they matter? When did I get my cat food?

I. Think. I. Know. What's going on. I'm in a conundrum. But how?

Then I woke up in a big bed. But where? In my room at the annex? In my own time? No. I blinked my eyes. Mirgan was rubbing my fleas. I mean my head. Still a little disoriented, I guess. It was dark, and the room was lit by a fire blazing. As my vision cleared, I saw that her children were sleeping on the floor around her bed, peacefully covered with blankets. Her place.

Mirgan whispered, "I foresaw you coming here, but I was surprised when I found you inside lying on the floor. You were cold to the touch, so I stoked the fire and put you to bed, and climbed in to warm you." She was naked and so was I, and I was getting warm, but my mind was grappling with what happened. Then it came to me.

"Freddie wasn't me, but he was my ancestor, so he couldn't die yet, or I wouldn't get born."

"Be still and rest, you are not making sense."

"No, it makes perfect sense. The Grail was a McGuffin, something designed to move things forward but insignificant in itself. Freddie was incapacitated, so I had to replace him, or I wouldn't get *born* . . . The conundrum spit me out, but it's not random."

"Poor boy, but you *are* Freddie."

"No, I'm . . . " I couldn't remember.

"Here, let me make you feel better . . . " She slid her hand across my chest and started to kiss me. My energy surged, and then she pulled me on top of her silently so as not to wake the children. Our eyes locked, and a beam of light seemed to connect them and gradually expand into an explosion. Then I fell asleep immediately.

I woke up early, just before dawn, in time to see her stretch and yawn awake, the children still asleep. I felt totally healed and healthy but a little guilty.

"I'm sorry. You're my mentor and I'm engaged, and I'm not really Freddie."

She laughed, "I understand now what last night you meant because it came to me during our sarding, but don't worry. Our souls travel through many bodies, and I was your teacher here, but I'm also your lover and your friend."

"What do you mean?"

"Like you suspected, the Grail was unimportant. You were brought here because your ancestor was unable to be with me.

I failed to conceive with Agravain, so I had my eye on Freddie as another strong knight. But now I know you—this you—are more than the father of my next child but part of my soul family. So I have something for you."

Wow. Soul family? That sounded really good. But . . . I need to know . . .

"Before you do that, wait—What's going to happen with Cantmell? Do you know?"

"Yes, it will fall to Kent after eight days' siege."

"When it runs out of food. And Arthur?"

"He is dying. We will start a rumor that Mirdynn takes him away, to keep his name alive."

I nodded.

She reached into a pouch and after a moment's fumbling, brought out a tarnished silver ring.

"No," I started to say, but she interrupted.

"It's not what you think, look carefully."

It reminded me somehow of the weird cylinder thing I got from St. Germain and never threw out. Where was it? Who knows. Hopefully it won't come back to haunt me. I reached for the ring and turned it over in my hand. It appeared to be a snake eating its tail.

"It is the serpent Ouroboros. An ancient symbol of death and rebirth, and mystical knowledge given to me by Mirdynn. I wear one myself." She showed me her right hand. It had one that was identical but even more tarnished. "Even the tarnish is important, the symbol of the wear on our souls as we journey through life over and over again."

"I think I've heard of it." I recalled that the German chemist August Kekule claimed that his dream of a snake biting its tail inspired his discovery of the benzene molecule's circular structure. And I vaguely remembered a Robert Heinlein story that one of the research assistants brought in about a time traveler who . . . I didn't remember, but something like what just happened, I guess. And he had that ring.

I put it on. "Who started the Ouroboros thing?"

"Mirdynn says centuries ago, Cleopatra the Alchemist."

"*The* Cleopatra?"

"I don't think so, another."

"And what's it all about?"

"Two things: Reincarnation, as I've said. And the transmutation of the serpent force for awakening the third eye."

"How did yours awaken?"

She laughed. "I'm not going to tell you, but you can guess . . . "

"No, but tell me this . . . What do you mean when you say, 'Hold to the light'? You and Mirdynn said that to me, and it was also said by another wise man."

"The light is the truth. You can know it in your heart if you are still enough. The darkness is the moods and urges that quench the light in most people."

"And the words that I repeat help me reach it, the mantras?"

She nodded.

"And is Aelfhere in my spiritual family?"

"Of course. She's been in your other lives, right?"

"The three that I know about. But then, in this one, did she betray me?"

"Yes, but in service to what she felt was a higher loyalty."

"I don't think I understand loyalty . . . that's what the first jailer told me."

"But you do. At least now. I inwardly saw how you stood for the King, even at the cost of a more painful death and though he failed to save your life. The light in you made you understand."

"Yet I originally just wanted to be loyal to Aelfhere and the Queen . . ."

"You were blinded by your love for Aelfhere, to not see her full nature . . . even though you knew the Queen was no good," she added after a pause.

"I guess it's like the difference between blind faith and a truer one." She nodded.

"And what about marriage? I was engaged to her, but in my other life engaged to another."

"You know the answer to that."

I reflected. "We have many lives and many loves to teach us the lessons of both bonding and detachment?"

She nodded again, "No one owns our souls."

"Will I see her again?"

"You know you will, as you will see your Elisabet, and you will see me. And you and I will always be lovers, friends, and fellow sojourners on the path." She leaned forward and gave me a kiss. It started softly and then got more intense. Just as my head felt like it would sizzle, I heard a rustling at the window behind me. I broke away and turned my head. There were two people outside

.

"Get a room," Talmo said, smirking.

"Haha, you're a barrel of laughs—We're *in* a room."

"Just kidding," said Lamo, "But we need to get a move on. Are you coming?"

"But where?"

"You'll see . . ."

## Chapter One—A Quark in The Park

"Do you want to take this baby for a spin?" Talmo asked me once we cleared the Moon's orbit. I was still wearing my medieval tunic and loose pants after being rousted from bed with Mirgan the witch. After a cosmic night of *sarding* (substitute that for another four-letter verb). Following almost burning at the stake by Sir Lanslod's minions for not returning the Holy Grail. Which I'd stolen in order to cannibalize a part to make the ship space and time worthy.

That was because Lamo had forgotten to bring a certain spare part—which is something you can never do when you travel backwards in time. If you go forward, there's always a space/time spare parts shop—usually with many upgrades for just a nominal fee.

Talmo and Lamo are my space bros from Venus. They are blond, lanky, spandex-wearing outlaws doing the Lord's work trying to save humanity, while occasionally toking up on the sly. In fact, they look almost like brothers, but Talmo, who I think is the leader of the two, might be a half inch taller. He also has a tiny bit of a crooked smile and can raise a single eyebrow, like Groucho Marx. Lamo is a bit more chill, and his eyes have the slightest violet tinge to their blue. They'd picked me up in Sedona, Arizona, in modern times and saved me from a pointless and feckless life after I'd lost my job and girlfriend, so I owed them everything.

On the other hand, I did help Jesus H. Christ obtain the emerald tablets, which possibly saved humanity. So maybe you owe me something. If you are reading this on Earth—and not a different planet. Then I did something or another in King Arthur's time, though I'm not sure what, except for nearly getting burnt at the stake. I am also supposed to be benefiting from these journeys which I probably am, since I was such a loser it's likely that practically anything would have helped.

"Really, you'd let me do that?" I responded to Talmo's request to drive the ship. "Isn't it pretty complicated?"

Talmo flashed a crooked smile. "The math is. Well, that is if you want to actually arrive anywhere. But that's what the computer is for. And the computer will adjust as long as you don't hit anything in the meantime."

I looked out the view screen, and nothing seemed too threatening. "What do I do?" I asked because there wasn't a steering wheel, pedals, or anything similar to what I'd recognize in a cockpit or driver's seat.

"Just visualize a trajectory and say, 'Show'." I did, and the trajectory appeared on a screen in front of me. It didn't appear to collide with any planets, comets, or other spacecraft. Which reminded me. "Why don't we see you guys from Earth if you're always tooling around like this?"

"That's because we're decomplexified, remember?" I nodded. Decomplexified is the state you always want to be in when you travel to other planets and other times. So you don't get crushed by higher gravities or blow up in anti-matter time-travel. Talmo added, "Looks good. Now say 'Go'."

"Before I do that, can you tell me what the time is?" He looked at his watch.

"Sure, it's 690 AD."

"I was wondering about that. And how fast are we going?"

Talmo raised his eyebrow and made a funny expression. "About two solar distance units per time unit. Why?"

"How much is that in mph?"

"Four million miles per hour."

"Dang, that's fast. How close are we to time travel speed?"

"Not that close. Need to get to 670 million mph, but we can't do that until we get a hundred million miles out. Fortunately, the solar system is kind of flat, so we can just make a vertical turn instead of going all the way past Pluto. That's so we don't create a black hole that sucks in a few planets."

"Wait," a voice piped up from behind me. It was Doltly, the Android. He was named after the first law of robotics, which is that computers are dumb.

Talmo turned to him. "What's the problem?"

"Time Police at 45 degrees, three o'clock!"

"Do something!"

"Yes, boss," he replied. Talmo smirked guiltily and started to say, "I love it . . ." when Doltly pressed a large red button that had suddenly appeared in his palm. Everything went weird.

Then dark.

When I regained awareness, I was on the floor. Talmo and Lamo were sitting at their usual places in front of the view screen, looking a little ragged, but Doltly was puttering around totally normally.

"Do you want to play ping-pong?" Doltly asked me in his silky George Clooney voice.

"His memory bank recorded that we played ping-pong last time you were aboard, but I have to remind you . . . . he never loses," Lamo inserted.

"Hard pass," I said, fighting off a slight tinge of nausea. "Where are we, and what happened?" Doltly pouted as I said it.

"We're about fifty million miles above the plane of the solar system. You can see it over there." Lamo pointed upwards, which meant we were upside down, not that it matters in space. He shook his head, apparently trying to clear it.

I did the same. "Doesn't look like much," I commented.

"That's because it's mostly space. Everything is a lot like peas on a football field. Except for the sun, of course. What happened is that Doltly followed procedure and pushed the panic button which instantly decomplexified us another ninety-nine percent and then sent us at on a trajectory toward the last departure point in space/time."

"Which is?"

"Earth 1975."

"Oh," I said, for lack of a better word.

"Apparently, too, there's something there we left undone."

"Why do you say that?"

"Well, since everything is predetermined, it means it was no accident that we saw the Time Police and had to bail."

"So what are we going to do?"

"Look around and see what doesn't seem right. And then try to fix it."

"I know I'm still hungover from the decomplexification, but I'm pretty sure I never figured out how predetermination jibes with what you guys do." Gallivanting all over eternity sticking their noses in everything.

"It's really very simple." I tilted my head expectantly to hear. "But your brain is too small to understand it." Great, a put down.

"It's the same size as yours, as far as I can tell."

"Right, but that's because you can't see inside. Our brains are totally optimized due to our longer evolution, and have four times the capacity and processing speed as yours."

"Oh," I said, for lack of a better brain.

"But don't worry, you are right where you are supposed to be." He patted me on the shoulder.

"Because it's all predetermined?" I ventured.

"See, even at one quarter mental power, you do just fine."

To fill you in, my story started with a failed suicide attempt after I'd lost my graduate research position in the social science lab for not finishing my dissertation in time, and then my girlfriend threw me out. I drove to Sedona on a whim to look for UFOs, but *they* found me. They took me to meet the leader of the world's currently largest religion, of whom you may have heard of, Yashua Ben Yosef of Nazareth, who I liked to call Josh, mostly behind his back. He was one cool dude, definitely worthy of being the founder of a religion, even though he had no desire to do so. You know, the line *I come to fulfill the law not to change it*, which I allegedly wrote down, though I don't remember doing it. Yeah, I was St. Matthew. For a few months. That's 'cause my dudes accidentally knocked the real him off, so they picked me— Matt's reincarnation—to fill in for a bit. Remind me to double check everything they do. That Martian weed they smoke is heavy duty, for reals.

After that, I went to King Arthur's court as a knight, Sir Escobar. The only Jewish knight, I'm pretty sure. Oh, and I almost forgot, I spent a few weeks in pre-Revolutionary War France where I got to meet Saint Germain, Cagliostro, and Robespierre while practicing my fencing skills. I managed to have romances in each of those time periods. Which is emotionally a little confusing. I always thought of myself as a one-woman man, but that's rare if you look across lifetimes. In fact, it would be hard to grow if you were always with the same person. And that's why I don't believe anymore in soulmates, twin flames, and all that romantic nonsense. We're here to love, learn, and be detached. Because nothing is permanent except that which we develop inside. But I have to say, I'm feeling little pangs at leaving Mirgan the witch, who was the wisest woman I ever met, even though I only slept with her one night. Before that, it was Aelfhere in King Arthur's court, and Elisabet in Joshua's time. I can't think about them too much though, or my feelings will get scrambled. I have olive skin which helped me fit in back in Joshua's era but not so much in Arthur's, plus curly dark brown hair and a very elegant nose. Or so *I* think.

Pre-space/time-travel, I was a lowly grad school dropout, raised by a mixed faith family that abandoned me as a teenager—my mom for a Jesus cult and my dad for a new family.

Dumped by my girlfriend, I had nothing to lose except my mind, and maybe I did, and this is all a hallucination and I'm locked away in a padded cell. On the other hand, maybe I'm not, and I'm having the adventure(s) of a lifetime. I'm going with the latter.

"Dudes," I said, on a little high from that realization, "we've done two missions now— so how do you think I'm doing?"

Talmo glanced over. "Not bad, making some progress but still have a lot to learn . . ."

"Aww, come on . . . Give me a break. Lamo, what do you think?"

Lamo scratched his temple. "I'm going with what Talmo said," he replied.

"No, really, don't you think I've come a long way? I mean, I started out as a total loser who coped by making jokes to avoid confronting reality. But I learned to trust myself. Plus, I learned a lot about loyalty in my visit to Arthur's court. You guys just can't see it. Too close, maybe."

Lamo considered for a second, then answered, "Why don't you ask Doltly then. He's totally objective, you know."

I turned to Doltly, "Okay, Doltly, lay it on me. How am I doing?"

Doltly tilted his head in an almost human fashion and then held forth in a slightly robotic version of George Clooney. "You are making progress but still have a lot to learn."

Talmo and Lamo snickered.

"Fine, name one thing!"

Doltly tilted his head again and said, "First and foremost, you doubt yourself but then rarely listen to feedback you receive."

"No way!" I practically shouted. "I'm very receptive to feedback, I just never get any good advice."

"Oh really?" Talmo stared at me, bemused. "Tell us more."

"Well, people's advice is so superficial. What do they know anyway? I'm very complicated, you need to realize that …"

"What about us advanced beings from the future with brainpower four times your own?" He struggled to suppress another chuckle.

"Well, in theory, yes. But you're from another planet, you don't understand. You don't get me."

Lamo sighed. "What about Joshua and Saint Germain? They're from your planet."

"Yeah, but they were from the past. People are much more complex these days, that's totally obvious."

"And how about Doltly? He's from the future and totally objective."

"Yeah, but you programmed him, so he's got your bias."

Talmo winked at Lamo who shrugged and replied, "Who knows, you might be right."

Of course, I'm right. Who knows me better than myself? My God, don't you think I wouldn't have figured it out by now? I tried to catch their eyes to keep the argument going, but they looked away pretending to look at some screen readouts. I always take advice if it's any good. Which it typically isn't. I know I sound defensive, but only because I hate it when people presume to know what's best for me when they don't know me at all. Why don't they just shut the eff up? I huffed off to a corner and started to fiddle with some knobs.

"Stop that!" Talmo shouted. "You'll blow us up!"

I stopped.

See? I *do* accept feedback.

After some time grumbling in the corner, I returned to the bridge, where the two of them were gazing at various screens with intense concentration. Doltly was also intensively hitting buttons off to one side and scrutinizing something. Lamo looked up, acknowledging me with a nod.

Seeking to distract myself from my awkward feeling, I threw out a question: "The headset told me early on that there were seven sexes on Venus. Yet you two seem like regular males. How does that even work?"

Lamo replied, "Now's not the best time for that question, but briefly—Sexes on Venus are a continuum. From 1-7. Most feminine to most masculine. The best sex happens between complementary numbers 1 and 7, 2 and 6, etc. Talmo and I are both fives. Since we're normally gasses, we can totally merge with a partner in a way you couldn't imagine. But there's a risk that we could get too merged, which is why we like to get a third party—a number four—to watch as a witness. Is that clear? Because we really are pretty busy right now."

"Yeah. Got it. Totally. Is there anything I can do to help?" I meant with the ship—not a threesome—knowing it was unlikely. More like inconceivable. He shook his head. Maybe I'd do better in the threesome.

I sighed and sat down behind them. In modern times, this would be when I started playing with my phone. But I'd lost my phone, probably when I got thrown into King Arthur's dungeon. Not sure, I wasn't really keeping track since we used these souvenir pens instead as communication devices. But they don't have games on them. Technology really went backwards on them. Well, except for the part where they can communicate with spaceships.

For lack of anything else to do, I closed my eyes and started to repeat a mantra. I was torn for a minute about which one to choose. It was between *One* and *I Am*, both of which have the euphonious consonant that produces the pure sine wave vibration needed to enter an alpha state. After a moment or two debate, I went with the latter, as I felt the need to assert my individuality which is actually not at all the point of meditation, but then I wanted to cut myself a break since no one understands me. After another moment or two, I felt myself exhale, and then I remembered I was on the adventure of a lifetime, even though my companions didn't get me at all despite their high IQs and whatever. Oops, let that thought go. Back to the mantra, haha.

After a while I was sufficiently chilled out and I opened my eyes. The three of them were gathered over a screen showing the North American continent. There were a couple lights showing over the East Coast, one near the Mississippi River and one in Northern California.

"What're those lights?" I asked.

Doltly responded, "They are sources of possible anomalies."

"What kind of anomalies?"

"People. Either ones who've had a forbidden space contact, or through some unusual form of mental illness have tuned into something that gives them great personal power and the ability to sway history in the wrong direction."

"What're you finding?"

"We've narrowed it down to a few hundred at this point—all twenty eight-year-olds—but I think we can get it down to a dozen or less. Then we will need to meet them to ascertain who and figure out how to fix the anomaly."

He went back to studying the screen. Pictures of individuals started to populate the screen. After a few minutes, Talmo leaned over and pointed. "That one, that one, and that one. And one more. Next screen."

Doltly pushed a button.

"Yes there, fourteenth from the left." A light went on in the upper right corner. "We've got it. Just four, fortunately."

"So who are they?" I asked.

"You'll maybe recognize some of their names. Bill Clinton, George Bush, Donald Trump and Winston Mysteriak. Should we take bets on who the culprit is?" Lamo asked.

"Absolutely," Talmo said.

"I pick Donald Trump," I jumped in, eager to get first dibs.

"Why?" Talmo asked.

"My God, it's obvious. He became a billionaire, then president, then got impeached twice and tried to start an insurrection. If that's not swaying history in the wrong direction, I don't know what is!"

"What about George Bush?," Lamo replied. "He was a doofus who got elected on a fluke, started a decade long war on false pretenses, and crashed the world's economy."

Talmo nodded. "Bill Clinton?"

"A sleazeball, maybe a rapist. Not quite in the same league. Plus that's the kind of person that usually gets ahead in this country. No help needed from any anomaly," I answered.

"Winston Mysteriak?"

"I got nothing," Lamo said.

"Nothing," replied Doltly.

"Me neither. Great name though," I couldn't help adding.

"Well," Talmo concluded, "We will investigate them equally without fear or favor." The rest of us nodded.

"Where first?" I asked.

Talmo pointed and said, "New York City."

# The Time Wanderer Series

BY ROBERT MANIS

- **The Emerald Tablets  (Or How I Saved the World with Help from Time Pirates from Venus**
- **The Grail and the Saucer**
- **The Serpent and the UFO Factory**
- **and COMING FALL 2025 - The Venusian Prisoner**

# About the Author

Robert Manis has a Ph.D in Sociology and was once asked to join the CIA. Despite declining, he remains an international man of mystery, occasionally surfacing in Las Vegas. His current research involves cloning Elvis Impersonators and using time travel to win at Roulette. Many people have experienced life-changing epiphanies from reading a single paragraph of his books. (Past results do not imply future epiphanies).